T0266421

ADVANCE PRA[illegible]

Beautiful Ill[illegible]

"A love letter to the razzle-dazzle of '30s San Francisco and the wonders of Treasure Island."
—Kirkus

"Christie Nelson's *Beautiful Illusion* is a breathtaking journey back in time to San Francisco, 1939, for the building of Treasure Island, the site of the world-class Golden Gate International Exposition, built in hopes of promoting peace among nations across an increasingly stormy Pacific. *Beautiful Illusion* follows a young reporter, Lily Nordby, who eagerly covers the Treasure Island story and in the process unwittingly unravels some secrets from her own past as she becomes tangled in espionage and romance. Beautifully written with rich details and stunning dialogue, *Beautiful Illusion* is a real treat! A fast-paced, intriguing read!"
—Michelle Cox, author of the award-winning Henrietta and Inspector Howard series

"Nelson's dazzling portrayal of Treasure Island's world fair and the late 30's San Francisco, blends the fast pace of a thriller while transporting us back to an era of pre-WWII enthusiastic innocence. Cub reporter Lily shows her moxie through the rise of the grandest San Francisco fair, ever. Her complicated attraction to the shadowy Imperial Japanese diplomat, Tokido, parallels the country's deference to Japan, even as their violence loomed across the Pacific. Set against Lily's conflicted relationship with the scholarly dwarf, Woodrow, and her own dodgy family, the novel revels with authenticity and historic figures."
—J. Macon King,
Publisher of The Mill Valley Literary Review

"Christie Nelson's tale is a loving valentine to the end of a San Franciscan incarnation. The two new bridges and WWII changed the city forever. Soon, ease of travel about the bay and the passage of hundreds of thousands of G.I.'s bound for the Pacific theater obliterated the small town feel that the story evokes. Told with a vivid attention to detail and populated with local characters, it illuminates the spectacle of the Fair, which was a last chromatic burst of fireworks, before the darkness set in."

—Will Maynez, Historian, Diego Rivera Mural Project,
City College San Francisco

BEAUTIFUL ILLUSION,

Treasure Island, 1939

BEAUTIFUL ILLUSION,

Treasure Island, 1939

A Novel

by

CHRISTIE NELSON

SHE WRITES PRESS

Published May 1, 2018
Printed in the United States of America
Print ISBN: 978-1-63152-334-2
E-ISBN: 978-1-63152-399-1

Library of Congress Control Number: 2017957970

Book design by Stacey Aaronson

For information, address:
She Writes Press
1563 Solano Ave #546
Berkeley, CA 94707

She Writes Press is a division of SparkPoint Studio, LLC.

Beautiful Illusion, Treasure Island, 1939 is a work of fiction. All incidents and dialogue, and all characters, with the exception of some well-known historical and public figures, are products of the author's imagination and are not to be construed as real. When real-life historical or public figures appear, the situations, incidents, and dialogues concerning those persons are entirely fictional and are not intended to depict actual events or to change the entirely fictional nature of the work. In all other respects, any resemblance to persons living or dead is entirely coincidental.

Historical Photos Courtesy of SAN FRANCISCO HISTORY CENTER, SAN FRANCISCO PUBLIC LIBRARY.

Night View of Japan Pavilion Courtesy of California Historical Society.

In memory of my parents,

Phyllis Kathleen Fryer

Arthur James Nelson

"One day, if I go to heaven, I'll look around and say, 'it ain't bad, but it ain't San Francisco.'"

—HERB CAEN

Dredging the Bay

George Smith, W. Kent Dyson, Leland Cutler Sink the Flag

CHAPTER ONE

Lily

After the heaviest rainstorm in over a decade drenched San Francisco, Lily Nordby, twenty-three and hardly green, jumped puddles and hopped on a crowded cable car rattling down Powell Street. The grip man, decked out in a serge, charcoal-gray suit, and a cap pushed back on his head, gave her a big-toothed grin. "Good morning, miss!" he called and rang the bell to a silvery rendition of "Happy Days Are Here Again."

She grinned back, stepped onto the running board, and held on to the grab bar as the cables in the street hummed beneath her feet. Suddenly the sky opened up in a downpour and a flock of pigeons took flight from the curb, soaring up and over the roof of the car.

At the turnaround on Market Street, she leaped off. A paperboy waved the February 11, 1936, *Examiner* in her face. Leland Cutler, the president of the Golden Gate International Exposition, had rowed out to the shoals with two cronies and sunk a flag into the soupy muck that proclaimed, SITE OF THE 1939 WORLD'S FAIR. Every day, stories about the city's claiming its right as the gateway to the Pacific made headlines.

Citizens quaked in a fever of excitement. For months, Lily had gathered on the Embarcadero with other onlookers and peered through the salty spray of waves slapping the shore to dredges huffing and puffing like beasts of burden as they clawed silt and mud into buckets and burped it onto the four hundred acres that were fast becoming Treasure Island right in front of their wondering eyes.

She could wait no more. A hurly-burly, never-die optimism had swept through town, lifting up every man and woman by their lapels. Two engineering marvels had occurred: the San Francisco Bay Bridge, linking downtown to the East Bay, had risen from caissons sunk into bay mud forty-eight stories high like upside-down skyscrapers, and the Golden Gate Bridge, the longest single-span bridge that could never be built, was swinging above the treacherous tides like a giant's erector set, aimed north toward the tip of Marin County.

She marched down the sidewalk of the wide boulevard, alongside men in suits and fedoras and women in coats and cloche hats stuck with pheasant feathers, who had all answered FDR's clarion call to rise out of the Depression. San Francisco had been born as a brawny port city with a back-

File cabinet drawers, left half open, bulged with folders and papers. Cigar smoke hung in the airless room. Toth, a florid-faced man with a lantern jaw, gave her the once-over. "Who in the hell are you?" he growled out of the side of his mouth.

"I'm Lily Nordby, reporter with the *Buena Vista Gazette,* and I can cover any beat you'd toss my way."

"Goddammit, you're the dame Adolph Schuman keeps pestering me about."

"Yes, sir!" She clutched the bouquet to keep her hands from shaking.

"How in the hell can you see anything with those goddamn flowers in your arms?"

"They're for you!" She laid the bouquet on his desk.

"What for?"

"Your birthday."

"It isn't my birthday, so don't expect to sweeten me up."

"Look at my stories." She tossed him the envelope.

"That two-bit rag."

"Yes, sir, but if you take a look, you'll see I can write."

He scowled but then shoved aside a stack of papers and shook out a fistful of columns. He raced through the first one before he slapped it down and went to the next. He raised his eyes, glaring at her from under a brow that had more wrinkles in it than a flophouse sheet.

"Your beat is local art and entertainment."

"I can cover anything: politics, business, baseball—"

"Is that right? Well, you're a go-getter. I'll give you that. But you've got to show me more than these puff pieces if you want to work here."

"Mr. Toth, I'm asking for that chance." Her cheeks were so hot, she thought they'd explode.

He ground out his cigar in a brass ashtray the size of a spittoon and fixed an unblinking stare on her. "What about the women's page?"

A flood of relief coursed through her chest. "With my eyes closed."

He leaned so far back in his chair that it squealed. "Gladys is up to her ears in a backwash of social events and contests."

"Right up my alley." She couldn't tell him she had her sights set on covering Treasure Island. He'd boot her out on her fanny.

"Tell you what. This is your lucky day, Nordby. Take the load off Gladys, and you can have the morgue beat all to yourself."

Whoopee, she said to herself. The sight of a broken body in the street didn't concern her. But she knew herself well enough to dread the prospect of coming across a small-time hood she'd recognize laid out on a slab, or, worse yet, her old man.

"What's the salary?"

"The first week, you work free."

She flinched. *Take it,* she told herself.

"When and *if* you measure up, we'll talk salary."

"When do I start?"

"How about now?"

"Why not?" It was all she could do not to leap into the air.

"And those high heels you're wearing?"

"Yes?"

"Ditch them. You'll break your neck. Mac out there will introduce you to Gladys. Take these goddamn flowers to her. They stink! She'll love them. Good luck, Nordby."

* * *

FROM THEN ON, every day at the *Examiner* was like slamming down orders at Woolworth's lunch counter. Gladys commanded her post from a desk piled high with magazines and papers and tossed assignments to Lily like "Twelve Tasty Macaroni Recipes," debutante balls, and charity drives by the Holy Sisters of Mercy. When Lily wasn't at her desk, writing stories to make deadline, she was hoofing around town to interview people and attend functions. She couldn't blame Gladys. It was easy to see her health had worn down. Between the job, smoking too much, and taking care of a sick sister, Gladys looked like she was held together by safety pins and a wish. Her bunions were the size of boiled onions.

Lily worked the morgue detail with grim determination. She wrote about grisly murders and unidentified suicides. If a cop had been on the scene, she'd call to pump him for details. Quickly, she caught on to the banter and traded quips with the best of them. She developed a fondness for every cop she met. When a naked, bloated female body wrapped in barbed wire washed up on Ocean Beach, she called a locksmith and had a dead bolt installed on her apartment door. Even though she lived in a single-room-occupancy walk-up on Ellis Street, down the hall from her best friend, she was spooked. She chewed Beeman's gum to choke down vomit at autopsies. If she was lucky, she got wind of a juicy affair, like a jilted wife shooting her husband before the crime desk got hold of it, but that was rare. Her worst fear—confronting her old man—never materialized.

She made friends with the secretaries and switchboard girls. She learned how to drink the acrid coffee from a stained electric urn near the water cooler. She flirted with the legmen, the reporters who dug up the stories and phoned the details back to the rewrite guys in the newsroom. Dudley McGee, one of the junior photographers, took a shine to her. They'd run into each other in the lunchroom and talk shop. He was like a kid brother she'd never had, a college student who'd fallen in love with Ansel Adams's photography, until he'd had to drop out of college to earn a buck.

Dudley and Lily covered flower exhibits, pie contests, and dog shows. They both loved to dance. When the Benny Goodman, Artie Shaw, and Tommy Dorsey orchestras played in dance halls downtown or at Sweet's Ballroom in Oakland, he never missed a chance to invite Lily. Nearly every Saturday night, they jitterbugged until they couldn't stand up anymore.

By summer, Lily knew the ropes and knew the players. On a late afternoon in August, she got wind of a groundbreaking ceremony on Treasure Island.

She nabbed Dudley in the coatroom. "Are you shooting Merriman and Cutler on TI tomorrow?"

He tipped his hat back off his forehead. "Yeah. The big dogs are burying a time capsule. I guess the slop is firm enough that the shovel won't submerge and float out to sea."

"Who's the legman?"

"Suppose to be Poletti, but I just saw him limp out the door a mite green around the gills."

Lily glanced over her shoulder, lowering her voice. "Take me. I'll write the story."

Dudley shook his head. "Front office won't buy it, Nordby."

"Come on, Dudley. Who's your friend?"

"Aw, shit, you never give up."

Governor Merriam and Delegation Break Ground

THE AUGUST DAY dawned, fog-banked, dank, and bone-chilling. Lily and Dudley caught a ferry at the dock on the Embarcadero and crowded elbow to elbow onto the boat with a contingent of Boy Scouts from Old St. Mary's Church in Chinatown, an honor guard, and a marching band. Steamy anticipation rose off the shoulders of the young boys and men, and the howl of voices made it nearly impossible to understand a word of what was being said.

As the ferry came abreast of the island, the wind ripped through Lily's coat. When she stepped off the gangplank, the soles of her rubber boots slipped on the mushy soil. Dudley, oblivious to the cold, charged ahead and began clicking a Leica strapped around his neck. Flash bulbs pinged in the murky gray light. Lily firmly tucked her trouser cuffs into the tops of her boots, straightened up, and ran after Dudley.

Not a hundred yards from the shore, a patch of damp earth had been groomed and flattened. Sailors in white caps ringed the outer perimeter. The Associated Press's loudspeakers hissed and crackled. Off to one side, military flags draped a dais upon which dignitaries and onlookers had assembled. The honor guard stood at the ready. Boy Scouts shuffled, shoved at each other, and then reassembled. Ahead, a ring of two dozen international flags, carried by female flag bearers wearing the costumes of their countries, flapped in the stiff wind.

Dudley and Lily pushed forward.

"Dudley, look. There's a black-and-red swastika of Nazi Germany flying next to the red rising sun of Imperial Japan."

"Yeah, I see it."

"Gives me the heebie-jeebies."

"Tell that to the do-gooders over at the Institute of Pacific Relations."

"Are they blind to Hitler's summer Olympics?" Lily protested. "He won't stop at anything to prove the supremacy of the Aryan race."

"My bet is on our University of Washington rowing team. They'll upset the führer's applecart!" Dudley rubbed his hands together. "Those boys are tough."

"Fat lot of difference that will make," Lily said. "Meanwhile, Germany is carving up Europe and Japan is slaughtering the Chinese and we're waving flags."

"The US is not in that dogfight. Yet. Anyway, keep moving, Ace. This is your big chance. Pageantry and spectacle. That's what Toth wants. That's what we all want."

The brass marching band, stepping in formation, struck up "God Bless America" and moved forward. They halted in front of Governor Merriam, who gripped a gold-plated shovel. Beside the governor, Mayor Rossi sported a white carnation in his lapel amid a bevy of mayors, businessmen, and diplomats, each of whom represented countries that were planning to participate in the Exposition. Merriam handled the shovel, praising the lofty purpose of peace in the Pacific on the greatest artificial island in the land, upon which a magic city would be built. The loudspeakers boomed. Then the ensemble trooped off to watch Leland Cutler sink a redwood chest filled with plans of the Exposition into hallowed ground.

Beside him, Ito was silent.

"And so our work begins," said Okamura, as they passed under the massive structure.

But it was not the demands of construction that occupied his thoughts. The site was assured, the architectural plans fine-tuned, the crew superior by all measure. Upon Tokido's bidding, the emperor would send his own gardeners to oversee the installation of the gardens. Emissaries from the Japanese consulate stood ready. Daily telegrams from Consul General Moto had flooded his office, informing Okamura of their preparedness. The Japanese American community was turning out in vast numbers.

No, there were other matters of sensitivity, such as the presence of the Chinese village that was being financed and built through the efforts of a San Francisco businessman, George Jue, at the request of the Chinese government. Jue would save face for the homeland at all costs. *When will the Chinese nationalists cease their useless opposition to our guidance?* Okamura thought. *Don't they grasp how their resistance has no place in the inevitable tide of progress?* Yet protocol would require impeccable respect. He had been counseled to proceed with the utmost caution. There were factions of the American government and citizen organizations on guard. They could not afford an incident of any nature.

The barrage of social gatherings and political meetings and the months stretched ceaselessly ahead. He would miss the small pleasures of life that marked his days—the ginkgo trees lining the stone path to his two-story wooden home, the exquisite porcelain perfection of his wife's face, the laughter of his young children, the sumo-wrestling events he attended, and the ritual at the end of the day that awaited him in the bathhouses.

Okamura removed a pack of Cherry cigarettes from his pocket. Ito withdrew a lighter, cradling the flame in the nest of his palm, offering it to him. The tip of the cigarette ignited, the taste of it bitter in his mouth.

In the distance, Treasure Island appeared like an apparition rising out of vapors.

"We will be the first foreign ship to drop anchor at the Port of Trade Winds."

"*Hai,*" Okamura said. "It is well to mark this achievement in the land of the gaijin."

CHAPTER THREE

Woodrow

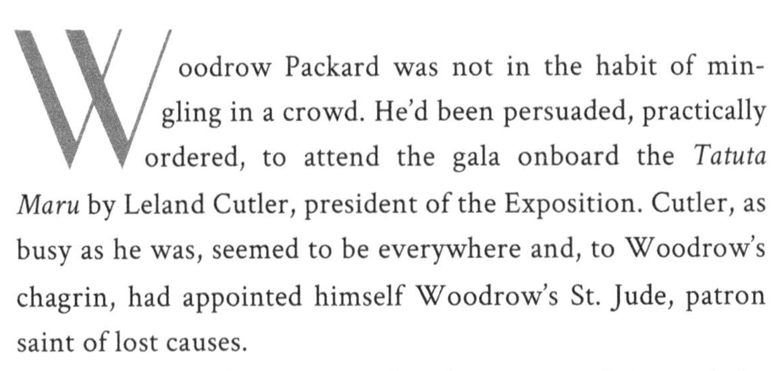

Woodrow Packard was not in the habit of mingling in a crowd. He'd been persuaded, practically ordered, to attend the gala onboard the *Tatuta Maru* by Leland Cutler, president of the Exposition. Cutler, as busy as he was, seemed to be everywhere and, to Woodrow's chagrin, had appointed himself Woodrow's St. Jude, patron saint of lost causes.

The gaiety of the event called for action and demanded a certain panache that was entirely abhorrent to Woodrow. He could hear his father's admonishment: *Good God, Woodrow. Pull yourself together. You may be a dwarf, but you're still a Packard. Stand up straight.*

He couldn't exactly fade into the background. Lord, he

wished he could. The curious stares of assembled dignitaries pained him tonight. The Japanese, at least, knew how to avert their eyes. Confrontational behavior to them was inherently dishonorable.

Woodrow adjusted his top hat—a miserable idea to begin with—and glanced through the trouser legs of gentlemen and politicians, past the petticoats of wives, and at the occasional rippling silk of kimonos that skimmed the floor. The grand Georgian dining room of the *Tatuta Maru*—soaring trompe l'oeil ceiling, ornate curved balcony, and Palladian gewgaws offered no refuge. Above the noise, he heard Mayor Rossi's gravel voice over whiskey-infused baritones. Beside Rossi, the slight frame of Toshito Moto, Consul General of Japan, bent like a delicate willow in the blunt force of wind.

Just then, the *Tatuta Maru* listed and the Persian carpet underfoot seemed to slip sideways. Woodrow felt a strong hand under his arm hoist him upright. He grabbed his hat and craned his neck over his shoulder. Timothy Pflueger, lead architect of the Exposition design committee, scowled down at him. "Hang on, old man. The night is young."

Woodrow regained his footing, wrenched away from Pflueger, and stuck his hat back on his head. Pflueger's belly, stuffed with one too many pork chops, seemed to precede him, and yet his piercing eyes punctured Woodrow's disguise.

"Say, I read your paper on the sculpted reliefs and murals of the Mayan temples in the Yucatán. Damn interesting stuff. What an experience being with the Carnegie team at Chichén Itzá."

Woodrow mumbled his thanks. Pflueger reminded Woodrow of his uncle, a man of annoying gusto, spit and polish, and undeniable brilliance. At the mention of Chichén Itzá, a flash of memory shot through Woodrow: a shaft of light filtering down through a narrow, dark opening; his hands grasping a ladder lashed with twine; the verdant jungle, the screech of monkeys, the buzz and click of insects fading; his feet finding purchase on the chalky ground; the static, bottled air of Mayan gods rushing into his nostrils. With shaking fingers, Woodrow had lit a miner's lamp and the Temple of the Warriors' inner chamber had flared into view.

"I've wanted to go," Pflueger said, "but projects here keep me chained to the drafting board." He wasn't boasting—his hand was stamped on every important building project in San Francisco. He peered down at Woodrow without sacrificing the impervious demeanor of a statesman.

Woodrow heard himself saying, "The next time I go, I'll advise you. Perhaps you can make time for a short trip." *What am I thinking?* he wondered. He couldn't tolerate being stuck with Pflueger in a jitney on the endless road from Mérida to Chichén.

Pflueger leaned in conspiratorially. "Tell you what. Some of the gents and I get together for a game of poker every week. Why don't you join us?"

From the balcony came the clinking of crystal, and all eyes turned toward Leland Cutler, who cleared his throat and beamed down at the assembled guests. Moto stood beside him. Mayor Rossi's face bloomed beet red. From publicity photos, Woodrow recognized Tokido Okamura, the diplomat sent to oversee the Japanese Pavilion, standing between Moto and Rossi. Okamura's gaze swept over the room, his bearing proud and erect. Officials from city hall and the Japanese embassy crowded behind.

Pflueger hurriedly broke away from Woodrow and bolted toward the stairway to the balcony. Woodrow peered closer. At the bottom of the stairs, a group of reporters had gathered. One of the reporters, a woman in an elegant peacock-blue cloche hat and coat, turned around toward the audience. Woodrow started. It was the reporter, Lily Nordby, whom he had met on the island. She had successfully disguised her beauty beneath the mannish outfits she wore on the job, but not here, not now. He had been dodging her calls for weeks. He glanced around for the exit. The official ceremony was on the verge of beginning.

"Ladies and gentlemen, assembled guests, Mayor Rossi, and Honorable Consul General Moto," Cutler began, "it is indeed an honor on this day of October 13, 1938, to welcome our esteemed Japanese guests to Treasure Island in celebration of the Golden Gate International Exposition, as we join together in peace and goodwill. It is no small . . ."

Cutler's speech would drone on and on. A nationwide radio hookup and short-wave transmission to Japan crackled from a corner. Woodrow was certain that Imperial Emperor Hirohito and the Japanese propaganda machine would take every advantage to herald the fair as a symbol of the West's admiration of Japan as the Light of Asia.

Woodrow shuffled from one foot to the other, studying

the assembled guests. *Men of means and ladies of leisure to a one,* he thought. *When will this end?* At last, Cutler concluded his address and, after rousing applause, Moto took the microphone.

Blinking rapidly, he cleared his throat. "Greetings," he began, bowing slightly. "Japan's eager acceptance of America's invitation to participate in the Golden Gate International Exposition is an expression of Japan's abiding friendship with the United States, as well as a manifestation of her fond hope to perpetuate lasting peace among the various nationals bordering on the Pacific."

A chill ran up Woodrow's back. *Murderous thugs,* he thought. *Moto is just warming up.*

He hungered to return to his house on Telegraph Hill, where his leather chair, books, and brandy awaited his return. He could catch a ferryboat, hop a cab, and walk through the door within an hour. The prospect of immense quiet and the loveliness of gliding on the bay practically made him groan. Ah, the smell of the sea and the pull of the cool wind. He tipped the brim of his hat down, angled his shoulder, and broke away.

Just as he reached the gangplank, he heard footsteps behind him.

A voice called, "Mr. Packard, Mr. Packard, wait!"

He increased his pace; footsteps grew closer. A hand touched his shoulder, and he swung around to face his pursuer.

Lily Nordby stepped back, clutching her hat in her hand. "Mr. Packard, why are you leaving so soon?"

He could see she was really a child behind her feminine beauty.

"I've been trying to interview you for weeks. Won't you stay so we can talk?"

His temper flared. Her doggedness might serve her well in her profession, but it was a hindrance to him and a trait he found extremely annoying.

"My dear, why won't you leave me alone? Certainly there are others to occupy your search for authenticity and valor here on the island, but hear me when I say I'm not that person!" Then he turned on his heel and left her with her mouth open and an expression of dismay in her wide eyes.

CHAPTER FOUR

Lily

Lily picked her way over ribbons of track that had been set for a steam engine to haul steel from one end of the island to another. Buildings and towers had been going up at lightning speed. Construction workers donned hard hats, their steel-toed boots thudding on girders as they maneuvered around the structures with the agility of rock climbers. The ripping of electrical saws, *rat-a-tat-tat* of rivet guns, and banging of hammers sang out a discordant hymn into the salty, stiff wind.

She pulled her hat down low over her ears; she was constantly cold. Her eyes watered, her nose dripped. She passed by carpenters moving in tight synchronicity, unaware of her presence. Their boots and pant legs were caked in mud as they laid foundations on top of driven piles. They had attacked stacks of lumber: spruce for flooring, pine for walls and scaffolding, Douglas fir for towers. The framing of the magnificent structures that would become pavilions and palaces and towers gleamed like golden bones when the sun broke through November's gloom. The barren outpost, framed by the Golden Gate Bridge, the East Bay hills, the Bay Bridge, and the city, had been designed with lofty architectural aims—nothing less than an imperial city, neither classically Greek nor Roman, but a fantastical polyglot of Cambodian, Mayan, and Pacific island styles that defied categorization.

In the distance, a group of men gathered at the base of two rows of huge cubes stacked one on top of another in ascending order, higher and higher, culminating in stylized, block-shaped elephants at the top. Lily fished a map out of her pocket. These structures could be only the giant Elephant Tower gates, inspired by the temples of Angkor Wat. Passing through these gates, which also housed wind baffles to shelter fairgoers from lusty west winds, into the Court of Honor, Lily saw the slender, 392-foot Tower of the Sun positioned in the court's center, piercing the gray sky. From this landmark, buildings followed a north–south, east–west axis, with interior courtyards, fountains, and ever-changing gardens.

She trudged off in the direction of the men, her boots as weighted with mud as the workers'. As she drew nearer, one man held the attention of the others. He was turned away, gesturing toward the opposing walls of the cubes. The flap of architectural paper snapped in his hands.

In the group, she recognized Timothy Pflueger, architect and head of the design committee, and Donald Mackey, architect of the Elephant Towers. She had been trying to interview both men for months. At their office on Bush Street, she could never get by the secretaries, who blocked her every attempt.

She caught Pflueger's eye. The men watched her curiously. Marching up to the lot of them, she smiled. "Sorry for the intrusion, gentlemen." She held out her hand to Pflueger. "Lily Nordby, reporter for the *Examiner.*"

He stepped forward and grasped her hand. "Yes, I know your work."

"Well, that's a start." She reached into her bag for a pad and pen. Her fingers were so cold, she was certain they'd fall off. "I'd like to feature you, Mr. Pflueger—and, of course, each of the other architects, if possible." She glanced around the circle, meeting each inquisitive gaze. Her eyes dropped to the man whose powerful voice had boomed out over the din of construction noise. It was Woodrow Packard.

Pflueger interjected. "Packard is the man you should interview."

"Yes, I know," she said.

"He's our Mayan art expert and an authority on the bas-reliefs of Chichén Itzá."

"Which of course are referenced throughout the island," Lily commented.

Woodrow was silent. Head down, he sketched a pencil drawing on the margin of the plans. The other men broke away and began to talk among themselves.

She leaned forward, observing the image of a stylized jaguar head that was flowing from Woodrow's hand. "We meet again," she said.

"It seems to be unavoidable." Woodrow raised his eyes, peering into the distance. They held a terrible beauty, as if he needed to arm himself against a world that pitied him.

"Then, in that case, here's my card. You can call me anytime."

Woodrow mumbled something unintelligible.

Pflueger touched her elbow, escorting her a few steps away. "Say, I wonder: By chance, are you from the city?"

"Yes," she answered, eying him inquisitively.

"There's a Nordby Plumbing on Twenty-Fourth Street. Are you related?"

She cocked her head. The fine hairs on her arms stood up. She could lie, but why? Pflueger had already figured it out. "Yes. He's my father."

"Hmm, I see. I thought so. I've lived in the Mission all my life."

"Even now?"

"It's home." Pflueger tipped his hat. "Love the neighborhood. Wouldn't consider leaving it."

"To each his own," she said.

"Yes, well, if you'll excuse me, I need to get back to our meeting."

"Wait," she said. "When can I interview you?"

"Call me at my office."

"If you'd give your secretary my name, I'd appreciate it. She guards your time like a bulldog."

Pflueger laughed. "Of course." Then he stepped away to rejoin the other gentlemen.

In her peripheral vision, she saw Dudley running toward her. He raised an arm in greeting. "Hey, Lil, let's get a photo!"

Stepping over the earth grooved by tire tracks, she stopped him. "Not now."

"Never known you to turn down a photo op. You sure?"

"Perfectly sure."

"What's the deal?"

"It's a long story. Come on—let's see if Stackpole is working at the Court of Pacifica." She flagged a flatbed truck that was barreling their way. "Hey, mister, can you give us a lift?"

* * *

LILY LAY FULLY dressed on a narrow bed under a quilt. Chills assaulted her body, and a size-ten headache had rendered her immobile. Below, the sounds of traffic on Ellis Street buzzed through the window. Then a knock sounded on the door.

"Come in," she mumbled, peeking out from under the quilt.

Maxine Pavich stepped through the door. Munching on a paper sleeve of roasted, salted cashews from Morrow's Nut House on Geary Street, she tiptoed toward the bed and laid her hand on Lily's shoulder. "What's up, kiddo?" she asked. "That time of the month?"

"Nope. I've got a lousy cold."

Maxine lifted her hand as if she had touched a cockroach.

"Ew! That's bad. I'm not surprised. Winter is breathing down our necks, and you're out tramping around TI day and night." She turned toward the hot plate on the counter of a small cabinet across the room. "Is there any soup I can warm up?"

Lily blew her nose on a tissue. "That'd be swell. All I had today was coffee and a doughnut."

"Sounds nourishing to me." Maxine picked her way through a maze of books and magazines arranged in stacks on the floor. Rummaging around in the cabinet, she came up with two Campbell's cans. "What'll it be? Tomato or chicken noodle?"

"You choose," Lily said.

Maxine opened the can of chicken noodle, plopped the contents into a small pot, added water, and turned on the burner of the hot plate. A pint of bourbon sat on the countertop. "Mind if I drink your booze?"

"What's mine is yours."

"Spoken like a true friend." Maxine stirred the soup with one hand and poured a shot of bourbon into a water glass. "So, what's the latest at the Expo?" she asked, sipping the drink.

"Huge structures are rising out of the mud like lotuses. I've never seen anything like it." She propped herself up with a pillow and blew her nose again. "I met Timothy Pflueger today. He's a big-shot architect. He's from the Mission, like us."

"So?"

"He figured out who my old man is."

"Bully for him."

"It bothered me. Like I'm marked or something."

"That's nonsense. Anyone who knows you thinks you're first-class. Who else from our neighborhood landed a job at City of Paris to sell gloves? Then Adolph and Bunny Schuman hired you to model their suits and you ended up running their business. Let it go, Lily. Nothing good comes from worrying about something you can't change."

"You're right. Still, I don't know." Lily rubbed her eyes. "What's up with you?"

"Same old stuff. Secretarial pool at Fireman's Fund. We're like trained seals. Our chief skill is typing sixty words a minute, hour by hour, day by day." Maxine poured another bourbon. "By the way, I need your talent."

Lily groaned. "For what?"

"I locked myself out."

"Again?"

"Slept in, woke up with a hangover, dressed in the dark, figured my keys were in my purse, and ran out the door." Maxine ladled the soup into two bowls, walked across the floor, and offered a bowl to Lily.

Lily inhaled the steamy liquid and slurped a spoonful into her mouth. "This hits the spot."

"Drink up," Maxine said, leaning against the cabinet and cradling the other bowl in her hands. "You need your strength. You know, if you're too sick, I could spend the night. Right here on the floor."

Lily groaned again.

"On the other hand, you're so good with a bobby pin. It'll take you two shakes to pick the lock." Maxine drank directly from the bowl. "You can't say that your good-for-nothing step brothers didn't teach you an indispensable skill."

"All right!" Lily exclaimed between sneezes. "Do you mind if I finish the soup?"

"Take your time," Maxine said, pouring another finger of bourbon. "I'm in no hurry."

CHAPTER FIVE

Tokido

A tap sounded on the door of the cabin. Tokido, seated at his desk, glanced at the clock: 7:17 a.m. Off the bay, morning light cast watery reflections that flickered across the ceiling and walls. The *Tatuta Maru* held steady in her berth in the Port of Trade Winds as the cries of seagulls pierced November's sunless air. The remains of breakfast—green tea, miso soup, slivers of *maguro* and cucumber—lay nearby on a tray. "*Hai*," he answered.

Kiyoshi Inoue, Tokido's secretary, opened the door. "Okamura-*sama*, a newspaper reporter is on the grounds of the pavilion."

Tokido frowned, momentarily perplexed. "What?"

"She is asking for you."

"Did she give her name?"

"No. Ishikawa-*toryo* requested that she wait for your arrival. But she would not be deterred."

"I will come now."

"We have meetings at ten this morning at the consulate, an appointment with the ambassador this afternoon, and a formal dinner with the mayor this evening."

"*Arigatou.* I will be ready."

The door closed softly. The frown on Tokido's brow deepened. The cigarette in his fingers had burned to a nub. He took a final drag and snuffed it against the edges of an ashtray where each extinguished cigarette was arranged in a row.

His morning ritual was to reach for a slim volume of Matsuo Basho's haiku. When dawn had breached the black sky, he had read:

an ancient pond
a frog jumps in
the splash of water

Well, he thought, *we shall see about this frog.* It was entirely unacceptable for anyone to roam unescorted through the pavilion site. He screwed the top of a fountain pen into its shaft and placed it alongside a leather-bound notebook.

The pages of the notebook were divided into columns. The columns were ruled across the page with the headings "Date," "Event," "Persons," "Title," "Location," "Type of Facility," and, finally, "Necessary Action." The writing was precise, the details exact. Every event he attended, every person he met, every facility he visited, was recorded into the notebook. He placed the notebook in the top drawer of the desk, locked it, and slipped the key into his pocket. He removed the navy-blue silk kimono emblazoned with white cranes that he wore over his day clothes, pulled on a black leather jacket, and left the cabin.

A Sankyo military motorcycle was parked at the dock. He revved up the engine and jammed it into gear. By foot, it would take him at least twenty minutes on rough ground, dodging trucks, equipment, and workers, to walk from the south end of the island to the eastern site of the pavilion; by motorcycle, it would take less than five minutes.

He sped away from the dock, around a pool in the Enchanted Garden, and directly toward the Tower of the Sun. He found the campanile, with statues of adventurers embedded in its base and winged, naked female spirits poised in its high niches, particularly distasteful. The spear-like tower had no relation to nature, no proportion, no restraint. Its only attribute was to fix in a visitor's eye the gates that led into or out of the Exposition.

In a further insult, all the palaces, courts, and malls on the island had been given majestic names, save one: the serene Moon Court into which he drove. High, arched walls rose up on either side of him. At the far end, a classically formed female statue, *Evening Star,* sat atop a fountain. He had been told that azure lights would illuminate her in the evening. Her beauty wiped his vision clean; he would never tire of her grace.

He continued through the Court of Reflections, past two long, rectangular pools that reflected walls of hanging vines. Tall Siamese ceremonial light standards that mimicked tiny umbrellas ringed the pools. He passed under the ninety-foot Arch of Triumph into the Court of Flowers. Zooming around a circular basin that contained a three-tiered fountain topped by a robed female figure reaching for a rainbow, he shifted into second gear. At the Lake of Nations, he made a sharp left and roared up to the site of the pavilion. The architecture was patterned after a feudal castle and, within the stronghold, a noble, seventeenth-century samurai house. The main tower rose to 125 feet, and the grounds were the largest of any foreign pavilion's.

Lloyd Brown, superintendent of construction, stood in a group of men wearing hard hats. As Tokido approached, Brown waved a hand in salute. Beyond them, Japanese builders swarmed the site. Dressed in indigo *noragi* jackets, *monpe* pants, and *tabi* socks, they seized stones from a carrion and aligned them along the foundation of the main building. From the road, a formal entry led to a series of rooms and halls, and the second floor accommodated private meeting rooms and ample space for storage.

Around the grounds, as far as could be seen, stacks of lumber, bamboo, posts, and beams were neatly assembled. Trees, shrubbery, and ancient stones were cordoned off. In the distance, another group of men furiously lashed sections of bamboo scaffolding together with rope.

Tokido hurried forward, stopped beside Brown, and offered his hand. "Good morning."

Brown shook his outstretched hand. "I'm impressed. I've never seen such outstanding materials assembled in one place. Your people are skilled and quick."

"The preparation was long. Our craftsmen will build the ancestral way they've learned from the masters."

"Not a nail used, I've been told."

"Correct," Tokido answered. "Wooden spikes ensure that structures hold for centuries, as they do in the Japanese empire."

"In that case, I hope you have plans for the buildings after the Expo closes. Otherwise, the craftsmanship is wasted."

"We do things as we do them. There is no other way."

"When the roof beams came off the ship, they were perfectly carved, shaped, and finished."

"Allow me to compliment your work," Tokido said. "In Tokyo, I saw the plans. Now I see the execution. Very well done. The transport of our supplies to the site is appreciated, and I look forward to speaking with you further." He paused. "Excuse me. Did you see a woman pass by?"

Brown raised his eyebrows. "You mean that dame from the *Examiner*?"

"Miss Nordby, I believe?"

"That's her. We saw her a while back. She disappeared into the site."

Tokido nodded and bade the men good-bye. Moving away, he heard Brown say, "She's trouble," and then muffled laughter.

He clenched his teeth and passed by workmen who swept over the site like soldiers claiming territory after battle. No patch of earth was wasted. Guttural shouts and the crack of mallets on stone filled the air. At each clearing, his eyes moved restlessly back and forth. Dust blurred his vision. He circled the site and ended up in the place where he had begun. His frustration turned to urgency; urgency turned to anger.

He backtracked to a hut in a clearing on the edge of the site. Here, architects laid out plans on planks and the lead foreman, Ishikawa, staged the phases of construction.

Ishikawa looked up from a brazier where he was warming his hands. A pot steamed on the grate. "*Ohayo gozaimasu.* May I offer you a cup of tea?"

"*Arigatou.* I don't mean to interfere."

"No interference taken."

"The woman who was here earlier."

"*Hai.*"

"Have you seen her again?"

"No, Tokido-*san.*"

"If you see her again, escort her off the site immediately." Tokido bowed and stepped out of the hut. He checked his watch—8:35—and hurried back toward the road.

That was when he saw her, standing ahead of him, inside the site, on a mound of rubble. But he had to squint. She hardly resembled the woman he had met onboard the ship at the gala. She wore trousers, a navy-blue coat, and boots, and her hair was tucked up under a brown hat. He walked rapidly forward and tapped her shoulder. She spun around.

"Mr. Okamura. You startled me."

"What are you doing?"

She looked puzzled. "I beg your pardon?"

"This area is cordoned off to the public." He pointed an accusatory finger back toward the site.

Her unblinking gaze followed his finger and then returned to his face.

"It's unsafe for you to be on the grounds when construction is in process, and—"

Her cheeks flushed, and her eyes flashed indignantly. "I've been on this island since it was a sinkhole. I've seen acres of topsoil laid, piles driven, concrete poured, electrical panels installed. I've watched towers go up, palaces fabricated, courtyards engineered. As a member of the press, I have a responsibility to see everything and know everyone."

"Please understand. You'll be my guest, or you're not welcome."

She stepped back, inhaling sharply. A thin sheen of perspiration glazed her upper lip. "Oh, I see. I've offended you."

"Not at all," he replied. "You must understand my position. Safety is essential."

"Of course." She appeared to be studying the ground between their feet. "I had hoped we could talk today. Perhaps another time?"

"Yes, I agree. Now, if you'll please follow me." He offered his arm, from which she shrank as if it were an insult.

They walked in silence until they were clear of the site, back on the road. He found himself reluctant to look at her. "If you'll pardon me," he said, the words halting and stiff in his mouth, "I must attend to other business."

"Of course," she answered.

He jammed his hands into the pockets of his jacket and jogged toward the motorcycle. On impulse, he turned and walked back to her. She watched him approach with an expression of nonchalant distain.

"There will be a press preview of the pavilion well in advance of opening day. I assume you're on the list?"

"Of course."

"Excellent. We'll meet then. May I give you a lift to your next stop?"

"That won't be necessary."

"As you desire." He bowed slightly. "Good-bye." He noticed then that her eyes, more green than blue, shone with the unmistakable glint of defiance. Their brilliance would haunt him throughout the day, and in the evening, just before he laid himself down to sleep, her eyes would be the last image in his conscious mind.

CHAPTER SIX

Woodrow

Woodrow liked to come early to the island, sometimes at dawn, when a mist lay over the salty bay, seagulls *caw-caw-caw*ed, and pastel light rose over the Berkeley hills. A byway of constant motion, the bay was alive with vessels—barges, military ships, fishing boats, sailing craft, and ferries. It was from here that he had first seen a barge delivering trees from San Francisco's Balboa Park to the island. As it moved over the water, it looked like a floating green forest.

Woodrow learned that the gardeners, led by brilliant chief of horticulture Julius Girod, were tasked with growing trees, shrubs, and flowers at the Mission Terrace's twenty-eight-acre site. Girod devised a scheme to heat the cool, damp soil with electrical cords to sixty degrees, to ensure vibrant growth. Residents joined in the effort. From all parts of the area—the East Bay, up and down the peninsula, and Marin County—citizens donated trees they grew in their backyards. In '37, Girod employed 350 gardeners; by '38, there were 1,200. Woodrow became one of their ardent admirers.

The planting of four thousand mature trees soon fascinated him. He watched as the packed black soil was leached of salt and then spread with good topsoil. Men dug holes, cranes lifted trees, gardeners shoveled soil into the holes and watered each new occupant. By and by, Woodrow learned that flowers of every variety would be propagated and planted according to their bloom time in an ever-changing palette to coordinate with the colors of the courts.

He found the number of bulbs alone staggering: 250,000 tulips, 20,000 irises, 20,000 begonias, and 10,000 hyacinths. The coup de grâce was the twenty-five acres of multicolored ice plant on both sides of the Elephant Court and throughout the island. Girod determined it alone could survive the force of wind and seawater on the west side of the island. Woodrow could not wait to see that sight. Girod described it as a "magic carpet"; Woodrow came to think of it as a Persian prayer rug. If only he could lie down on it to invoke the gods, his prayers would pour like honeyed wine.

One morning, unable to sleep, he arrived earlier than usual. As he stepped from his apartment, Telegraph Hill was cloaked in fog. Streets were wet with moisture, cable car tracks silent, light standards dimmed to golden orbs against the black sky. A taxi drove him over the Bay Bridge, onto

Yerba Buena, and down the Avenue of the Palms to the edge of the ice plants, glistening under the great expanse of night.

A few engineers on the island had devised a way to install a motor on a child's bicycle for his transport, for which he was grateful. He guessed they grew tired of watching him hobble around with mud and dirt up to his knees. And what a joyous mode of travel it was. He kept it tied inside one of the gardener's shacks. He hopped aboard but soon realized that, without a light to illuminate the ground, he would be foolish to ride too far. He carefully made his way onto California Avenue at the south end, closest to the Port of Trade Winds. Not a sound reached his ears, save the lapping of waves, the moan of foghorns, and an occasional horn blasting from a ship crossing the bay. Small boats rested in their berths along the dock.

The *Tatuta Maru* was anchored along the jetty, sleek and stately, dark except for marker lights port and starboard, fore and aft. He parked his bike and tucked into the Enchanted Garden, pulling his coat and scarf around him more tightly, and sat with his back against a low wall facing the Port of Trade Winds. The faint, herbaceous scent of Girod's plantings intermingled with the sea breeze, tickling his nose. He watched as Treasure Island, embellished with a wealth of greenery, prepared to awake to another day.

Over the water, he noticed the headlight of a small vessel approaching. As it drew closer, the faint *putt-putt* of the motor slowed and the craft slid up to the jetty. Woodrow pulled his knees into his chest and shrank down. The beam of a flashlight swept over the ground. Muffled voices carried from the deck. A figure jumped to the ground. The flashlight illuminated the face of the man, who had landed no more than a hundred feet from where Woodrow rested. He saw a cap pulled low on the man's forehead, binoculars around his neck, and suddenly the unmistakable profile of Tokido Okamura flared into view. Woodrow stopped breathing. Okamura quickly walked down the jetty, up the gangplank, and disappeared into the *Tatuta Maru.* The skiff pulled away. Woodrow didn't move a muscle until dawn crested the East Bay hills.

CHAPTER SEVEN

Lily

"Tell me," Lily asked Adolph Schuman, "why is Japan pulling out all the stops to build the most extravagant pavilion on Treasure Island?"

They were standing off to one side of the Grand Ballroom at the St. Francis Hotel mobbed with San Francisco's elite, swells and hacks, highbrows and politicos. Couples danced to Freddy Martin and His Orchestra, and waiters balanced trays of canapés as they wove through the crowd. Brisk air blew in through high transom windows. Adolph kept his arm protectively around Lily's bare shoulders as she sipped champagne from a crystal flute and shivered in a green satin gown.

"What do you think?" Adolph asked.

"I can't figure it out." Lily adjusted a diamond comb in her upswept hair. "They jumped at the chance to accept San Francisco's invitation. Their budget is one million dollars. That isn't chump change."

Adolph pursed his lips and nodded. "Propaganda, my dear. Clear and simple. They arrive bearing gifts of goodwill and heralding peace. Their pavilion will reflect ancient arts, pastoral and tranquil. Yet their modern society rejects Western ideals. There is no equality among its people—certainly not women, even if they present a feminized concept of beauty."

"You can say that again. I was banished from their building site. Their diplomatic envoy, Tokido Okamura, dressed me up one side and down the other because I dared to enter without him. He said it was for my safety. But I'm not so sure."

Adolph frowned. "Here, our Japanese American community lives in harmony. But in Japan, the people feed on a will of superiority. Their military has occupied Manchuria and Korea, and they're sweeping though China. They're conquerors. No doubt about it. The pavilion is smoke and mirrors."

Goose bumps rose on Lily's arms. "The newswires hum with news of Japan's aggression. Yet we dedicate a whole island to Pacific unity and continue to uphold isolationism. The conflict abroad feels like a world away. When will it end?"

"FDR isn't asleep," Adolph said, drawing Lily away from the revelers toward a secluded corner and lowering his voice. "He's got one eye on Hitler, who's rolled over Czechoslovakia, and another eye on Il Duce's fascist hammerlock in Italy. Vincent Astor is motoring on his yacht, the *Nourmahal*, cruising the South Pacific. Astor is reporting back to FDR on Japanese activity in the Marshall Islands."

Lily cocked her head and regarded Adolph with keen attention. "Tell me more."

"There are American people here and abroad who may learn information of vital importance to our country's safety." He paused, dipping his mouth to Lily's ear. "You may be one of those people."

"What do you mean?"

"Once all the pavilions are built, a reporter like you may come and go with impunity. You may be in a position to come across intelligence that's significant."

"Are you suggesting that I snoop?"

A smile creased his cheeks, but his eyes reflected a somber reality. "Hardly. Just keep your eyes and ears open. Let me know if you come across anything of interest, and I'll pass it on to the right people."

"Really, Adolph, you surprise me."

"But one caution: We've invited snakes into our backyard. We can't expect not to get bitten." He tapped his temple. "Watch yourself."

Just then, a radiant and bejeweled Lillian Schuman, nicknamed Bunny, approached through the throng. "Look at the two of you," she said, embracing them both. "Heads together and no doubt discussing world affairs."

Lily laughed and hugged Bunny back. "I feel like a new woman in your marvelous gown. I wouldn't have been able to come if you hadn't sent it. And the diamond comb. You shouldn't have!"

"Nonsense. We won't have you missing a night like this. Especially when we hardly see you anymore. My goodness, you're as rare as hen's teeth."

"I keep meaning to call."

"Every morning, I tell Adolph we'll read a story of yours in the paper, and, sure enough, you prove me right. I want to hear all your news, but first there are a few people you must meet." Bunny threaded her arm through Lily's arm and glanced at Adolph. "I'm stealing her from you."

"I would expect nothing less," he said, winking at his wife. "Did you invite her for Thanksgiving?"

"No, darling, but you just did!" Bunny patted Lily on the arm. "There—that's settled, so don't say a word."

The women glided along the edge of the polished parquet floor, past the sway of dancers doing the rumba. As they walked, Bunny snared a glass of champagne from a waiter and another for Lily.

"There's Ted Huggins, the PR wizard of Standard Oil, smack in the middle of the big wigs, paying homage to W. R. Next to him is Clyde Vanderberg, mastermind of the island's publicity machine. They're parading a long-legged dancer, Zoe Del Lantis, dressed in a pirate costume and a big smile, across the country to publicize the Expo. He's with your editor. Oh, look—Simon is nodding at you. They're smoking those ghastly cigars. Have you met Hearst yet? Well, you will. W. R. loves pretty women. There are two people in particular whom I want you to meet. Let's see. I saw Monsieur Reboul a moment ago."

"You mean the owner of the Pink Palace? Really, Bunny,

I'm perfectly happy on Ellis Street. Anyway, I'm hardly there except to sleep."

"Don't be ridiculous. You've been in that drab little walk-up too long. Monsieur's boardinghouse is ideal for the both of you. Oh dear—there's Leland Cutler's wife in a gaggle of women. She's perfectly fine, but she can talk my ear off. Don't look. Keep going."

Suddenly Bunny spotted a tall, distinguished gentleman and waltzed up to him. "Claude, I'm so happy to see you."

"*Bon soir,*" he said, kissing Bunny's outstretched hand.

"Allow me to introduce my dear friend Lily. I've been telling her about your residence. Your wife tells me that there may be a few openings."

"*Oui,* this is so. Are you anticipating a move, Miss Lily?"

"Not exactly, but Bunny can be very persuasive."

"Ah, this is true. If you're curious, perhaps the best thing is to visit. We're on Scott Street at Green. We think of ourselves as a family." Claude twinkled. "A French family, although everyone is welcome, especially if you like French food."

Lily's mouth began to water. *Perhaps I shouldn't be so rash,* she thought. "May I bring a friend who might want to be my roommate?"

"*Mais oui.* We have a nice, large room available soon. Perfect for two young ladies."

She thanked him and, despite her resistance, found herself warming to the idea. Monsieur Reboul gave her the name of the manager and suggested she visit on a Sunday.

Bunny triumphantly guided her away. "There. That's done.

Good. Now, let us find the most fascinating and unusual man I've met in a long time."

"Who?" Lily asked.

"You'll see."

"Why all the secrecy?"

"Be patient. Let's roam a bit more. He tends to hide from the crowd. We'll probably find him behind a palm."

As they rounded the corner and passed into an alcove, Bunny squeezed Lily's arm. There, seated against the wall, alone, looking downhearted, balancing his top hat on his leg and refusing a glass of champagne, was Woodrow Packard. His eyes registered their approach, and a faint smile—or was it a grimace?—parted his lips.

"Woodrow," Bunny said, swooping up to him. "I've been looking for you everywhere. Please, don't get up. We're dying to sit." Without hesitation, she drew two chairs forward, tucked aside her gown, and sat facing him. "I've been wanting to introduce you to the smartest young woman I know."

Woodrow gave Lily a look of sheepish recognition.

"Bunny, we've already met," Lily said.

"Why didn't you say so? Well, I should have known. Don't hover, dear. Please, sit down."

Woodrow looked from one woman to the other and, with an air of resignation, exclaimed, "Of course. Join me. Clearly, I'm the odd man out at an event like this."

"Well, I won't insist you spin me around the dance floor," Bunny said mischievously.

Lily blanched. Woodrow started, as if shot by a dart, and

then began to chuckle, sending Bunny into trills of laughter that rivaled musical scales.

"Lily tells me that she's tried to interview you but you're impossible to pin down."

Lily sighed. "Don't embarrass Woodrow. He's a busy man."

Woodrow shifted in his seat, his feet dangling above the floor. "Forgive me. My social skills are lacking."

"Believe me, Woodrow," Bunny said, "you're heads above most of these stuffed shirts in striped trousers."

That remark set them all to laughing again, until Bunny added, "Now that we've got that out of the way, tell us what you've been up to of late."

Woodrow cleared his throat. "I'm like a tourist on holiday."

"Whatever do you mean?"

"Poking around the island, uncovering this and that. It's in my blood."

"What have you found?" Lily asked.

"The foreign pavilions are of infinite variety," Woodrow said. "There's no end to their inventiveness."

Lily sat up straighter, another question on the tip of her tongue, when the conversation veered off course. Woodrow explained that although his design work had formally concluded, he had been asked to help draft some of the PR materials in the island brochures and booklets about the Mayan architectural motifs. "They've also suggested I sit in on some of the meetings with Jesse Stanton, the color architect, and A. F. Dickerson of General Electric as they finalize the night lighting. I think they're trying to keep me occupied. I'm happy to wander and watch the trees and gardens being planted."

"They're choosing nineteen colors drawn from a Pacific palette," Lily added. "Pagoda yellow, Hawaiian emerald green, Imperial Dragon red, Death Valley mauve—all exotic and alluring."

"We like more subtlety in some of the buildings," Woodrow explained.

"I agree. But, given the plans, subtlety may be sacrificed," Lily said. "Blue spotlights, pink fluorescent tubes, and ultraviolet black lights will be hidden in every shrub and in the creases of the Cambodian towers. Fountains will change color, stucco walls flecked with iridescent mica will shimmer, and statues will spring to life. Even Ralph Stackpole's undulating metal prayer curtain behind *Pacifica* will change from dark blue to apricot."

"I heard the budget is one and a half million dollars for night lighting alone," Bunny said. "Imagine! The Exposition corporation may be filled with fat cats, but none who ordinarily open their pockets to siphon off the cream. I smell financial disaster."

"World's fairs aren't meant to make money," Lily added. "Still, the mind boggles at the sums that are tossed around like flapjacks. The idea is, we'll lure fairgoers across the country to San Francisco. Have you seen the railroads that are offering special travel packages? The head office is working on this like crazy. They're speculating we'll entice New Yorkers away from their fair to ours."

"Another pipe dream," Bunny said.

"Whatever the outcome, the island will glow like a crown of jewels in the middle of the bay," Lily added.

Woodrow regarded Lily shyly. "From the windows in my apartment, I'm watching an ancient city rise from the sea."

"How wonderful. Where do you live?"

"On Telegraph Hill."

"That's perfect. The lighting will cast a path across the water to your doorstep."

Woodrow gazed at Lily, his eyes softening. "The truth is, I've become enamored of your city. It's starting to feel familiar."

"Listen to the two of you," Bunny said. "Romantics at heart. What I want to know is, was either of you listening to the radio the other night when *War of the Worlds* aired?"

"Some of the gals in our apartment went nuts," Lily said. "They ran up and down the hall, screaming about a martian invasion. They were listening to Charlie McCarthy on *The Chase and Sanborn Hour.* When programming switched to music, they spun the dial to *The Mercury Theatre.* Maxine and I were listening from the beginning. We knew the show was a drama. The gals thought it was real."

"What made it authentic," Bunny said, "and believe me, we knew it was Mischief Night, was the newscaster's voice announcing, 'We interrupt this program to bring you a special bulletin.' Then he became hysterical, like the newscaster when the *Hindenburg* crashed—those screams and moans and shrieks. Out of nowhere, the airwaves went dead. It curdled my blood."

"Pure poppycock," Woodrow said. "Green men slithering out of black holes in New Jersey? Fields bursting into flame and people choking on gas? An invading army from Mars? The country is already apprehensive about Hitler. We're all sitting on tenterhooks."

Absorbed in conversation, they didn't notice Timothy Pflueger as he strolled up. "Good evening, Woodrow, Miss Nordby, Bunny. You've sequestered yourselves in a cozy corner."

"Lovely to see you, Timothy," Bunny said.

"You as well. Say, Woodrow, nice to have you join us the other night at our poker game. You managed to fleece us handsomely."

"It was my pleasure."

"You owe us a chance to even the score."

"Don't be too sure of that," Woodrow said.

Pflueger looked at Lily. "Miss Nordby, may I speak to you privately?"

Lily felt a frown knit her brow. He offered his arm. She stood and nodded at Bunny and Woodrow. "Excuse me. I'll be right back."

He drew her aside, his hand resting lightly on the small of her back, several paces from the alcove. "I had a chance to speak to my aunt. Usually I don't see her very often, but she came to a family reunion. I told her I had met you."

Lily's throat went dry. The sounds of conviviality, tinkling glass, and laughter receded to a distant hum. "Why is that?"

Pflueger paused. "My aunt prides herself on knowing everyone. As a matter of fact, she remembers you as a child."

Lily's heart started to race, and she felt a pressure in her ears, as if the altitude had changed. She stared at Pflueger. His broad face and clear eyes broadcast a mixture of friendliness and concern.

"She knows your father."

"Really?"

"And she remembers your mother."

"My mother?"

"My aunt knew her."

"My mother is dead."

He spoke so quietly that Lily leaned closer. Pflueger's breath was moist on her cheek. "You should know that your mother is very much alive."

The floor descended, as if Lily were in an elevator crashing down a shaft. Pflueger's face seemed to melt. "I need some air," she said, reaching out blindly. She stumbled toward Bunny and Woodrow. The music and the chattering of voices dissolved. Darkness seeped into the edges of her vision with dizzying speed. Pflueger caught her before she slumped to the floor.

CHAPTER EIGHT

Tokido

By day, in the Japanese consulate on Post Street, phones jangled, official documents were stamped and dispatched in haste, and cables flew back and forth over the Teletype with the urgency of birds in a rainstorm. Now, in the hush of night, behind closed doors in the consul general's office, the shoji windows were latched against the darkness.

Tokido, dressed in a charcoal suit with black pinstripes, a white dress shirt, and a gray striped tie, composed himself upon a rosewood high-back chair drawn up to a black lacquered table. A blue-and-white porcelain teapot, two teacups, and a plate of rice cakes were placed in the center. A vapor of steam rose from the spout of the teapot.

He waited. Memories of home surfaced. He heard the tinkling of wind chimes and felt the snap of crisp, cold wind. He envisioned the ginkgo trees, stripped of yellow leaves, lining the quiet stone paths. The scent of pungent grilled fish and chicken yakitori sold from wooden carts filled his senses.

He imagined walking to his two-story wooden house through the maze of alleyways and hidden gardens in Yanaka, the only district in Tokyo that had survived the 1923 earthquake. His boys would be playing inside while his wife prepared dinner. Her presence, without fail, penetrated the stillness. A classic beauty—white skin, clear black eyes, crescent moon eyebrows, bow lips painted red—she never failed to stir him.

Without warning, the door clicked open and the consul general, Toshito Moto, hurried forward. Diminutive in size but potent in energy, he projected an air of imperturbability. Like a cat, he could jump one way or the other and land so swiftly that an opponent never saw the move coming.

Tokido stood and bowed low. "*Domo arigatou gozaimasu,*" he said.

Moto answered in kind and took the seat opposite Tokido. He cleared his throat. "My visit to the pavilion last week was most impressive." He opened a pack of cigarettes and offered one to Tokido. Leaning across the table, Tokido struck his lighter and lit the cigarette.

"I'm pleased you witnessed our progress," Tokido said. "The visions of the architects, Tatunae Toki and Yoshizo Utida, are springing to life."

"One seeing is better than one hundred tellings," Moto

said. "The architecture, grounds, and garden promise great refinement and beauty." As he spoke, he poured the tea, its roasted, grassy scent lacing the air. "Please," he said, nodding at Tokido's cup. "You are my guest."

Tokido lifted the delicate cup to his lips. "All preparations signal our readiness to open the pavilion on the same day as the opening of the Exposition."

Moto fastidiously bit into a rice cake and slid the plate across the table. "Excellent. We have slightly more than two months to complete our tasks."

"We will proceed with efficiency and purpose," Tokido said.

"Tonight there is an opulent ball at the St. Francis Hotel. Holiday festivities have begun." Moto raised his eyebrows. "Perhaps a sampling of Glenlivet is in order?"

"How appropriate," Tokido said.

Moto stood, walked to a tall *tansu,* and removed two crystal tumblers and a bottle. Returning to the desk, he sat and poured the whiskey neat into both glasses. Sitting back down, he offered one to Tokido.

"To our success," Tokido said, savoring the powerful, spicy mash, which went down hot in his throat.

Moto threw back a mouthful and appeared to relax. "All nations will be represented, though none as grand as ours." Across Moto's face flickered a grin so fleeting that Tokido wondered if the expression was from indigestion, rather than pleasure.

"Is it not agreeable to pause and anticipate opening day?"

"Most agreeable," Tokido responded.

"A parade will be conducted up Market Street to city hall. The Japanese American community is building a float that will be festooned with cherry blossoms, lanterns, and lights." Moto sat back, lacing his fingers together. "Geishas in traditional costume will dance on the deck. Marching alongside the float will be hundreds of schoolgirls dressed in kimonos and wearing hats woven with flowers. In the afternoon, dignitaries will lead the celebration at the pavilion."

"We are honored in many ways," Tokido agreed.

"*Hai.* Just as we have planned."

As they sipped the whiskey, smoke curled in lacy patterns above their heads.

Tokido wondered how long it would be before Moto arrived at the true reason why he had been summoned.

"I'm gratified that a blending of Oriental and Occidental styles will be displayed in the Tea Room," Tokido offered. "In the Silk Room, round-the-clock demonstrations of silk production will be conducted."

Moto sipped the whiskey, eyeing him intently while refilling the tumblers.

Tokido pressed on. "The furnishings will include Western carpets and armchairs alongside a *tokonoma,* a recessed alcove for display of ikebana and art objects and folding screens. A replica of a modern Japanese room behind a glass wall, inhabited by mannequins of a mother and her two daughters, will also be on display."

Moto snuffed a cigarette into an ashtray and smoothed his tie. "Let us speak freely."

"By all means," Tokido replied.

"Your surveillance of the bay is essential. We want you to continue that. Also, investigate the northern headlands at the mouth of the bay. There is increased chatter about powerful weapons in a new battery."

"*Hai.* I was briefed on this development."

Moto's eyes burned with fierce intensity. "Our primary emphasis in all we do is to promote favorable public opinion about our homeland."

"Exactly," Tokido said.

"At the pavilion, we are in a unique position to directly present the ancient arts and architectural beauty of Japan." Moto paused, sucking his teeth as if to dislodge a sesame seed. "However, we face caustic criticism about the China war." He lowered his voice. "You are aware that our consulates across the United States have engaged in a top-secret plan to employ American journalists?"

Tokido paused before answering. He looked directly at Moto without blinking. "I am."

"In San Francisco, we have some cooperation. Harry Cotkins, the foreign editor of the *San Francisco News,* has agreed to write favorably about Japan. However, the journalists from the three other papers could not be enlisted."

"I see," said Tokido. "What do you propose?"

"Use your influence to gain favor with other newspaper reporters, especially those who are covering the Exposition."

"As a matter of fact, I'm awaiting a more propitious moment to engage a reporter from the Hearst paper."

"Wait no longer," said Moto.

"You understand my reason?" Tokido asked.

"How far along is the Samurai House?"

"The work will be completed in a few days."

"Proceed quickly."

Tokido rose and bowed. "As you wish."

Moto bolted to his feet. The chair skidded out from behind him. The teacups rattled; the tumblers jumped. "Remember, Okamura-*san,* a mighty river is fed by many tributaries."

CHAPTER NINE

Woodrow

Woodrow couldn't take his eyes off Lily, even as Pflueger led her away. She was a charming creature, so fresh and unaffected, that he wondered why he hadn't noticed her attributes before that evening. *My rush to judgment is often a wretched gauge of human nature,* he thought. Suddenly he watched her sway, falling to the floor. In a flash, he was on his feet and running, with Bunny at his heels. Woodrow skidded to his knees beside Lily, nearly knocking Pflueger down.

Lily lay as still as a sleeping child, her gown fanned out and crumpled underneath her. His fingers probed her neck, finding a pulse, slow and steady. With his body, he shielded her from people who were streaming by, their eyes curious and probing.

"What in the hell happened?" Woodrow demanded.

"Bit of bad news, old man," Pflueger explained, leaning over and fanning her face with his handkerchief. "I'm genuinely sorry. Didn't know she'd take it so badly."

Bunny had dropped on the other side of Lily and stared up accusingly at Pflueger. "Whatever you said, I could wring your neck."

"What can I do?" he said helplessly. "Shall I call the hotel doctor?"

"No, for God's sake. Be useful. Find some water," Bunny ordered, stroking Lily's brow.

Pflueger dashed off, muttering to himself.

"She's out cold," Woodrow said, cradling Lily's head in his lap.

"I've got just the thing," Bunny said, withdrawing a small square of lace from her bodice and passing it under Lily's nose. "Lily, Lily, dear, wake up. Wake up."

As Woodrow held Lily gently, the floral scent of Joy, which his sisters had worn, wafted by his face, bringing with it a rush of memories. Then, all at once, Lily's eyes popped open. She peered up at Woodrow and then at Bunny as if she were awakening from a dream.

"Lie still," said Bunny. "Whatever Timothy Pflueger said, you dropped like a stone."

"No, no, I'm all right. It was nothing. Too much champagne on an empty stomach. Please don't make a fuss."

Adolph appeared, clutching a glass of water, while Pflueger stood sheepishly behind him. "Golly, kid," Adolph said, "you had us worried. Here. Drink this."

Woodrow propped her up, and she gulped down a few swallows. "Woodrow, would you help me up?"

He took her hands and pulled her to her feet. Adolph steadied her as she rearranged her gown, and Bunny hurried back to the seat and grabbed her silver fox jacket. She immediately returned and draped the fur around Lily's shoulders.

"Darling, I wish we could take care of you. But we're expecting a mob for a soiree we're hosting. The whirl of holiday parties has already begun." She stood close, her arm wrapped around Lily's waist. "Timothy will get you a taxi. It's the least he can do."

"Of course," Timothy said, slinking away. "Straightaway!"

Woodrow spoke up. "I'll take Lily home."

"Would you, dear?" Bunny asked.

"It's my pleasure."

"I'll take care of myself," Lily said. "Really. This is so embarrassing."

"That's ridiculous, Lily. You look like you've seen a ghost. I won't allow it."

"Nor will I," said Adolph.

Woodrow stepped between the three of them and announced. "Take my hand, Lily. I'll see you home."

They left Bunny and Adolph waving at their departing figures. He ushered Lily through the partygoers and under the chandeliers, amid the frenetic rhythm of the orchestra and dancers twirling in arcing circles, out into the carpeted hall, down the elevator into the lobby, and out onto the street. It was pulsing with lights and pedestrians, the whoosh of traffic and blare of horns. Pflueger was nowhere to be seen. The doorman hailed a Checker cab, and in seconds they were inside the sanctuary of the car. The cabbie flicked down the ticker, pushed back his hat, and asked over his shoulder, "Where to, mister?"

"What's your address, Lily?"

"I don't want to go home."

Woodrow squinted at her. "You don't want to go home?"

"Not tonight."

"Where shall we go?"

She bit her lip, and her fingers worried the skin between her eyebrows. "Your apartment?"

Woodrow startled. He shook his head, as if to clear it and adjusted his tie. It was then that he remembered his hat. *Forget it,* he thought. *A damn nuisance anyway.* In a clear voice, he ordered, "Telegraph Hill. Filbert Street steps, right under Coit Tower."

In minutes the cabbie whisked them across town and wound up the twisted, dark road, past houses and adjoining lots overgrown with blackberry vines, low-hanging trees, and ivy, to the top of the hill. Woodrow paid the fare while Lily waited. The gray majesty of Coit Tower rose against the misty sky. Wide stairs were built into the steep hillside. It appeared as if a giant's hand had flung cottages and houses in glee down the embankment. November's mild temperatures had encouraged a mélange of morning glories and nasturtiums, which wove through the trees overhead. Leaves glistened, dripping fog.

"Watch your step," Woodrow said, leading the way.

Electric lights tucked into shrubbery and stone niches illuminated the stairs to his front door.

She followed him into a woodland, damp and fragrant with greenery, tender shoots, and birds' nests. Furry creatures skittered and chirped in the undergrowth. Ferns draped over the stairs, their fronds reaching out to brush her ankles.

Soon he turned onto a narrow path and stopped in front of a high wood door intricately carved with birds. He fished in his pocket and pulled out a key. The door fell open. A flight of narrow stairs led upward. The treads complained under the weight of their feet. Burnished light glowed on wood paneling. The scent of pipe tobacco, smoke, and something sweet, like the sandalwood of sea captains' chests, laced the air.

At the top of the stairs, a room distinguished by diminutive appointments opened into yet smaller nooks. All the furniture was scaled smaller than usual. Threadbare Oriental rugs were scattered over worn floorboards. Bookshelves lined one wall. A miniature fireplace embellished with a marble surround and mantel stood against another wall.

"Make yourself comfortable," Woodrow said, nodding toward a worn, lumpy couch of indeterminate color and a tufted leather club chair near a leaded window that was black, save lights twinkling over rooftops all the way to the bay and the dim but unmistakable shape of Treasure Island. Had he known a woman would be visiting him tonight, he would have done a little housekeeping—at the very least, straightening the pile of books that lay scattered around his chair. But it was too late, much too late, to do a thing. "Take the chair or, if you like, the couch. I'll make a fire."

Wordlessly, she chose the couch and settled into its deep folds. Slipping her arms out of the sleeves of the jacket, she draped it over her body. Woodrow dropped to one knee to build a tepee of kindling and logs on the grate. The improbability of this moment made his blood race. By God, she was a beautiful woman, and a woman who had had a shock. He was glad to lend some assistance. There was nothing thus far to suggest that she looked upon him as deformed. But surely she would. How could she not?

Carefully, he chose the wood from a copper bin nearby. When he struck a match to the kindling, embers crackled and spit, until soon, in a pyrotechnic display, the logs burst into flame. "Now," he said, standing and dusting off his hands, "the fire will warm us in no time. What may I get you? I'm afraid there's not much to offer. I do have tea."

"Tea?" she asked.

He regarded her apologetically.

"Do you have anything stronger?"

"I have Armagnac."

"Is that like cognac?"

"Better by far."

He disappeared around a corner and soon reappeared, holding two snifters. He swirled the amber-colored brandy before passing one to Lily. She accepted it with a sigh. He poked at the fire, put two more logs on the top, and, stepping first onto a footstool, climbed into the club chair beside the couch.

"To you," he said, raising his glass. The silky, fruit-infused taste hit the back of his throat and warmed a smooth passage into his stomach. Perhaps now he could relax.

"And to you," she said, tasting the brandy. "Mmm—delicious." She sank farther back into the cushions. "I feel like I'm in a hobbit's house." She blanched. "No offense meant."

"No offense taken. I'm a great fan of Tolkien's."

"Yes, I see that," she said, nodding toward his side table, where a copy of *The Hobbit* sat. "I, too, have the book in easy reach." She sighed in wonder. "My one-room apartment is frightfully dull compared with this house. Bunny is trying to induce me to move to a French boardinghouse. Perhaps I should take her up on it." She pointed at the ivy that had raucously broken through the seams of the wood battens and attached its tendrils to the walls. "Nature is claiming her right. How in the world did you find this place?"

"A friend from the Carnegie Institute knew the woman who built this cottage. She was a landscape architect at Golden Gate Park. Luckily for me, she was unusually small and, as you can see, designed everything to fit her size. I believe she was no taller than four feet. Even I can reach the kitchen counters. Not that cooking is my strong suit." He smiled, stuck his nose into the bowl of the glass, and inhaled. "I haven't done a thing to change it. I like it just as it is."

"Even the ivy growing through the walls?"

"That, too." He chuckled. "While it's true that there are many significant reasons for living in San Francisco, the least of them is this cottage." He motioned to the bookshelves. "After a splendid day at Treasure Island, in this chair, with my library, I can go anywhere and still feel perfectly at home.

Next to living in a hacienda on the outskirts of Chichén Itzá, where I spent many fine hours with colleagues, I haven't been happier anywhere else."

"I've wondered about your work there. I have so many questions."

He regarded her quizzically. "What do you know?"

"None of this is God's truth, mind you." She sat up a little straighter, stroking the nap of the fur jacket on her lap. "Only what I've been able to dig up."

"Go on."

"For starters, in '25, Earl Morris, the field director for Carnegie, invited you to join the staff to investigate the main temple. Earlier, you had developed a brilliant skill for deciphering the ruins at Persepolis. Your interest in glyphs bordered on obsession. Word got around that you had your eye on the research being done at Chichén Itzá. That, and a reputation for geniality among archeologists and scholars, offered a winning combination for Morris to take you on."

He pursed his lips and smiled. "Aren't you the sleuth?"

"What's a newspaperwoman to do when a subject is evading her every attempt to give her a story?"

Woodrow blushed. *Is she flirting with me?*

"You were a great success," she continued. "After the discovery of the Temple of the Warriors and its principal altar area, you assisted in copying and translating the sculpted reliefs and murals of the inner chambers." She stopped. "Am I sounding too academic?"

"Not at all."

"By '31, you had contributed significantly to the body of

work in the publication *The Temple of the Warriors at Chichén Itzá, Yucatán,* copublished by Ann Morris and the artist Jean Chariot. This achievement sealed your authority and world-wide acclaim."

"You make it sound so grand," he said.

"Wasn't it?"

"Well, yes and no. Actually, it was bloody hard work, intolerably hot and bug infested. But I loved it."

"Tell me what you loved," she asked. "What was it really like?"

"Are those things diametrically opposed? I suppose not." He shook his head.

"Please. Go ahead and indulge me."

"I'd awake to the smell of mold in the pillow under my head. When there wasn't a moon, I couldn't see my hand in front of my face. The rain coursing down through leafy canopies obliterates every sound. I'd stumble to the cottage window to try to catch the yellow glow of a jaguar's eyes in the undergrowth, which of course I never did. They're far smarter than to come around human activity. Then I'd light the kerosene lamp and struggle into my clothes, damp as a dishrag wrung out by a scullery maid."

"Did you wear a pith helmet, like Sylvanus Morley?" she asked.

"Gracious, no," he guffawed. "Surely an affectation. Most of us wore wide-brimmed canvas hats. The sun can scorch you to blisters. My canvas pants were as stiff as sails, and leather boots up to my knees. Scorpions and snakes, you know. I'd set out for a brisk walk along the slick cottage paths well before dawn. By then the cicadas were chattering like a band of mariachis. Never would I tire of the pale sight of the great cream-and-pink limestone walls rising thirty feet to timbered ceilings, the arched passageways, and the splendid expanse of red-tiled balconies. The roosters were crowing, and the Mayan cooks were setting out pots of rich, fragrant coffee and platters of eggs, mango, papaya, and tortillas, served on the veranda. We feasted like ravenous dogs. Then it was time to pack our tools, mount the horses, and hack our way through the jungle, to return to our work in the ruins."

She sighed longingly, "I suppose I'll never travel there."

"It is a long journey and hardly civilized for a lady like you."

"Is that so? You must think I'm made of glass."

"And if I do?"

"Then I'll have to show you otherwise." She paused, as if to concoct a way in which she was made of heartier stuff than Woodrow presumed. "One of the things I love about the Expo is the vast number of foreign pavilions going up. So many nations will be represented that it may feel a bit like an adventure. I'm especially intrigued by the Japanese Pavilion."

"Why is that?"

"Possibly because our Chinatown and Japantown, although less dense, are the strangest places I ever visited. Live birds squealing in cages, carcasses swinging from hooks, bent old men and women in costume, the scent of sandalwood incense, tiny pink plastic dolls that urinate into the air when you squeeze their bodies. Forbidden and at the same time exotic. By the way, do you know Tokido Okamura, Japan's diplomatic envoy?"

"No, not personally. Why do you ask?"

"He ordered me off the site when I tried to have a look around. I found him arrogant and insufferable."

"I'm sure there are far more interesting people to pursue," Woodrow hastily suggested. *If only she knew what I know,* he thought.

"There's something fishy about him that I can't shake. Anyway, how will Japan favorably present its culture when it's ransacking China? I wasn't surprised when China declined to build a pavilion. But now that the Chinese community here has taken over that task, there may be fireworks."

"All the fireworks will be in the sky. None of our Asian friends will want to lose face."

"You're right. Well, now that we've gotten to know each other a bit, I hope you'll allow me to write a story about you."

"Perhaps. Let's save that topic for another time."

She swirled and sipped the brandy. Silence settled around them. "I had a shock tonight."

"Obviously. Not good news?"

She shrugged. "I'm not sure I want to talk about it."

"Of course. Whatever you wish." Stepping first onto the stool, he extracted himself from the chair, stoked the fire, and returned. Shadows danced on the ceiling. They sat quietly, as if sealed in a cocoon.

"It's just so unexpected, the furthest thing from my mind. Earlier, you and I and Bunny had been laughing about the preposterous notion that green aliens from Mars could have landed in New Jersey."

He sat quietly, not laughing, watching her face.

"Have you ever been told that someone you thought was dead . . . is alive?"

He shook his head. "No, never."

She swallowed the last of the brandy.

"Someone in your family?" He shifted slightly in the chair, continuing to hold her gaze, her eyes revealing a vulnerability that he hadn't seen before.

"My mother." The soft, sibilant sounds of those two words spilled from her lips. "I only remember living with my father. Well, that's not exactly true. He put me in an orphanage. The smell of Pine-Sol to this day makes me ill." She shuddered, passing her hand over her eyes. "Then a foster family wanted to adopt me. I was about two and a half, or maybe three. Apparently, that's when my father's paternal instincts kicked in. He brought me home to Guerrero Street. Back then, it was just the two of us. Aunt Jenny, who eventually told me about this, lived down the street. She was kind and soft and smelled like cinnamon. I would sit on her lap and stroke her arms, and we'd make cookies. She always wore an apron imprinted with tiny red and green apples. The wallpaper in her living room was a pattern of pink roses tied with a green ribbon. She was the one woman I learned to trust, and when she passed away, I had no one."

His brow knit with concern. "And your mother? You never knew her?"

"I have one memory. I saw her at the end of the hall in a fur coat that stopped above her ankles. The glow from a bare lightbulb hanging from the ceiling cast a halo around her dark hair. I'm not sure if we were at Aunt Jenny's or Pa's house. Her high heels tapped on the floor as she came toward me. Overcome with shyness, I could only look at the floorboards until her shoes came into view. She placed her hand on my head and stroked my hair. The aroma of something sweet, like gardenias, hovered around her. When she said, 'Lily,' I looked up into her face. She was more lovely than anyone I had ever seen."

"And?"

Her eyes glistened in the firelight. "That's all. I don't remember anything else. I'm not sure who told me she died or if I made it up. Children have their own way of making sense of a world they don't understand."

He let the minutes pass between them, not because he didn't know how to respond, but rather because he wanted his words to give her comfort. When he finally spoke, his voice was low. "I have a bit of experience in that realm, too, although not the loss you've suffered. I can't imagine how difficult it was for you to grow up without a kind and loving mother or a father who protected you. The blows I endured came well after childhood."

Silence enveloped them; the only sound came from the fire, which had burned to embers. She looked at him with such tenderness that he held his breath. "Oh, Woodrow," she said, her voice trailing off, "we've both known hardship." A wan smile glanced her lips and faded; her eyelids drooped. The glass in her hand loosened, her head rested back on the cushions, and her eyes fluttered shut.

He wanted to hold her, to stroke her cheek. He wanted to offer her a secure landing ahead, as if there were refuge beyond the profound sadness that she had endured. If her mother was alive, why hadn't she taken Lily with her? What possible reason could she have had to abandon her? How could she have left her in the care of a father who had no decency in his heart? He was sure if he moved a fraction of an inch, the moment would be lost. He waited until her breathing was rhythmic, and when he was certain that sleep had claimed her, he slid off the chair and, one by one, slowly removed her shoes. Lifting a blanket from the edge of the sofa, he laid it over her legs, took the glass, and climbed back in the chair, and he, too, closed his eyes.

CHAPTER TEN

Lily

Lily filed a story about Treasure Island's Musée Mécanique and traded shoptalk with Dudley, checked in to say hello to Gladys, and evaded Mac's daily attempt to pinch her backside before she ducked out early. On Market Street, she boarded a swaying streetcar occupied with weary passengers bundled in overcoats. They snoozed, chatted, or rested in upright seats in stony silence, as if grateful for a respite from the day's duties.

She found a seat next to a gentleman who was reading the *Examiner*. His cheeks were smooth, and he exuded a faint scent of lemony aftershave mixed with the sharp smell of newsprint ink. The paper was folded lengthwise to a single column. She glanced sideways. He was reading her story "Exposition Artisans Like Their Jobs—Building Dreams." The stranger tipped his chin and smiled. She smiled back.

"Great coverage on TI," he said. "A carpenter in this story talks about building a never-never land. He says in order to bolt the last panel into the top of the Tower of the Sun, his buddies had to lower him head down by his heels. Think of that!"

"You looking forward to the opening?" she asked.

"You bet. Who isn't?"

"They're working like gangbusters to finish. It will be spectacular."

"You sound like you know what you're talking about."

She smiled again and stood, gripping the handrail and stepping into the aisle. "My stop is next."

"Nice to chat," he said.

"See you at the Expo!" she called.

Standing on the streetcar island as traffic sped by, she paused, waiting for the light to change. When it turned green, she hurried up Grove Street to the Office of Births and Deaths in City Hall. In front of a Dutch door with a small ledge, she paid fifty cents to a poker-faced clerk who didn't make eye contact.

As the minutes ticked on in the drab hallway, she paced, her shoes echoing off the polished floors. Finally, she pulled off her gloves, chewing her cuticles until they stung, and, in disgust, drew her gloves back on.

Mercifully, the clerk reappeared. "Here you go, Miss." He held out a sheet of onion paper. She stepped up to the window and hesitated. "Do you want it or not? I haven't got all day."

Wordlessly, she took it.

Outside on the street, clouds rolled by, casting shadows over the sidewalk and onto the flimsy page that she held in her hands. She tried to focus her disbelieving eyes.

PLACE OF BIRTH
City and County of San Francisco
Lane Hospital

FULL NAME OF CHILD: Lily Claire Nordby

SEX OF CHILD	LEGITIMATE	DATE OF BIRTH
Female	Yes	September 7, 1913

FATHER	MOTHER
FULL NAME: Christopher Nordby	Sadie Friedlander
RESIDENCE: 2865 Folsom Street	2865 Folsom Street
COLOR OR RACE: White	White
AGE: 25	17
BIRTHPLACE: California	Lithuania
OCCUPATION: Plumber	Housewife

Her eyes fastened on her mother's name and equally on her birthplace. Sadie Friedlander. Born in Lithuania. How could this be? Until this moment, Lily had not once heard her mother's maiden name or birthplace spoken.

No matter how many times she repeated "Sadie Friedlander" to herself—sometimes just "Sadie," other times in conjunction with "Friedlander"—it was like hearing a foreign language. What ethnicity was she? Was Sadie a nickname for

Sarah? Had she landed on Ellis Island, and how in the world had she gotten to California? Had her parents brought her here? Why would she have married a man eight years older than she was—a man like Lily's father, blunted by drink, grease under his thick fingernails, and a booming laugh that assaulted the ears?

Urgency rose up in Lily and gathered momentum. There was no choice. She had to see the house on Folsom Street for herself. She ran for the bus.

* * *

NOTHING ABOUT THE broad-shouldered Victorian, adorned with handsome bay windows and rising three stories from the street, or the bold numbers 2865 emblazoned in gold on the transom above the high door, suggested her father's hovel on Guerrero Street, where Lily had spent her girlhood. This residence suggested respectability, refinement, class, and culture. How could her father have fallen from such lofty heights? She wasn't sure she wanted to know. What she wanted, what she needed, was to find her mother. The last person she'd ask was Chris Nordby. She wouldn't put herself in his line of fire. He'd make demands, ride her like one of his miserable, cowering dogs. The only warm-blooded creature he cared about was his parrot, Loretta, whom he paraded around on his shoulder. As for Timothy Pflueger or his aunt, she'd sooner dance naked at the Burlesque Follies than ask for their help. And she wasn't sure she wanted to ask anyone, not even Maxine or the Schumans, for advice. It was enough that, only days earlier, she had confessed to Woodrow the disgrace of her family and the shame she carried.

Or she could walk away now, she reasoned, but instantly knew she could not. She walked across the street, stopped at the foot of the stairs that led to the front door of 2865, and looked up into the windows, hung in Irish lace, silent and chaste.

At the top of the stairs, she rang the brass bell: *zing-zing.* Its tinny echo faded. Frozen in anticipation, she rang again. Every muscle was tuned to the ragged hope that someone would come to the door. Someone who could tell her anything about her mother. Inexplicably, she recalled the forty-four-bell carillon, imported from Britain, that had been installed in the Tower of the Sun. She was in the crowd when it was first tested. Everyone stopped in his or her tracks, heads titled backward, mouths agape. The sound rendered a celestial chorus that split the blue sky, bursting all hearts in gladness.

Here on the step, the air was dead. She pressed her nose to the cold glass of the door. Steps carpeted in scuffed, rose-patterned wool led upward. She turned and touched the cool metal mailbox affixed to the wall. The little frame that was suitable for a name card on the face of the empty mailbox was blank.

She glanced up and down the street. A beat policeman strolled by and tipped his hat. Children rode by on bicycles, hooting and calling to one another. Women, smiling and chatting in twos and threes, hurried along, cloth bags hanging off their arms. One maroon Studebaker rolled by.

On the opposite side of the block, at the corner of Twenty-Fifth Street, a black-and-white-striped awning, imprinted with block letters, read HERMAN'S MARKET. Wooden crates of red and green apples stacked under the plate glass windows marked the entry. She crossed the street, opened the door, and walked in. A bell tinkled in greeting.

At first she didn't see anyone. The store was immaculate: a wooden floor swept clean; vegetables neatly bundled in a crisper along one wall; a glass meat-and-poultry case stocked with a meager but neatly arranged selection of raw chicken parts, stew beef, cutlets, and fish fillets. Along one aisle, Lily noticed the shelves were lined with tins of Hills Bros. coffee and Carnation canned milk, boxes of Bisquick, Quaker Oats, Jell-O, and jars of Beech-Nut baby food.

Just then a little man, wire-rimmed eyeglasses perched on the brim of his nose, appeared from a side aisle. A fringe of frizzled gray hair ringed his bald head. As he hobbled toward her, he wiped his hands on the tails of a stained white apron stretched over his belly.

"Hello," he said. "May I help you?" Traces of an Eastern European accent thickened his speech.

"I hope so," Lily answered. "Have you been here long?"

"Many years, my dear."

"Then you must know the people in the neighborhood."

He squinted at her. "They're my customers, my regulars. I know them all. Are you new here?"

"Not exactly." She offered her hand. "I'm Lily Nordby."

He took her hand in both of his. "Nice to meet you. Herman Oronoffski." He pushed his glasses back up his nose, and squinted at her. "By chance, are you related to the plumber Chris Nordby?"

"Yes. He's my father." A slow blush rose from her collarbone and spread up her throat and into her cheeks. "But I'm not here because of him."

"Ah, well, I see his truck in the neighborhood. He comes and he goes. Sometimes he stops in here for one of my pastrami sandwiches."

"Did you know him when he lived across the street at 2865?" She turned and pointed out the window. "He lived there with my mother in 1913. Do you remember her?"

Herman's black eyes, set into a face crisscrossed with a map of wrinkles, bore into her own.

A shopper rolled a shopping cart down the aisle, pushed the cart up to the narrow wooden counter, and began placing items on the countertop.

"Hello, Maud," Herman said. "I'll be right with you. Excuse me," he said to Lily, touching her arm gently. "This won't take long."

"I'll wait."

"One moment, dear. Now, don't go away."

Lily stepped back and tried to collect herself. Was it folly to think that she was a breath away from some kind of knowledge about her mother from this kind old man?

Painstakingly, Herman rang up each item, filled a straw basket with the purchases, counted out the change in coins, and led the customer to the door.

He stutter-stepped back to Lily, removed his glasses, and dabbed his eyes and the corners of his mouth, filled with ruinous teeth. "Let's see. Where were we? Ah, yes, your mother. Sadie," he said softly. "She was born in Vilnius, the capital of Lithuania, like me."

Lily felt an electrical current shoot from the soles of her feet, up her legs, through her body, to the roots of her hair.

His face became pliant, the wrinkles of his deflated cheeks smoothing, a sweet smile lifting his careworn features. "I remember you as a baby. You look just like her. She'd roam the aisles, singing, with you in her arms—waltzes, folk songs, love songs to break your heart. A voice like an angel's."

Involuntarily, Lily touched her cheek.

"You see, she came in every day. I knew her well—at least, as much as a grocer can know his clientele. Let's say I knew what she liked. Always making stews. She'd bring me halvah, a sweet white concoction made of sesame butter and honey."

"Was she Catholic?" Lily managed to ask.

"Heavens, no. She was a Jew, like me."

The specter of pogroms struck Lily's soul. Only weeks before, the newswires had been filled with horrific stories of Kristallnacht, the Nazi attack on Jews in Germany and Austria. She was suspended between an ancient past and an uncertain future. Everything she knew as solid and real was collapsing. Since her mother was a Jew, that made her a Jew. What did this mean? Her lips refused to move. Perspiration drenched her blouse, and her runaway pulse thudded in her ears.

Herman dragged a chair from behind the counter. "Sit down," he said. "You look unwell."

She waved him back. "No, I'm all right. Give me a minute."

"Please, dear. I've upset you."

"No, no, not at all." She reached out and squeezed his frail arm. "You've been so helpful." She leaned over and kissed his bony cheek. "I need to go now, but I'll be back. I promise."

CHAPTER ELEVEN

Tokido

As was his custom, Tokido stole a moment of solitude in the gray light of dawn. He was chilled to the core, taut nerves humming from lack of sleep. The imperative to draw strength from words written 250 years earlier drew him irresistibly, like a beacon. He reached for Basho's *Journal of Bleached Bones in a Field* and, thumbing through the pages, read:

> dew trickles down
> in it I would try to wash away
> the dust of a floating world

These words, written when Basho began a journey on foot from Edo to roam westward nearly eight hundred miles and circle back a year later, touched Tokido's heart and soothed his restless spirit. His clothes lay on the floor of the bath, still damp and stiff, saturated by salt spray. The opportunity to record the previous day's activities would have to be delayed. He had dressed hurriedly and barely had enough time to compose himself before the day began. His morning meal, set beside him on the table, was untouched, except for a steaming cup of tea, which he cradled in his hands and sipped slowly.

The endless night had been arduous. The skiff, signaling three long and one short blasts of light, had swept alongside the *Tatuta Maru* at exactly 2:00 a.m. on November's turbulent seas. Tokido boarded swiftly and took his station alongside the nameless pilot. In the faint reflection of stars, Tokido could easily see that he was of mixed Japanese and Caucasian blood.

They crouched in the stern, binoculars hung around their necks, poised to hoist the lenses to their eyes, and sped off. Tokido was often unsure what direction they were headed until the pilot navigated a course communicated through guttural commands. He read the contours of the vast San Francisco Bay, its tides, channels, and shoreline, like a hound tracks the scent of its prey. Here, the prey wasn't a warm-blooded animal. It was the steel silhouettes of military transports, submarines, and destroyers. Tokido was schooled in the different types of ships, their shapes and gun sizes. The pilot was schooled in where to find them along the waterfront: the military bases at Fort Mason, Hunters Point, Mare Island, and the Benicia Arsenal.

The pilot steadied the skiff as close to the massive prey as was safe and idled the motor. He spotted and Tokido recorded the type and number of each ship. Often they would observe a military transport setting out under the Golden Gate, lights flashing, carving a curl of white foam in its wake. At the close of the hunt, when Tokido was dropped off at the *Tatuta Maru,* the pilot departed in the skiff, carrying the intelligence, dubbed Blind Warrior, in a pouch strapped to his back.

* * *

THE MORNING LIGHT had turned brighter. Tokido stood, placed Basho's book on the table, and left the cabin. Kiyoshi was waiting for him in the library. They would review the names of members of the press who had responded to the invitation to preview the pavilion later that morning. The list of those who had been invited had been culled from confidential sources, which had identified journalists and newspaper reporters sympathetic to Japan's quest in the Far East and opposed to America's entry in the Sino-Pacific war. Tokido had studied their credentials and read their articles. Most important, he had Consul General Moto's assurance that the majority would favorably present the wonder and excellence of the pavilion. Of course, they had also invited members of the local press who did not fit into this category—the "lightweights," as Tokido had come to think of them. Their inclusion was unavoidable. They wrote feature stories about social issues of the day or popular figures in the news.

He would curry their favor as required and avoid any further unpleasantness, especially with the brazen female reporter who worked for the Hearst paper.

When Tokido entered, Kiyoshi leaped to attention. His back was as straight as bamboo, his eyes clear, a sheaf of papers at the ready, pencil sharpened to a point like the tip of a dagger.

"Let us quickly review who we can expect today," Tokido instructed. "The group will be gathering, and we must arrive well in advance of their arrival."

"Of course," Kiyoshi replied.

He read from a list of names, of which Tokido nodded approval. At the conclusion, he confirmed that hostesses at the pavilion were in the process of preparing tea, which they would serve, and would then be available to act as guides for the remainder of the tour.

"*Hai*," said Tokido. "Stay by my side today." He slipped his arms into a jacket and tied a silk scarf around his neck. "As a precaution, I have also spoken with Chizu, our most trusted senior hostess, whom I have instructed to attend to any reporters who stray or need attending. We can never be too careful."

"As you wish," Kiyoshi said, dashing behind Tokido, whose voice trailed off as he rushed forward into November's biting grip.

* * *

FIFTEEN JOURNALISTS AND reporters had gathered at the entrance to the pavilion, bundled against the cold, hats pulled low over their eyes, coats buttoned to their chins, and scarves knotted around their necks. Mercifully, it was not sleeting rain but the blustery wind that tore tears from their eyes and kicked up dust devils at their feet. All across the island, the din of heavy machinery, the flurry of trucks crisscrossing the roads, and the frenzy of workers engaged in a Herculean effort to meet final construction deadlines was reaching a crescendo.

Schedules were crucial; any delay or error could prove catastrophic. Yet an air of calm emanated over the pavilion's site. When Tokido opened the pavilion's center doors precisely at 9:00 a.m., the reporters stamped their cigarettes under the soles of their shoes and pressed forward.

"Welcome," Tokido nearly shouted. "Please enter. We're serving tea in the Tea Room. Our hostesses will lead you there."

In the group that streamed past, he recognized several faces from photographs and prior events. Prominent among them was David Warren Ryder, an attorney and columnist for the conservative quarterly *Controversy*, and Henry Cotkins, foreign editor of the *San Francisco News*. He studied their expressions and shook their hands. He was somewhat startled to see Ralph Townsend, a far-right author and prominent advocate of nonintervention in the Far East. His best-selling book, *Ways That Are Dark: The Truth About China*, openly supported Imperial Japan's position of domination. Tokido instantly understood that the consulate had employed persuasive efforts to secure Townsend's appearance.

"Good to see you," he said to Townsend, pausing and bowing slightly, before turning to the next person.

A small, leather-gloved hand was proffered, and when he looked up, he was peering into the face of Lily Nordby. He grasped her hand, and she returned the pressure equally.

"Good morning," she said coolly.

He was prepared to comment that he was pleased she had come, but she whisked by. He watched her depart, the hem of her long coat snapping against the backs of black boots, and a pheasant feather tucked into the brim of her hat, which bobbed above the crowd.

Behind Lily, the young waterfront reporter for the *San Francisco News,* Katherine Meyer, stepped forward. He quickly mentioned to her his interest in labor relations with dock-workers and unions. She peered closely at him and admitted surprise. "Contact me, if you like," she suggested. "I'm always in the office." As the last reporter streamed past, Tokido entered the pavilion and nodded to Kiyoshi, who closed the high wooden doors.

In the long and elegantly appointed tearoom that adjoined a veranda looking out to a garden under construction, Tokido mingled among the guests seated at Western-style tables and chairs, drinking steamy green tea. The shoji-shuttered windows cast a soft, natural glow upon the gathering. Red tassels dangled from paper lanterns, grassy-scented tatami mats covered the floor, and lovely, kimono-clad hostesses moved with ease between the tables. When he was satisfied that everyone was served, he began to speak.

"Welcome to the Japanese Pavilion. The displays within

these walls are not yet finished, and we ask for your patience now to imagine what is to come but is not yet installed. Rare art pieces, national treasures, and technological advancements will be represented." The words rolled off his tongue effortlessly. "It is our wish to show the beauty and modernity of our country to enhance the significance of the Golden Gate International Exposition. We are honoring this occasion to join with all voices that declare San Francisco is truly the gateway to the Pacific." He was attuned to any discord that might descend without warning, especially in the midst of newspaper reporters whose probing eyes were hungry for a breaking story.

"My assistant, Kiyoshi, has prepared a press packet for each of you," he continued.

Kiyoshi stepped from behind Tokido and began to distribute gold-embossed folders into the hands of reporters.

"Today we have asked that no photos be taken because of the unfinished nature of the rooms. Instead, we're providing photographs for reproduction, should your papers wish to publish them." Tokido's gaze swept over the room. His eyes met Lily's as she appraised him openly. She was seated at a table near the rear windows with Miss Meyer and two other women. "If you have any questions, I'm at your disposal."

A hand shot up from the same table. A tall woman in a wide-shouldered coat and tortoiseshell glasses stood. "Florence Higgins, staff reporter at the *Chronicle*," she said. "Your efforts are impressive. There is no doubt that your pavilion will be a standout among other foreign pavilions. It certainly has cost a fortune to construct. The Chinese nation has withdrawn its participation because of the war it is fighting against your country's oppression in Mainland China."

A murmur rippled through the crowd.

Miss Higgins pressed on. "The Chinese American community here in San Francisco has stepped into the breach and is building a pavilion to represent their motherland. How will you handle this potential conflict?"

"Our efforts in San Francisco are to engage in peace and brotherhood," Tokido answered. He kept his expression placid to belie the fact that the back of his neck bristled at her affront. "Indeed, that is the theme of the Exposition. To that end, we pledge cooperation and diplomacy with all nations."

"Have you encountered any hostility from the Chinese Americans?" Miss Higgins asked.

An air of expectancy hovered in the room. Some reporters turned to one another with raised eyebrows; others whispered. Everyone looked to Tokido with upturned faces. Pressure constricted in his temples.

"The Chinese community has extended the hand of friendship," he answered with civility. "We have returned the sentiment."

Ralph Townsend lumbered to his feet. A big man, he seemed to unfold in sections from the chair, and, as he came to his full height, he folded his long arms across his thin chest. "Miss Higgins, may I suggest that this is neither the time nor the place to engage in political debate? We have forums for that discourse, and they are certainly not here. Mr. Okamura and his staff are graciously providing an opportunity to preview the pavilion. I, for one, would like to see and hear what they have to present."

As Townsend finished, a voice rang out. "I should like to suggest," Harry Cotkins said without standing, "that our job in this room at this time is to focus on the goodwill represented here and stay out of the conflict across the seas. The purpose of the Exposition is to generate peace and understanding. This is the message from the mayor, civic leaders, and citizens of this great city. This is why we have come together today."

Miss Higgins sat down abruptly, her lips sealed in a thin line of disapprobation.

Tokido broke the uneasy silence. "Thank you, ladies and gentlemen, for your comments." Had any of the reporters leaped to his or her feet and demanded justification for the imperial emperor's honorable imperative to rescue Asian countries from under the crushing boot of Western imperialism, Tokido's retort would have been unthinkable. He rushed on. "Please, join us now. Our hostesses will accompany you into the adjoining room. We are ready to begin the tour."

As the reporters gathered in the immense hall and clustered in small groups, he cleared his throat. "The Travel Hall is a lofty tribute to our country's diverse regions. As you see, I'm standing in front of a fountain." He gestured to the pool of sparkling tiles. "The statues of three girls stand in the fountain. Soon water will surround their figures. We have a typical Japanese girl in a traditional long-sleeved kimono." He braced himself. There was no turning back now. "A Korean with a high sash, and a Manchoukuo with a fan in her hand." His remark was met with a cool reserve that he had lately observed when speaking to American audiences. Cotkins, Ryder, and Townsend formed a core in the middle, while Florence Higgins, flanked by other female reporters, glared at him from the edge. Lily was obscured from view, and then he spotted the pheasant feather in her hat, riding at the back. She had been circulating in and out of the group like flotsam caught in an eddy. She was never in the same place twice. Tokido caught Chizu's eye. He slightly tipped his chin toward Lily. Chizu faded away. If he could see her brightly patterned kimono, he could be certain Lily had not wandered off.

Tokido soldiered on. "Against the wall, a panoramic map in wood has been created. We are still in the process of painting the map, which will show in elaborate relief the many travel routes between Japan, the United States, and China. There are more steamship and railroad lines than are shown on this map, which indicates only the main lines." He pointed to the cities served by airlines and then drew the audience's attention to two large *komainu*, Korean dogs, that flanked either side of the fountain. "These legendary animals are usually found on both sides of an entrance to Shinto shrines in Japan. They're thought to keep evil spirits away from holy places."

He stepped away, walking quickly across the wide floor to an opposite wall. The reporters followed. He stopped in front of elaborate silk paintings recessed into the wall. "Here are four masterpieces of embroidery, measuring nine feet square and made entirely by hand, using silk." He pointed to one panel at a time: "Mount Fuji and Miyaima, of Japan proper; Mt. Kongo in Chosen; and the mausoleum of a Manchu emperor in Manchukuo." Several of the reporters, murmuring, "Elegant, beautiful, magnificent," drew closer to examine the handiwork. Tokido nodded and exchanged smiles and, like a herder guiding a flock, led the group toward the rear of the hall.

"Lastly, we have an information office." He motioned to an area where several of his staff stood behind a counter. Above the counter, against a high wall, circular discs were mounted and imprinted with large letters that read THE ORIENT CALLS.

"For visitors' convenience, we will maintain this office for the duration of the Exposition," Tokido explained. "Illustrated travel literature is available, and we extend a sincere invitation to all who wish to visit Japan."

He heard a gasp; the rise and fall of agitated voices, like water flung on hot coals; and deeper voices, calling for restraint. Unexpectedly, Lily surfaced at the front of the group. "Mr. Okamura," she asked, "are you suggesting that *now* it's wise to travel to Japan, much less China?" The tone of her voice was accusatory, the pitch ascending with each word.

"Miss Nordby, we extend a most cordial invitation to visit Japan, where you can see for yourself the beauty of our country and also can visit Manchukuo, which reflects a new optimism of Asian ideals. Our country has an abiding friendship with the United States, as is evidenced by its being the first foreign country to accept your invitation to this enterprise. We join you in celebrating the achievement of building two gigantic bridges across the San Francisco Bay and in the perpetuation of lasting peace in the Pacific."

"I fail to see how—"

Ralph Townsend shuffled forward. "Miss Nordby," he interrupted, "both Mr. Cotkins and I have traveled extensively throughout Japan and Manchukuo. There, we have been enlightened by their economic stability and 2,500 years of classical tradition. May I also remind you that San Francisco's great port is looking forward to additional trade and increased shipping in lumber, grain, and goods between our countries?" He added, almost apologetically, "It is well to keep an open mind at this time."

Miss Higgins popped up beside Lily. "May I remind *you,* Mr. Townsend, that not all of us share your opinion?"

Tokido brought his clasped hands to his lips and, parting his hands, palms up, with dignity, quietly commanded, "Ladies and gentlemen, may I suggest we resume the tour? I'd like to show you several more rooms as we wander toward the front. Your time is valuable. For those of you who wish to continue the sharing of ideas, I'm available afterward."

The air of agitation deflated like a pierced balloon. Arm in arm, Lily and Miss Higgins folded into the group. It was as if the reporters woke up to the fact that they weren't in a newsroom, sleeves rolled up, hands balled into fists. Everyone followed respectfully behind Tokido. They were still in clusters that corresponded to their political beliefs, but there was a resignation that suggested they would neither insult their host any further nor degrade one another to prove a point.

In the Silk Room, Tokido explained the process of silk making that would be demonstrated. In the Industrial Arts Room, he reviewed the sixty-three examples of arts and crafts that would be featured. In the Transportation and Communication Room, he pointed out the displays that would chart the progress of Japan in the modern world. All along, he kept watch for Chizu's figure, and it wasn't until the end of his presentation that he lost sight of her. As he stood in the hallway by the door, saying good-bye to the reporters and thanking them for their participation, out of the corner of his eye, he glanced Chizu, strolling down the hallway beside Lily.

As they drew nearer, Chizu, demure and gracious, smiled. "Miss Nordby finds our pavilion's architecture to be of great interest."

Tokido looked carefully from Chizu to Lily. "We have taken great care to blend the aspects of a feudal castle and a seventeenth-century samurai house. It's really one of a kind in that respect. Is there some element that you're particularly curious about?"

"There is attention to detail everywhere I look, and yet back there"—she turned around and pointed toward an opening between the Silk Room and the Industrial Art Room —"that corridor leads to nowhere."

"Ah, yes," Tokido answered. "We are still completing final details." He glanced at Chizu. "Are you in conversation with the architect about that area? I believe you were hoping for a storage area."

"I have, Tokido-*san*. We're discussing the advisability of

building a small office at the end of the hall to better serve you and your staff."

"Ah, a most useful solution." Tokido addressed Lily: "Our main office and meeting rooms are on the second floor. I would prefer to be closer to the public."

Chizu responded, "We'll still be able to install shelving along the walls for the overflow of ikebana vases and tea implements."

"Thank you, Chizu. Don't let us keep you."

She bowed slightly. "If you'll excuse me, I must attend to other duties."

"Of course," Tokido answered, holding her gaze until she padded away in the direction of the tearoom.

A cold breeze from the open door blew into the hallway. Outside, Tokido heard Kiyoshi speaking to some of the departing reporters. He had wanted to engage a few in further conversation before they left, but he was highly aware of Lily beside him. She seemed unwilling to amend any of the remarks that she had flung in his face before, and he wouldn't defend his position. *Best to let sleeping dogs lie,* he thought. Her behavior, true to course, was impudent and rude. As she started to walk toward the door, he searched for a parting remark.

"By the way," he said, "I've been invited to Forbidden City in Chinatown."

She stopped and regarded him. A puzzled look fell across her face.

"Would you be my guest?" No sooner had the question left his lips than he wanted to retract it.

They both seemed pinned to the spot. His invitation was preposterous, dangerous, out of bounds. He was certain she'd laugh. To his amazement, a coy smile lit up her face. Had he noticed before how radiant she could be, or had it just dawned on him?

"I've never been," she said. "Call me. You have my number."

With that, she turned on her heel, the hem of her coat flapping against the backs of her black boots, the pheasant feather stuck in the brim of her hat riding above her head.

CHAPTER TWELVE

Woodrow

Timothy Pflueger dealt five cards facedown to the men who were gathered around a burnished game table in the cask room of Hotaling's warehouse. Woodrow picked up his hand, tightly fanning the cards: two aces, two tens, and a deuce. Lady Luck had finally smiled on Woodrow. He laid the cards back on the table and sipped Hotaling's spicy whiskey from a tumbler. His expression remained the same: thoughtful, patient, good-natured. If the group had mistaken him for a rube during their first game, their impression had rapidly faded.

Woodrow occupied the catbird seat, directly to Pflueger's right. After the evening when he had laid a bomb at Lily's feet, Woodrow wasn't entirely certain of Pflueger's motives.

Had the man acted out of genuine concern, or was he up to something fishy? Woodrow couldn't really say. Right now, Woodrow's chips had dwindled down to a modest amount, despite his betting wisely, and he had to clear his mind.

Cigar smoke curled over the heads of the players, veiling the umber glow from the lamps stationed on the high brick walls between the massive banded casks. Woodrow raised his eyes to the first bettor, a real estate kingpin by the name of Moe Shirley. Shirley had a smile that blasted out of his mouth like he had fifty teeth. Right now, he wasn't smiling. His stack of chips had shrunk to practically nothing. He flipped open his wallet, drew out two Ben Franklins, and pushed them toward Pflueger, who shrugged and counted out forty chips, sliding them to Shirley.

"I'm in," Shirley said, tossing down four chips. A nice bet. Twenty bucks total.

Simon Toth matched the bet wordlessly. Woodrow watched him closely. Toth had been drinking heavily. His neck was stuffed into a tight collar, the skin at the back bristling a porcine pink and slick with sweat.

Adolph Schuman, impeccably dressed and cool, tossed in six chips. "I'll raise you two." Woodrow admired the man, whom he had met at a posh dinner when he had first arrived in the city, and he liked him even more after the night at the St. Francis Hotel. Schuman and his wife, a stunner and wickedly smart, made a brilliant pair.

Next to Schuman was Ted Huggins, Standard Oil's genius public relations man, known as the Father of the Exposition. He had spearheaded the movement to mount a world's fair back in '33 and guided it to reality. Widely recognized for his acumen and energy, Huggins was a force and regarded highly by both men and women. His charm was undeniable.

Huggins smiled amicably. "I'm in." He set down six chips.

The bet went to Woodrow. He nodded, fingering six chips and then two more. "I'll raise you two."

Pflueger whistled. "Excellent, Woodrow, my man," he said, and pushed in eight chips. He looked to Shirley.

Shirley's tongue poked into his cheek. He peeled off four chips and set them down.

Schuman and Huggins each added two chips. The pot held at $240, the largest one yet in the first round of betting.

"Gentleman," Pflueger said, "the pot is right." He looked to Shirley. "What'll it be?"

Shirley flung down two cards. "Hit me." His hand, as wide as a paw, the top of which was pelted with black hair, scooped up the cards, and as he splayed them open, his heavy brow twitched and his eyes blinked in rapid succession.

Woodrow calculated quickly. He figured Shirley had gone for an open-ended straight draw. Shirley couldn't stand to be sidelined. Put to the test, he'd bluff rather than quit. If the response of Shirley's nervous system was any indication, he'd just lost the gamble.

Toth asked for two. Woodrow wasn't certain about his state of sobriety or, at this late point in the evening, his judgment. More than likely, he was holding a pair with a high face card. He mouthed the cigar in his mouth like a kid sucking on a wad of black licorice.

Schuman asked for one. Woodrow estimated he was

looking for a flush or an inside straight draw. Both risky, both improbable. Smooth as a seal, Schuman cradled the cards and peered at them. His eyes glistened.

Huggins asked for two cards. Possibly, he held three of a kind. As he glanced at the cards, Woodrow detected a slight deflation of his shoulders.

Woodrow extracted the deuce from his hand and laid it down. Pflueger pursed his lips and dealt him one card. Woodrow smoothly tipped the corner. An ace, proud and strong, smiled up at him, and what a beautiful sight it was: a full house—three aces and two tens. Deep within the recesses of Woodrow's memory, the voice of his prep school Episcopal reverend intoned from Mark 12:17: "Render to Caesar the things that are Caesar's, and to God the things that are God's." He folded the ace into his hand and laid it facedown on the table.

Pflueger dealt himself one card. The rounded features of his face, his skin as bumpy as a potato pancake, revealed nothing. Woodrow ascertained that Pflueger, like Woodrow himself, was looking for one card to complete a full house. With a flourish, Pflueger grasped the whiskey bottle by the neck. "As the immortal Charles Kellogg Field said, 'If, as they say, God spanked the town for being overfrisky, why did he burn his churches down and spare Hotaling's whiskey?'

"Perhaps, gentlemen, a little lubricant?" The bottle went around the table. Everyone partook.

This was the moment in the game that Woodrow relished. Unless the whiskey had dulled his brain, he was fairly certain of each player's hand except that of Pflueger, his erstwhile supporter and constant champion. Why, then, did he want to show him up? Maybe because of what had happened with Lily? Maybe because of Pflueger's constant good humor? Maybe it was a knee-jerk reaction to his father's unrelenting insistence, born in the long years of childhood and adolescence, that at every turn he'd take the bit in the softest places in his mouth and bite down? No matter—he'd take down Pflueger and the rest of the gents one by one, like ducks in a pond. There was no malice in his soul—just a pure white flame that burned in his belly as he stood on turf that was rarely the same for him as it was for other men.

Shirley started the final round of betting. He inspected his hand as if the cards would tell him something different than what he already knew. Finally, his eyes swept from player to player. "Let's get this thing going," he challenged, tossing down eight chips. His bluff was no different than it was on other nights, Woodrow surmised. His bonhomie masked an impulse to cinch the deal no matter what. If there was a toehold, Shirley would step into it.

Toth threw down his cards. "I'm out." He pushed back from the table, grabbed the butt of the stubby cigar, and staggered away.

"Taking the air?" Pflueger asked.

Waving over his head, Toth wove across the slick concrete floor between the casks and toward the front door, which opened onto Jackson Street, where the night's foggy wind routinely cooled the ardor of more than one man.

"Come back soon," Pflueger called.

Before the heavy door slammed shut, the blast of a horn

and shrill laughter echoed down the great room. The lamps flickered and then flared. Everyone halted until the disturbance passed.

Schuman resumed the pace. "I'll see you and raise you eight."

With a genial smile and a tip of his chin, Huggins surrendered his cards to the table.

Woodrow paused, more for effect than for a reason. "I'll see you and raise sixteen more."

"Well, well," Pflueger said, "our friend has upped the ante." He eyed Woodrow as he tumbled chips in his fingers, moving a bottom chip to the top with a nimble thumb and forefinger. He stacked a row of thirty-two chips and inched them forward.

A sweat had broken on Shirley's upper lip, and he swiped it away. "I'm out." He closed his lips over his teeth and tilted back in the chair, rocking precariously back and forth.

A hush fell over the table as Schuman leveled an unblinking stare at Woodrow. "I'll call you."

Woodrow returned his gaze and, with a little English in his wrist, laid down the full house, pretty as a picture.

Huggins whistled and broke the band of a Romeo y Julieta cigar.

Schuman relinquished a flush of spades. "Nicely done, Woodrow."

Pflueger spread out three queens and a pair of sixes, laughing as if he had won the bet himself. "You bested me as well."

Shirley strained forward, clicked his tongue, and shook

his head. "Take our money, you bugger."

"That he will," said Pflueger. "But not without payback. I suggest we round up Toth, wherever he might be, and take a hike up to a little nightspot where the scenery is resplendent. At the very least, Woodrow owes us a round."

The pot stood at $720. The money meant nothing to Woodrow. Although his satisfaction came in reading the cards correctly, a frisson of glory spread across his shoulders and rippled down his arms. He had beaten the men! The sensation flashed as brilliantly as a comet, then died just as quickly. As in all games of chance, he knew it was an educated guess that hit the mark.

Chips were counted, money pocketed; the bottle went around again. Chairs scraped on the concrete floor, and the men, grumbling good-naturedly at Woodrow, ambled past the night shadows and yesteryears' bubble of mash in the barrels, where the ghosts of firemen winked and jawed about how in '06, after the earthquake, as the city burned, they pumped salt water through hoses stretching eleven blocks from the Embarcadero to Hotaling's, the largest stash of whiskey on the West Coast, and saved the good citizens of San Francisco from going dry.

* * *

THE MEN MOVED up Jackson through the infamous district of the Gold Rush's Barbary Coast. As they rounded the corner onto Montgomery, they detoured past an electric sign arched over Pacific Avenue, proclaiming in bold letters IN-

TERNATIONAL SETTLEMENT.

Pflueger had positioned Woodrow by his side, protectively looping an arm over his shoulders, and hurried him along as if a lowlife would jump out with a long-bladed bowie knife and slit their throats.

"What was that?" Woodrow asked, craning his neck. Honky-tonk music spilled out over the rooftops, and drunken voices howled profanities.

"Sin City, my friend. Stay up with me. The place is still notorious for crime and prostitution. Back in the day, that's where you could buy your way to hell. It hasn't changed much. You don't want to try your luck there."

A seedy, faded air hung over the neighborhood. Even in the chill of night, the stench of urine and beer rose from the gutter. Hollow-eyed bums and bedraggled women hunched in doorways locked for the night.

Shirley kept calling, "Toth, Toth," until Huggins told him, "Shut your trap. You'll wake the dead." That set them to chortling and trading scandalous tales about upper-crust swells who had wandered into the International Settlement and never come back. A cold wind whipped through their clothing. Automobiles sped by. Toth appeared out of a doorway.

Shirley was on him like flypaper. "Where in the hell have you been?"

"What's it to you?"

"Not a damn thing."

"In that case," Toth said, "a hot tip on a nag at Bay Meadows doesn't interest you?"

"Aw, kiss off."

They fell into step, followed by Schuman and Huggins. Pflueger and Woodrow took up the rear and gradually fell farther and farther back, until the men ahead had gained a full city block.

Woodrow was out of breath. "Where are we going?" he panted. He leaned into the gusty wind and wiped tears from his eyes.

"To Sutter at Grant."

"That's at least ten more blocks."

"I'll hail us a taxi. We'll meet the boys there."

Pflueger stepped off the curb and raised his arm. A Checker cab pulled up smartly. They piled in, and Pflueger rolled down the window. As the cab sped off and roared by the men, he shouted, "See you at Forbidden City!"

* * *

A RED AWNING stretched over the sidewalk; above it, a soaring sign, FORBIDDEN CITY, flashed against the night sky. Woodrow tumbled from the cab onto the street, rearranged his tie and jacket, and combed his fingers through his wind-tossed hair. He had read about the club, intrigued about a cast of all-Chinese showgirls, whom he could picture as stunningly beautiful, although he could hardly imagine himself as a patron.

People stretched down the block and, as usual, gawked at him. Woodrow ignored their stares. Pflueger paid the cabbie and clapped his hand on Woodrow's shoulder, and together they pressed to the front of the line.

The doorman tipped his cap. "Good evening, Mr. Pflueger. Nice to see you!" With a grand flourish, he swung open the plate glass door.

"Thank you, George. Meet my friend Mr. Packard."

George smiled down at Woodrow. "How do you do, sir?"

Pflueger took George's elbow. "A few friends are right behind us."

"Yes, sir. I'll be on the lookout."

"I appreciate that," Pflueger said, and slipped a bill into his hand.

As they walked up a flight of stairs leading to the second floor, Charlie Low poised at the entrance to the club, greeting guests with genuine delight. He stood between a pair of red satin curtains tied back with gold braided sashes. Behind him, the floor of the club gleamed; lights dazzled the eye. A sea of round tables covered in black tablecloths stretched to a stage at the rear. In the center of each table, a candle flickered and danced.

When Charlie saw Pflueger, a wide smile filled his face. "Nice to see you this evening," he said, pumping Pflueger's hand.

"This is Mr. Packard. A very important person at Treasure Island."

Charlie bowed slightly and shook Woodrow's hand. "A friend of Mr. Pflueger is a friend of mine," he said, ushering them into the club. "We have your regular table tonight." He hurried them between the tables, filled with men in dark, elegant suits and ties and women in long, strapless gowns and fur jackets draped over their shoulders. They drank cocktails in glasses that tinkled and inhaled from cigarettes, smoke curling and twisting above their heads.

Charlie stopped in front of a table for six one row back from the stage. "Your lady friend is not with you tonight, Mr. Pflueger?" he asked, waiting while they sat.

"No, not tonight." Pflueger winked. "She's out of town."

"Of course." Charlie winked back. "Enjoy the show!"

An exquisite Oriental waitress, dressed in a long white cheongsam buttoned to the neck and slit up the thigh, stepped up to the table. A white orchid was pinned above her ear; her black hair was pulled into a smooth chignon. "What may I get you this evening?"

"Make it six Singapore Slings, my dear. That will get us started."

Woodrow was fascinated and slightly taken aback. He wasn't prepared for the glamour of the club. He hadn't hob-nobbed much in the city, and tonight was an eye-opener. There was nothing here remotely similar to the streets of Chinatown, where crowds pushed and shoved to buy vegeta-bles, break the necks of chickens, and carry off sacks of rice.

The men arrived and tumbled into their seats just as the cocktails were delivered. The band members came out and sat behind music stands off to the side of the stage. The lights dimmed, and Charlie Low escorted a couple toward a table on the opposite side of the club at the lip of the stage. Woodrow turned his head toward the pair. A black-haired man bearing an erect posture walked behind a woman whose hat brim dipped and shaded her face. A fur jacket was buttoned to her neck. As she sat, she peeled off a pair of black satin gloves. Woodrow squinted. The man turned to take a seat next to the woman, and Woodrow stared into the face of Tokido Okamura. The woman removed her hat, lifted her face, and nodded at Tokido. Woodrow bolted upright.

Toth, who sat next to Woodrow, exclaimed, "What the hell? That's Lily Nordby. What's she doing with the Jap?" Pflueger's eyebrows had shot up to his hairline. Every man at the table either knew Lily or knew of her, and every man had something to say.

Schuman caught Woodrow's eye and nodded a slight *no,* as if to say, *Don't touch this. I know something you don't know.*

Seven bewitching showgirls in exotic costumes and dazzling makeup rushed onto the stage as the lights flared and the band's brass trumpeted. The extravaganza on the stage had riveted everyone in the club. Everyone but Woodrow. His heart was beating wildly, and the havoc in his mind would not subside.

CHAPTER THIRTEEN

Lily

Maxine lounged on her bed in the room she and Lily shared in the French boardinghouse, one arm flung back, a Lucky Strike in her hand, a bourbon half-consumed on the bedside table. Bing Crosby's "White Christmas" swelled from downstairs. Gay voices carried up and down the hall; Saturday night's merriment could not be contained.

"I've got to hand it to you, Lily. You had to shoo me into this joint. I wasn't so sure it was us. You know what I mean?"

"We were ready, Max. We just needed a little push." From across the room, Lily wiggled into a gold-toned evening gown that cascaded in shimmering folds to her ankles.

"Monsieur Reboul can push me any which way he wants," Maxine said. "He's a doll."

"He's a little old for you." Lily shuffle-stepped to the bed. "Zip me up."

Maxine propped herself up on one elbow and drew the zipper up the back of the dress. "I don't know. I can be persuaded to make an exception."

"In his case, I wouldn't blame you. But remember, there are lots of fish in the sea." Lily slipped her feet into a pair of gold satin high heels. "So, what do you think?" she asked, peering over her bare shoulder.

"You look like a million."

"Thanks, Max." Lily grabbed a hat off the bureau and a fur jacket from the back of a chair.

"Hold it, kiddo. Where're you going?"

"I don't know."

"You expect me to believe that?"

Lily flashed Maxine a red-lipsticked grin.

"At least tell me the name of the lucky fella."

"My lips are sealed."

"What a bunch of horseshit. Dudley and I aren't going to stand for your disappearing act much longer. Good God, you skipped out on us at Thanksgiving, and Christmas is coming. Most of the time, you're nowhere to be found."

"I had Thanksgiving with the Schumans. I told you that."

"Are you deserting us for the upper crust?"

"I'm buried in work."

"That's nothing new."

"Toth is all over me to churn out more stories. As fast as I file them, he pushes me for more. Anyway, I've got to go."

Maxine's interrogation was getting under her skin. She

scooped up a black silk bag and a pair of black gloves studded with rhinestones.

"My mom is insisting I bring you to Christmas dinner."

"You know how I hate the holidays."

"That won't fly with her. She considers you her *other* daughter."

Lily pulled on the gloves. "We'll talk about it later."

"Promise?"

"Sure."

"Wait."

"What?"

"Turn down the brim of the hat," Maxine said.

Tentatively, Lily touched the brim with her fingertips and curved it toward one cheek.

Maxine leaped up off the bed. "A little more over your eye." With both hands, she smoothed the brim downward. "Like this."

"What would I do without you?" Lily asked, kissing Maxine on the cheek.

* * *

LILY SWEPT DOWN the stairs into the foyer, where a ten-foot Douglas fir tree was strung with colored lights and pearl tinsel. Red apples, ribbons, glass angels, and white candles, one for every month of the year, adorned its branches. A three-tiered, bubbling fountain stood in front of a floor-to-ceiling mirror. She heard catcalls through the open French doors of the dining room beyond the foyer. She laughed and waved over her shoulder. "Don't wait up for me." Her shoes skimmed over the marble floor as she pushed open the beveled-glass door and hurried down to a cab waiting on the curb.

The cabbie opened the door. "Where to, little lady?'

"Coit Tower."

"You got it. We'll be there in a jiffy."

Lily reclined against the seat, closed her eyes, and rubbed her forehead. She disliked concealing anything from Maxine, and yet the revelation that her mother was alive had separated Lily from everything she had known or assumed. She had been unable to act on finding her. She didn't know why. Although she had promised the kindly Herman Oronoffski at the market on Folsom Street that she would return, she couldn't bring herself to go back. Visiting the old neighborhood, even the warmth and loving company of Maxine's family, filled her with apprehension. Approaching Bunny or Adolph about the question of her mother's origins had seemed like a reasonable idea, but now that, too, seemed impossible. And, just as impossibly, she had to keep her destination tonight confidential from everyone. There was no way around it—she was wading into unknown territory.

The cab whisked along darkened streets where Christmas wreaths and lights twinkled in the windows of handsome homes, and on neighborhood corners the sounds of Salvation Army jingle bells blended with the clanging of cable cars. Christmas had come to San Francisco adorned in finery and the covenant of Jesus Christ, the son of God, to save sinners from damnation. Lily felt she hadn't admission to either the cathedrals of Christians or the synagogues of Jews. She was a stranger in her own skin.

The cab twisted abruptly up the tree-lined road to Coit Tower. Lily peered through the window as they rushed by the Filbert Street steps that led down to Woodrow's house. How long ago the night he had brought her to his home seemed; Lily felt a twinge of regret that she hadn't contacted him since then. The only glimpse she had of him was when he pedaled by on the island, atop the seat of his motorized bicycle.

The cabbie swung into the roundabout under Lillie Coit's tribute to her beloved volunteer firemen of Washington Square and pulled to a stop. The lights in the top of the slender-fluted column beamed red to celebrate the holidays. A hard wind buffeted the cab. "Clear as a bell up here tonight," he said, and flicked the flag up on the meter. He squinted out the window to a few cars parked along the edge of the pavement and then frowned at her in the rearview mirror. "You want me to wait?"

"That won't be necessary," she said.

"You sure?"

"Yes, quite sure."

"Suit yourself. That'll be thirty cents."

She reached into her purse and passed him two quarters.

"Thank you, miss! Watch your step."

She pushed against the door. Stepping out of the cab, she felt the cold, sharp wind whipping against her body, pasting the gown against her legs. Shivering, she clutched her hat. Stars hung bright in the black sky, and the working lights on Treasure Island shone from across the starlit expanse of the bay. The taillights of a limousine idling ahead winked. She hurried over the pavement to the waiting car.

The rear door of the Cadillac Fleetwood limo swung open. Tokido stepped out, the tails of his coat whipping in the wind. Holding out his hand, he reached for her elbow. She slipped into the backseat, and he hopped in beside her. The door slammed shut sealing them in the luxury of the finest engineered steel, pistons, and padded leather that Detroit could manufacture. A chauffeur sat silently behind a glass panel at the wheel, a jaunty cap atop his head.

"Good evening," Tokido said, glancing at her.

"Good evening to you." She reaffixed a hatpin that had come loose. The wind hadn't disturbed one strand of hair on his head, and he was impeccably dressed in a long black coat and black leather shoes. The collar and cuffs of a white shirt gleamed against his skin. A band of anticipation tensed her shoulders.

"You look lovely," he said softly.

The tone of his voice caught her off guard. Despite herself, she blushed.

"I trust this arrangement to meet hasn't been inconvenient," he continued. "Under the circumstances, I thought it the wisest choice."

"Not at all," she replied. She wondered what circumstances he was referring to. Was he protecting her from raised eyebrows at the boardinghouse because it was scandalous for a white woman to be seen alone in the company of a Japanese man? Or was he was using her as a foil to gain intelligence? *One way or the other,* she thought, *I'll find out.*

She had met him twice before, never in private but by invitation—once when the emperor's gardener had come to the Japanese Pavilion, and another time, when tea had been served at a lecture about Japanese porcelains. Afterward, he had shown her special preference by sitting next to her.

"Coit Tower is visible from my berth at Treasure Island, and often I have wanted to visit."

"This is your first time, then?"

"Yes. We have nothing quite like it in Tokyo."

"Do you miss home?"

"I do, but time goes quickly. While I'm here, I'm honored to represent my country." He paused. "We have time tonight before the show at Forbidden City. I'd like to take a drive."

"To where?" she asked.

"Across the Golden Gate Bridge."

"Tonight?" she asked.

"Is this not agreeable to you?"

He seemed unperturbed—not at all like the times when he had ordered her off the pavilion's grounds, or when she had questioned him at the press conference.

"I've been only under it, not across it," he said.

"I roller-skated across it on opening day."

Suddenly, he laughed. "What?"

"Oh, yes—it was Pedestrian Day, May 27. Twenty-five cents per person. People crossed on horseback, bicycles, sprinters, even a man on stilts."

"Please go on."

"The automatic counters shut down when the number hit one hundred thousand people, but the crowd kept coming.

Hot-dog vendors sold out. When we started, the sun was out, but by noon the fog rolled in under the deck of the bridge and rose like smoke blotting out the towers."

He peered more closely at her. "But you haven't been across the bridge by car?"

"Only a few times."

"Why not again?"

"Why not?" she replied.

Rolling aside the glass privacy panel, Tokido addressed the chauffeur, "Hayato," he began, speaking in Japanese. Their language had a reedy quality to it, punctuated by a quick expulsion of breath at the end of each word. The chauffeur smoothly shifted into reverse, backed up, shifted forward, and steered down the hill toward the bridge.

The cushions had the faint odor of leather and the feel of kid gloves. The limousine, with its long, low hood and curved fenders, seemed to glide like a swan on a pond. Pinpoints of light reflected off the polished windows and brilliant chrome. Lily had never been inside such an elegant automobile. Her father, rolling in dough from making bathtub gin during Prohibition, had bought a Stutz Bearcat, but she and her half brothers had steered clear of his beloved car, for fear of his leather strap.

Tonight, the city flashed past like a rolling tableau of architectural wonderment set out for its inhabitants' delight. Lily glanced at Tokido's profile. His expression was tranquil, and his hands lay folded in his lap. It wasn't until they floated past the spires of Saints Peter and Paul Church and the broad green of Washington Square that he spoke.

"This place is filled with people, like the Yanaka district at home. Where are we?"

"It's called North Beach, an Italian neighborhood filled with families that go back many years. The church we passed is Catholic. The parishioners worship and go to confession to ask forgiveness for their sins. Religious holidays are celebrated, babies are baptized, couples marry, and Mass is said for the dead."

"Not like the austere Buddhist temples of monks at home," he commented. "May I ask, are you Catholic?"

"Not one bit," she replied.

"Do you celebrate Christmas?"

"Christmas is for children," she answered quickly.

He looked at her strangely. A furrow wrinkled his brow. "Were your parents not religious?"

"You could say that," she answered. "Are you Buddhist?"

He pursed his lips. "It was how I was raised. We follow the customs of our ancestors. But please, tell me more about this neighborhood."

She told him about the restaurants that served platters of pasta, roast beef, and crab, and Chianti in straw-wrapped bottles. On Columbus Avenue, she mentioned the bakeries that made long loaves of sourdough bread and the delicatessens filled with the pungent, mouthwatering fragrances of salami, olives, and cheeses. When the chauffeur navigated up onto the broad expanse of Bay Street, they passed the Ghirardelli chocolate factory, whose sweet scent wafted into the limo. Along the Marina, she pointed out the sailboats bobbing in the little yacht harbor and the handsome homes on the boulevard, with views to Marin County.

"Where have you been that you like?" she asked.

"My business takes me to the consulate and often into homes for dinners. But I'm confined to Treasure Island. There is too much work to leave it."

Gradually, the limousine pulled off the city streets and rolled onto the broad approach to the bridge. Traffic was sparse. Headlights flared and faded. Wind buffeted the limo. They skirted along the periphery of the Presidio, the military base strategically placed on land at the mouth of the bay and above the Pacific Ocean's open waters. On the opposite side of the road, she pointed out Crissy Field, the army's airstrip bordering the sandy coastline inside the bay.

"When the *Tatuta Maru* came under the bridge, I saw seaplanes there on the ramp," he said, "but not any aircraft."

"Since the bridge was completed, the South Tower and anchorage have interfered with the flight path of aircraft taking off from Crissy Field." She watched him as she spoke. In the glow from the dash, his eyes remained the same, watchful and curious. She made a mental note of his questions, deciding that every answer she provided would be either public knowledge or already known to him and or his superiors. "That and the prevailing west wind make takeoff dangerous."

"Go on," he said.

"Large aircraft operations have been shifted to Hamilton Field in Novato."

"And where is this Novato?" he asked.

"It's a small town about thirty minutes north, straight up Highway 101."

All at once, the chauffeur slowed and they turned from

each other to look out the windshield. The tollbooth appeared ahead, and beyond it the roadbed onto the bridge. Tokido slid open the glass partition and spoke to the chauffeur.

The chauffeur maneuvered the limo into the thin line of cars and stopped at the toll taker's booth. The toll taker leaned out. "Good evening. One way or round trip?"

"One way," the chauffeur said in perfect English.

"Fifty cents, please."

Lily watched the chauffeur pass the coins to the toll taker. *Why wouldn't he have bought a round-trip ticket?* she wondered. Tokido seemed indifferent, his entire being enraptured by what was to come.

Gradually, the chauffeur accelerated and the limousine sailed onto the bridge. Ahead, the massive South Tower loomed into the black sky. The tower rose as one huge column with four openings, each section stacked one above the other, to its arched top. Beyond and through the openings, the silhouette of the North Tower appeared in miniature. Light standards strung along the deck glowed like misty beacons illuminating the brilliant orange paint that covered every section of the art deco design.

"Oh," she gasped.

Beside her, she heard Tokido's intake of breath.

To the east, the bay waters shimmered like hammered metal and cut a path to Treasure Island and the dim outline of the San Francisco–Oakland Bay Bridge. To the west, whitecaps pale as dove wings rippled from beneath the bridge to the ocean's darkened, misty horizon.

"This structure is magnificent," Tokido said, craning his neck to look up through one window and then the other. "The largest suspension bridge in the world. A daring engineering feat."

His voice held respect and reverence, and, although she dared not, an unexpected impulse to reach out and touch him rose up in her. "You can't imagine what it was like to see it go up."

"I wish I had. It was reported that the straits of the Golden Gate could never be spanned. Is it true that citizens protested that the entry to the bay would be ruined?"

"Vehemently," she replied. "And that's not all. Geologists and seismologists publicly argued about the bridge's safety. But the chief engineer, Joseph Strauss, and his team persisted."

Tokido shook his head. "Such skill and courage are admirable."

She thought twice about divulging any more structural information but relented because each question formed a pattern of suspect inquiry. "Under the South Tower, divers dynamited footings sixty-five feet down, and when the bedrock shattered, contractors dug thirty-five feet deeper and poured the base."

Just then, the limo passed the midspan and began to slow. The North Tower, monolithic and noble, came into view.

Lily explained, "Under this tower, four concrete anchor blocks, weighing sixty-four thousand tons each, pin the structure to the cliffs."

Tokido whistled and stared up into the tower, turning

slightly in the seat to look over at the landmass that rose sharply from the sea. "The *Tatuta Maru* passed by these cliffs when we arrived. Are they not inhabited?"

"The US Army occupies the headlands and the land along the coast, and there"—she pointed down and below—"what you cannot see is Horseshoe Cove and Fort Baker. Didn't the ship's navigational charts indicate these landmarks?"

"Our captain was in charge. My eyes were filled with the wonder of the bridge."

"Of course," she answered. "Do you know about the batteries in the cliffs?"

"Is 'batteries' a military term?"

She highly doubted that he was ignorant of the answer. "Precisely. They are fortifications that house arterial gun emplacements, crucial to protect the Golden Gate and the bay."

"I learn something at every turn." Tokido nodded. "I am in your debt."

"Not at all. My job is to know the facts."

The limo's tires clicked over the end of the bridge's roadbed, and the road curved slightly left and then right, rising steeply over the jagged promontory.

"Where are we now?" he asked.

"At the top is a tunnel. When we come through the other end, the road plunges down. At the bottom is a side road that doubles back to a little seaside hamlet called Sausalito, which is a graveyard for abandoned ships. Across the bay from Sausalito is the town of Tiburon, which means 'shark.' In its heyday, fish canneries lined its shores."

"Perhaps we can return someday. I would like to see such

places. Your description of Sausalito reminds me of the coastal villages I visited as a child."

"As you like," she said.

"But now I think it's best to return to the city." Tokido peered at his watch. "I wouldn't want to miss the show at Forbidden City."

"Nor would I," Lily answered. She breathed deeply, feeling as if she'd run a gauntlet.

Tokido leaned forward and spoke to the chauffeur, then closed the partition. The limo crested the highway, sweeping through the tunnel to the other side, where eucalyptus trees stood guard along the road, lashed and bent by a torrent of wet wind that poured over the craggy ridges of the headlands.

* * *

STEPPING FROM THE limo onto the sidewalk on Sutter Street, one block from the Chinatown gate, Tokido ushered her toward the club. Lily bristled at the disapproving stares of people around her. Some did a double take; some mumbled. One man spat, and her temper flared. She wasn't unaccustomed to witnessing racial insults, but this was the first time they had been aimed at her. Tokido seemed indifferent to their rudeness. He swept her past the club's glass display cases, featuring black-and-white photographs of glamorous dancers, and she felt his hand at the small of her back as they entered and climbed the stairs.

Garish paintings of Oriental scenes lined the walls of the

red-carpeted staircase. At the top, Charlie Low's grin was as wide as the twelve-note set of ivory piano keys.

"So pleased to see you. Yes, yes, George Jew has reserved a table for you. Hurry now, before the show starts." He parted red velvet curtains, leading them to a table.

Lily quickly scanned the room. Tasseled silk-and-gold lanterns cast dappled light onto tables packed with Caucasian men and women in fancy evening wear. She didn't see one mixed couple. Charlie Low led them to a front table at the lip of the stage.

Tokido waited for her to be seated and then drew his chair closer to hers. "Are you comfortable?" he asked.

"Very," she answered, slipping out of her jacket and gloves and removing her hat.

"What would you like?"

"The house specialty will do just fine."

"Of course," he answered.

A strikingly beautiful waitress appeared. She bent low toward Tokido as he ordered. Lily watched the polite ease with which he spoke to the woman, and her graceful response. The band struck up the chords to "One O'Clock Jump."

From the first note, the club burst into an uproar. Brilliant lights flooded the floor. Four female dancers dressed in pink-and-black ruffled costumes, showing plenty of leg and midriff, tap-danced onto the stage floor. Their long, dark hair was upswept into elegant hairdos. Their sultry eyes flashed, and their full red lips curved into teasing smiles. They tapped in tight syncopation, peeling off the line and coming back together in perfect rhythm, kicking, sliding, twirling. They spun so near to the edge of the stage that Lily could have reached up and plucked a sequin off their costumes. She had seen burlesque clubs down on Market Street, the hawkers who hustled tourists and down-and-outers through the door, the tawdry glitter that disguised gloom and loneliness. But this was something entirely new. Forbidden City had all the allure and glamour of Bimbo's 365 Club, but it also had something that Bimbo's didn't have: an all-Chinese cast. She was awestruck.

Two Singapore Slings, each garnished with a pineapple slice and a cherry in a frosty glass, arrived at their table.

Tokido held the glass and extended it toward her. "To the pleasure of your company," he toasted, looking into her eyes.

She lifted the cocktail and met his gaze. The cold, tangy mixture of gin, Benedictine, and cherry brandy laced with lemon and pineapple juice flooded her mouth. "Delicious," she murmured and took a second sip, the concoction flowing into her bloodstream.

The music halted, the dancers tapped off, and an elegant couple waltzed onto the stage floor. He was dressed in top hat and tails; she wore a curve-hugging silver gown that shimmered like a mantle of stars. They paused until the band struck up "And the Angels Sing." Taking the lady in his arms, the gentleman led her around the room, turning, dipping, swirling in sweeping arcs, in a number as stylish and sophisticated as any performed by Ginger Rogers and Fred Astaire.

Tokido leaned toward Lily. "Terrific," he said, clapping with the audience as the couple exited the room. "But I have to tell you that not all of the women in the first act are Chinese."

"Really?"

"Two of the female dancers are Japanese. And another is Filipino."

"What?"

"You can't tell, can you?"

"My ignorance is showing."

"It's to be expected. To Americans, all Orientals look alike."

"You're right. I try not to lump everyone together. Can you tell my heritage?"

"You look Scandinavian." He reached up and touched her cheek, drawing his finger from her cheekbone to her chin. "But there's something else that I can't identify."

"It's a secret." At that moment, second drinks appeared. She promised herself that she wouldn't have a third.

He studied her curiously. "Well, I'll tell you something I do know. Charlie Low is a master at packing a club. I can also say that the showgirls have disgraced their parents by revealing their bodies and dancing in public."

Just then, an acrobat in a pajama-like outfit took the floor. He executed somersaults, backflips, handstands—all in a flurry of showmanship that drew oohs and aahs. Next, the dancers returned, dressed in sexy burlesque getups that showed off their flawless skin, smooth arms, creamy décolletage, and long, shapely legs, with little fans pinned in their hair. They danced one number after another with dizzying speed.

The final act, "Dance of the Moon Goddess," was performed by Jadin Wong, who glided onto the floor in a costume with a long, trailing skirt and elaborate headdress. She gracefully arched backward, folding her arms crosswise across her chest and sliding one foot forward. The band started to play Debussy's "Clair de Lune," and she began to dance. Her beauty and skill were mesmerizing, and the audience was spellbound until she left the floor.

Around them, the crowd was standing. "Shall we call it a night?" Lily asked, gathering gloves and hat in her hands.

"Whatever you wish," Tokido answered. He reached for her jacket.

"Oh God," Lily said, looking across the room.

"What is it?" he asked, turning in the direction of her gaze.

"There's Simon Toth."

"Your editor at the *Examiner*?"

"The one and only. He's aiming right toward us."

"Here," he said, taking her arm. "Come with me."

"I can handle this," Lily said. "There's no reason to run."

"I insist." He wove her through the tables, past people standing in the aisles.

As they halted to file into line, Toth shouldered forward and held out his hand to Tokido. "Good evening. Nice to see you again."

He looked directly at Lily. "Out on the town, are we?"

"Of course. All work and no play makes Jill a dull girl."

He guffawed. "Good for you, Lily!"

"Miss Nordby has been gracious enough to accompany

me tonight," Tokido interjected. "I had an invitation from George Jew, who, unfortunately, couldn't make it. What a show."

"Yes, quite a show. The gents and I are painting the town ourselves." He pointed to a table, where Lily picked out the stricken face of Woodrow. Even from a distance, their eyes met and she felt her heart constrict.

"I want to thank you for the excellent coverage on our pavilion," Tokido said.

"Lily is doing a bang-up job. There's more to come."

"I've no doubt you are right. Now, if you'll excuse me, I'd like to get Miss Nordby home."

"You bet," Toth said.

Lily snapped to attention. "See you tomorrow, Boss!"

"Good night, Mr. Toth." Tokido escorted Lily through the red velvet curtains, down the stairs, and into the waiting limousine.

CHAPTER FOURTEEN

Tokido

Treasure Island was shrouded in shadow, waves lapping at the rock seawall, and, across the vast span of the bay, pinpoints of light from the far shores twinkled around the island like a necklace of diamonds. Tokido raced his Sankyo along the esplanade in a blur. The wind whipped in his face, and Basho's words came to him:

Cold first winter rain,
poor monkey,
you too could use
A little woven cape.

Only hours before, he had left Forbidden City; sleep did not come easily. Vivid images invaded his consciousness—

images that he fought to banish. At the center of each frame was Lily. Lily as she watched the show, her slender fingers nesting in her palms, the curve of her breasts pressing against the bodice of the gold gown, the floral scent of her perfume invading his senses. He was sure the perfume was French, but he couldn't place it. Certainly not a fragrance his wife would wear.

He wanted to touch this woman who had offended his sensibilities, driven him to anger, frustrated his intentions. This desire shocked his concept of personal responsibility and allegiance. When he dropped her off a block from the French boardinghouse, he was astonished to find himself bowing. Usually he suppressed this custom around American women. But not then. The gesture was pure; it could not be resisted.

He doubled-back toward *Evening Star* in the Court of the Moon, the architectural blend of modern Cambodian, Mayan, and Oriental styles that he usually found distasteful, and forced himself to focus. On a whim, he careened around the Court of Honor and whipped down the Court of the Seven Seas. At the far end, the haunting statue of Ralph Stackpole's *Pacifica* rose up against the backdrop of the metal prayer curtain. The curtain rippled in the wind, sending a vibrational tone out into the mist. Her elbows were bent at the waist, palms turned open in supplication.

He slowed and looked up into her face. *The serenity of her placid expression cannot be denied,* he thought. But he believed the ideal she represented in this place, at this time, did not exist. Across the seas, the world was at war. Hitler and Mussolini had roused the masses to a furor. His countrymen had occupied China. It repeatedly baffled him that thirty nations on this artificial island were each working side by side to bring about a fair devoted to peace. And even more perplexing was the hand of generosity from the Chinese community that continued to be extended to him.

Christmas was fast approaching, and he had no sense of what to expect, other than another round of dinners and political receptions that, however necessary, would divert his concentration. Then, in less than six weeks, the Exposition would open and festivities would start. There would be celebrations, dedications, parades, concerts. In many of the halls, art treasures would be on display. In buildings devoted to scientific discovery, modern technology would be demonstrated. Flowers, food, and music would win every visitor.

It will all be in vain, he thought. *It will all come to nothing.*

A blast from a passing ship's horn sounded, winter's air pierced his jacket, and he rode on. At the entry to the pavilion, he stopped and peered into the grounds. In the pond, the swans were sleeping. Around the garden, the raked paths were empty. He removed a ring of keys from his pocket, slipped one into the lock, opened the door, and locked it behind him. A trace of sandalwood incense lay in the air. Rice-paper lanterns emitted a dim glow in the hallway.

Passing by the Silk Room, he heard the faint sound of silkworms moving about the mulberry leaves in the demonstration cages. He turned into a smaller hall, where blue-and-white porcelain teacups and teapots were arranged in glass-fronted display cases that lined the wall. He stopped in front of a small door, unlocked it, and stepped into a windowless office. He flicked on an overhead light and double-locked the door behind him.

Three desks occupied the space, one for Chizu, another for Kiyoshi, and the largest one for him. A lamp and telephone rested on each desk. To the back wall was affixed a large, glass-fronted display case. Inside, a collection of netsuke was arranged in tiny wooden cubicles. The carved ivory figures, no more than three inches high, were happy Buddhas, rabbits, elephants, monkeys, dragons, bent old men holding walking sticks, skulls. The erotic couplings of naked men and women so valued in his country were absent. The case was trimmed in a bird pattern constructed from Japanese cypress.

Tokido ran his finger from the top of the trim down to the head of the seventh bird and pressed. The trim opened smoothly to reveal the edges of two panels. He grasped the first panel and pulled it out. A hydrographic map of the San Francisco Bay was pinned to a cork surface. The map depicted the water's depth, shipping lanes, navigation hazards, and aids, such as buoys and range markers, that delineated shipping lanes. Alongside it were black-and-white aerial photographs of the bay.

Suddenly, a low rumbling interrupted his thoughts. A clock on the wall said 4:12 a.m. He froze in place. Was it a Clipper taking off? An explosion from across the bay? The gardeners? They had been arriving earlier and earlier, their trucks and cranes delivering crates of plants. He cocked his head and waited. The rumbling faded.

He drank deeply from a container of water on his desk.

Plagued by headaches that began in his temples and marched up his forehead, he rolled his head and massaged his neck. Chizu and Kiyoshi would be arriving by 6:00 a.m. There was work to be done.

Walking back to the case, he pulled out the second panel, a land map of coastal defenses: batteries, gun emplacements, and army and navy bases within or bordering the bay. Pinned in the right-hand corner were black-and-white photographs of the batteries above the straits of the Golden Gate. He returned to his desk, took up a pen, and recorded in a logbook minute observations of all that he had seen when he had crossed the Golden Gate Bridge. He frequently lifted his head and regarded the map before he returned to his report. He didn't raise the pen from the page until he heard two quick knocks, a pause, and two more quick knocks. He slid both panels back into the case and secured the trim in place.

"Ohayo gozaimasu," said Chizu, as he unlocked the door. She bowed quickly and entered the room, carrying a tray laden with a pot of green tea, cups, and rice cakes.

Kiyoshi entered behind her and secured the door. They exchanged formalities. Chizu served the tea and cakes. They shared the repast in silence, until Tokido stood and walked to the display case.

"I have called you here at this early hour to discuss a mission that requires extreme caution." He paused, filling his lungs with air. "When the *Tatuta Maru* came through the straits of the Golden Gate and passed under the new bridge, it was clear to me that this structure is a potent symbol of American spirit, ingenuity, and freedom. Now, it has never been clearer." He lifted a pointer from the corner and set the tip on the map. "Here, the bridge spans the only entry to the bay. If the towers and the roadbed were dropped into the bay, the straits would be blocked and the military would be trapped. Commercial shipping, the lifeblood of California, would be stopped."

The faces of Kiyoshi and Chizu had turned ashen.

"Kiyoshi, I want you to find a way to secure the engineering blueprints and final calculations of the bridge."

"*Hai,*" Kiyoshi said, his unblinking eyes riveted on Tokido's face.

"Chizu, support whatever assistance he may need."

"Tokido-*san,*" she said, "I have a relative who works in the engineering firm that designed the bridge."

"Do you trust him?"

"I have known him all my life."

"Speak to him. Exercise caution. Our timing is propitious. The Christmas season and opening of the Exposition have the attention of all citizens."

Chizu and Kiyoshi stood in unison and bowed.

Tokido bowed in return. "Report back to me in one week. Proceed with discretion. Our mission is vital."

CHAPTER FIFTEEN

Woodrow

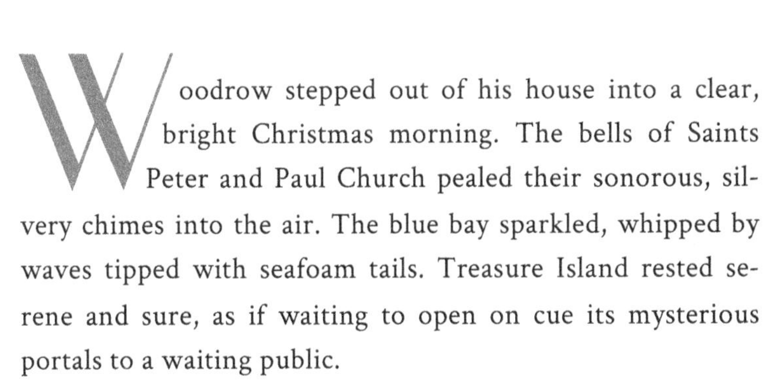

Woodrow stepped out of his house into a clear, bright Christmas morning. The bells of Saints Peter and Paul Church pealed their sonorous, silvery chimes into the air. The blue bay sparkled, whipped by waves tipped with seafoam tails. Treasure Island rested serene and sure, as if waiting to open on cue its mysterious portals to a waiting public.

Over his shoulder, he noticed a lacy curtain part at the window of Mrs. O'Brien, his elderly neighbor. He turned slightly, doffed his hat, and saluted. The curtain fell back into place. He reminded himself to leave a box of See's candy on her doorstep when he returned.

He climbed up the stairs onto Filbert Street, leaving Coit

Tower to the curious crowd that gathered even on this day to view the sights. The wind kicked up, and he pulled his red woolen scarf around his neck. The city spread at his feet. He paused to look out over the houses built cheek to jowl that spilled down Telegraph Hill to the snow-white spires of the church. The nearly two-hundred-foot twin spires towering above Washington Square were etched in gray against the horizon. The sight never failed to thrill him, and on this day, the feeling was especially poignant.

A Western Union telegram lay tucked inside the thrilling book, *Incidents of Travel in Central America, Chiapas, and Yucatan,* by John Lloyd Stephens, that lay on the table near the fireside.

> *Dear Woodrow,*
> *Merry Christmas. We miss you.*
> *We're all anxious for you to return. When are you coming home?*
> *Lovingly, Florence*

Her message filled him with a familiar yearning for the bully strength of his father, the tender hand of his mother, and the irrepressible good humor of his brother, Edward, and his dear sister. She was the one who shouldered the responsibility of caring for their aging parents. But Woodrow wouldn't make the trip back to Philadelphia anytime soon. He would write again and explain; they would understand. Perhaps he would send Florence a Pullman ticket on the Southern Pacific to journey to San Francisco for the Exposition, which she would relish with every bit of her adventurous soul.

He stopped on the steep sidewalk when a young boy ran out the front door of a two-story clapboard house that was festooned with holly wreaths studded with candles in its windows. The boy was dressed in a cowboy costume with a Boy Scout scarf tied around his neck and toting a six-shooter in his hand. He whooped and hollered on the sidewalk. Two little girls, outfitted in sailor hats and double-breasted coats, skipped out to join him, followed by their mother and father. Woodrow slowed his pace. The father locked the door and, as he turned, caught sight of Woodrow. Without hesitation, he tipped his hat and called, "Merry Christmas!"

"Merry Christmas!" Woodrow called back.

The man waved in return and caught the arm of his wife, and the family proceeded down the street. *What a fine morning,* Woodrow thought. *I shall make the best of it.*

He walked smartly down the hill, passing the homes and apartments, wandering by busy restaurants, shuttered bakeries, and shops and over the green sward of the square. The scent of roasting coffee, bracing wine, and sugary pastries laced the air. Long ago, cows had grazed on this boggy spot of land, which would regularly flood even as the city grew. *Just look at it now,* he mused. *The loveliest little park, dotted with benches. The good cheer of humankind written on all faces.* Couples strolled, families gathered here and there, and he noticed the baker of Liguria Bakery flying a kite with his young son. He ambled over to the steps of the church and decided to enter. Baptized and confirmed in the High Episcopal Church, he was no stranger to finding serenity in the house of God.

A side door was ajar. He removed his hat and peered through the opening. It took a moment for his eyes to adjust to the dim interior. At the far end of the nave, lined by vaulted arches from which filigreed lanterns were hung, he gazed at the high altar, carved from snow-white Italian Carrara marble. Red poinsettias adorned the steps to the altar, where the marble statues of Saints Peter and Paul flanked Jesus Christ on the cross, Saint Paul on the right. Above the altar, Christ All Powerful, in a dark orange robe, was painted into the dome. Stained glass windows cast a rosy glow on the polished wooden pews, which were empty save a figure here and there, heads bent in prayer.

The Mass had been offered, carols had been sung, and communion had been taken, and in its wake, the smoky-sweet scent of frankincense, myrrh, and sandalwood, burning on charcoal and swinging from the hands of priests from censers, lingered in the air. It reminded him of the music to "We Three Kings of Orient Are," and he hummed the melody softly to himself as he slipped into a pew.

From the rear, Woodrow heard the sharp *click-click* of heels on the marble floor of the side aisle. As the sound grew nearer, he glanced at the figure of a young woman passing by. Her face was obscured by wavy brown hair, her trench coat belted and cinched tightly. His heart leaped into in his throat. *Lily?* he wondered. As she turned to sit, he saw clearly that it wasn't she. But his pulse was thudding, and, trying to settle his nerves, he bowed his head in contemplation.

Thoughts of her would not cease. The look of vulnerability on her face as she'd sat opposite Tokido at Forbidden City had been shocking. How could she expose herself to him? She had confided that her instincts had warned her about Japan's intent in sending such a large delegation to build a pavilion on the island. Just as important, her vehement dislike of Tokido, which she had also voiced, echoed in Woodrow's mind. And yet there she had been with that very man at a nightclub! Didn't she realize how much attention they'd attract? A Caucasian woman with an Oriental man could cause a riot.

Woodrow's memory of Tokido's returning to the island on the skiff before dawn hadn't dimmed. News of Japan's aggression continued to roll over the AP wires. The Movietone black-and-white news clips of atrocities in China sickened him. At the club, Schuman's steely glance warned him off. After the show, Pflueger, Toth, and the gents had a fine time trading quips and innuendos. In the end, Woodrow concluded he would remain silent, keep his ear to the ground and his finger to the wind.

Abruptly he rose to his feet, shaking himself free of worry. *A man without illusions is a sorry creature,* he thought. *But the dangerous hope that a woman like her might come to feel for me something that she's found in a whole-bodied man is a fool's quicksand.*

Leaving the church, he consoled himself that he wasn't entirely unaccustomed to a male's basic means of expression. The charms of certain women—the silky softness of their thighs, their musky scent, their sex as potent as a drug—had been bestowed on him, infrequently but memorably, by the hearty arrangements of Edward. In the Yucatán, the Mayans revered him as a god, and so there were occasions when he couldn't turn away from the elaborate offers of female engagement.

Enough, he reminded himself, posing on the stairs of the church, readjusting his hat on his head. *Blessings on my family. Blessings on this troubled world. If I can do good or offer kindness, then I shall. The Exposition is about to open, and what a grand affair it will be. For now, there's a chop in the refrigerator, a bottle of fine claret on the sideboard, the Brandenburg Concertos on the turntable of the Philco, and a corking good yarn.* Off he set for home, head high, step purposeful.

* * *

AFTER DINNER, HE lit a fire, set a glass of wine on the table, reclined in the chair, and began to read. Logs crackled in the grate. A faint knock sounded at the door. He lifted his head. Was he hearing correctly? *Ah, it must be the wind,* he thought. The knock came again, this time louder. Tentatively, he hopped off the chair and walked down the stairs. *Who would be knocking on my door on Christmas?* He flicked on the porch light, unlocked the door, and slowly opened it.

Lily stood on the stoop, the collar of her fur coat turned up against her pale neck. The tips of the fur glistened in the light. Her gloved hands held a small box wrapped in glossy red paper and tied in a white bow. She smiled shyly down at him. "Merry Christmas, Woodrow."

He couldn't find his voice. He began to shake. *What right does she have to show up on Christmas unannounced? What presumption! Did she think I wouldn't have invitations? Did she think I'd be crying in my eggnog?*

"Are you all right?" she asked.

"Of course I'm all right," he snapped. "Why wouldn't I be? I'm having a perfectly fine Christmas."

Her eyes clouded. "Oh, well, I wanted to . . ." Swallowing, she caught her lower lip with her teeth.

"What is it?" he demanded.

She began again, her voice faint. "I wanted you to have this." She held the box out to him.

He looked at it with disgust. "I don't hear from you in weeks. Now you show up. Did you think I'd ask you in? That we'd sing a carol and share stories?"

"No," she whispered.

"What did you think?" He seethed with anger. "That I'd want to hear about your evening with the enemy? That I'd be overjoyed to learn what you did, where you went, the lies he told you?"

She stepped back, her face crumbling with dismay. "I thought we were friends."

"Think again," he said, slamming the door in her face.

Court of the Moon

Night View of Japan Pavilion

CHAPTER SIXTEEN

Lily

Woodrow's front door shook on its hinges, casting Lily backward. She stumbled and nearly fell. For an instant, she was catapulted to another Christmas, when she was no more than ten and had presented her father with a cigar wrapped in white paper imprinted with candy canes. Not just any cigar—a Cuban cigar she had confiscated at bodily risk from her stepbrother's cache of stolen goods buried in the cellar.

Her father had unwrapped the cigar, a scowl on his face. "Where're you get this?" he growled. His dark eyes bore into the softest part of her heart. Before she could move, he had unbuckled his belt and slipped it out of his trouser loops. It was useless to run. The slashing sound of the leather dropped her to her knees before the first blow lashed across her back.

Now she reeled, her feet finding purchase on the ground. Woodrow's path was scattered with winter's dead leaves. Their burned scent rose to meet her nostrils. The gift in her hands mocked her. She bent down and placed it on the mat. The immense quiet of the night draped around her shoulders. She turned blindly; her eyes stung with tears, running down her cheeks. Strings of red, yellow, blue, and green lights twinkled on Christmas trees hung with tinsel in the windows of the homes along the stairs. Through the dense foliage, above the rooftops, across bay waters, Treasure Island seemed close enough to touch.

She tripped down the steps, wanting to be as far away from Woodrow as she could get. On the edge of Montgomery Street, she leaned against the concrete wall and gazed at the new art deco Malloch Building constructed on the downslope. Silvery sgraffito figures, forty feet high, gleamed on the concrete of the facade. On a corner of the structure, she peered at an image of a bare-chested Spanish explorer with a telescope raised to one eye. Directly around the corner, a robed female, representing the spirit of California, was overlaid upon a map of the state.

A lacy mist dampened the air. At the dead end of the street, Julius's Castle had opened its doors to Christmas festivities. She could almost hear patrons in the restaurant, smell whiskey in the Manhattans, platters of fragrant roasted turkey, mounds of mashed potatoes slathered with savory gravy. She had never felt so alone. She stared back at Treasure Island. The Tower of the Sun was outlined against the black sky. The taste of defiance flooded her mouth. *Who is Woodrow to pass judgment on me?* she thought. *Neither he nor anyone else has any idea what I'm capable of.* She pulled her hat down low, slung the strap of her bag over one shoulder, tightened her scarf, and started walking.

* * *

LILY WATCHED THE lights of the island from the backseat of a cab as it *click-clack*ed over the Bay Bridge. Midspan, the cabbie veered sharply onto the turnoff to Treasure Island. At the bottom of the road, a lineup of ticket booths appeared, and beyond it the Avenue of the Palms. One booth was illuminated. Inside, a night watchman peered at Lily as she stepped out of the cab.

"Merry Christmas, Miss Nordby. What're you doing here?"

"Same to you, Eddie. Holiday or not, the presses keep rolling."

"No kidding. I read your stories every day. Gee, they're swell."

"Glad you like them. So, you're the one to pull guard duty tonight?"

"I don't mind. It's real quiet. The family celebrated earlier."

"Didn't you tell me you and the missus have a child?"

"You bet. Our daughter is a cutie."

"I'm sure she's a doll." Lily reached inside her pocket and pulled out a Heinz pickle pin and two matchbooks embossed with the Tower of the Sun and the Elephant Tower. THE PAGEANT OF THE PACIFIC, SAN FRANCISCO, 1939, was printed on the matchbooks. "Here's something to take home, the latest from the publicity machine. They're churning out souvenirs like Folgers roasts coffee beans."

"Gosh, thanks. My wife is keeping a scrapbook. She'll get a big kick out of these trinkets."

"What do you think about the Expo?" she asked, sweeping her hand toward the buildings.

"Don't know what you call the highfalutin architecture, but it sure takes the cake for flashy. And the flowers will be pretty, all right. Can't wait to ride on the Elephant Train and a rickshaw."

"Likewise," she said. "Me? I'm a pushover for Count Basie, Bing Crosby, Eddie Duchin. Oh, and parades—I love them. We'll be dizzy with parades. Well, I'll amble over to the press room." She flashed a key. "Working on a story about the preview tours that are starting."

Eddie nodded. "I'll call Fred. He'll escort you."

"That's not necessary."

"I can't let you onto the grounds alone."

"Come on, Eddie."

"Rules are rules."

"Bend this rule for me." She reached out and lightly touched his arm.

He hesitated. "Just looking out for your safety, Miss Nordby. Won't take a minute to get Fred." He plucked a walkie-talkie off the counter.

"To tell you the truth," she said, "it's been a rough night."

Eddie paused, pressing his lips together in concern. "Shucks, can't imagine a gal like you having trouble."

"Happens to all of us. Families are tricky. I'd like to take a stroll down the esplanade to clear my head before I pound the keys. You understand." She pointed over her shoulder. "I won't go far. Just to Clipper Way."

Eddie glanced at the lights strung along the road. The monolithic curved walls of the administration building gave way to the phosphorescent glint of the fountain in the Enchanted Garden just beyond it. Opposite the garden, the outline of the *Tatuta Maru*'s bow was barely visible. "You sure?" he asked.

"Absolutely."

Eddie put the walkie-talkie back on the table.

"There's a bed in the press room. I'll probably bunk there for the night."

"Okay, then. Just between you and me." Eddie said. "Off the record."

"Off the record." She saluted and stepped away.

"Thanks again for the souvenirs."

"Absolutely!"

* * *

BEFORE EDDIE COULD change his mind, she hurried away, hunching her shoulders against the damp cold. Bay water lapped at the seawall. Gulls screeched and sea lions barked. She halted and ducked back into the shadows, studying the *Tatuta Maru,* half as long as a city block. Flags strung along guy wires flapped in the wind. Thick, braided ropes, looped around stanchions, held the ship fast to the shore. Along the starboard flank, yellow lights glowed in portholes, and on the upper level of the ship, the windows were dark. The gangplank tilted up at a sharp angle to the shore. She clutched her collar and rushed away.

In the dim of the Treasure Garden, she glanced down to the Court of the Moon, where she made out the long, rectangular pool ringed with huge Ali Baba vases and Irish yew trees. Beds of flowers and plants slept in stilled silence. She pressed on, her feet seemingly knowing where to go, her eyes searching every crevice and corner. An otherworldly presence hovered along promenades, in courtyards, near alabaster sculptures. Unexpectedly, her neck prickled. She came to a sudden stop. Her eyes scanned the area. Had she heard a footfall? Shadows angled in a crosshatch of elongated shapes. Perhaps a bird had fluttered in a bush, or one of the rats that roamed the island had scurried along the path. Her stomach dropped. She had hardly eaten all day. Her hands felt clammy.

She picked up speed, turning at the Tower of the Sun, down the Court of Reflections, around the Lake of Nations. She alternated between sprinting and walking the final distance until she reached the Japanese Pavilion. Her breath came in short gasps. At the top of the wide stairs, underneath deep eaves, she folded into a corner and studied the grounds. The scene was as fixed as a woodblock. The frigid air seemed to hiss. She slipped her hand through the handle of the great front door and pulled. It didn't budge. She tried the next door. It, too, was as immobile as the gnarled trunk of an oak. She darted past the smooth, round columns onto the deck overhanging the lagoon. Rice-paper shoji extended along the length of the deck.

She crouched low, removed her gloves, and stuffed them in her pockets. As she crept along the floorboards, her fingers traced the shallow wooden grooves where the shoji frames rested. Every window was secured, except for one. The last one. It gave way, sliding in its track. Stock-still, she swiveled her head, her eyes sweeping back and forth.

The water of the koi pond licked against the underpinnings of the pavilion. A distant beating of wings sounded in the sky. In one fluid motion, she opened the shoji, hiked herself up, and jumped through the opening. Landing on her feet, she spun around and closed the shoji.

A calm, cool purpose settled over her.

In semi-darkness, she deciphered the tables and chairs in the tearoom. She tiptoed through the long room and into the passageway, past halls leading to other displays. When she reached the hallway that she had been told would lead to a personal office for Tokido and his staff, she inched along the passage, her fingertips glancing the shelves. Perspiration trickled down her temples. The door handle was cool in her hand, and as she turned it, she found that it was locked solid.

Without hesitation, she fished two hairpins out of her bag. With one hairpin between in her lips, she pulled the other apart until the legs formed a ninety-degree angle and bent the tip of one leg to form a pick. Holding the pick between her teeth, she bent the other hairpin to form a lever. Then she closed her eyes and listened. Dead quiet answered.

She dropped to her knees, slipped the lever into the

lower side of the keyhole, and turned it slightly, keeping pressure on the barrel. Taking the pick out of her mouth, she inserted it into the barrel and ran it back and forth under the pins. Meticulously, she tested each pin. The first two were loose; the third one was seized. Slowly and carefully, she forced it upward until she heard it click into place. "Ah," she exhaled. The next pin had seized, and, clenching her teeth, she forced it upward. It, too, clicked into place. Three more go to! Her pulse pounded in her ears. Two! One! The door opened. "I'm in!" she whispered, and stepped into the office.

The metallic face of an electric clock cast an icy green glow over the room. Swiftly, she closed the door and switched on an overhead light. Three desks were swept clean of the usual clutter of books, papers, and ashtrays spilling over with cigarette butts. A typewriter sat on the smallest desk. A black phone beside a blotter, notepad, and pen rested on each desktop. A bonsai pine bough and a spray of red holly berries in a shallow bowl was placed on the largest desk. *Ah, Tokido's,* she thought.

She pulled up a chair and slid open the slim drawer under the desktop. It was fastidiously arranged with writing implements, an engagement calendar, and an address book. There were no personal effects, photographs, or documents. She rifled through the pages, which were written in Japanese. The handwriting resembled inked bird scratches. She replaced the items as she had found them and turned to the deep drawers. She grasped the handle and pulled. Locked. A groan escaped her lips.

The contents of the other two desks were the same—almost identical and just as orderly. What had she missed? She returned to Tokido's desk, took out everything, and flipped the drawer over. On its underside, she stared at a small key taped to the wood.

She wet her lips, bent down to the first deep drawer, and carefully slipped the key into the keyhole. It wobbled. She wanted to scream. The key fit a much smaller lock, but to what? Her mind raced. She inspected a closet that held reams of papers, raincoats, an umbrella, black galoshes.

A display case on the wall caught her eye. She stood in front of it and stared through the glass front, which held ivory miniatures arranged in niches. Along the cabinet's edge, small birds, vases, and floral motifs were carved into the gleaming, dark wood. She ran her finger along the carvings, tracing their smooth shapes.

A buoy tolled on the bay. Her blouse was soaked through with sweat. The clock read 10:37 p.m. A calendar and architectural renderings of the pavilion and samurai house were pinned to the wall. What had she found? Not a goddamn thing. She replaced everything as she had found it, killed the lights, and carefully opened the door, straining to hear. A hush met her ears. She decided against resetting the lock, which would take precious time. She crept back to the tearoom and hiked out through the shoji window.

She left the pavilion as quickly as she had arrived, retracing her steps, deflated, hungry, and very cold. She felt like a fugitive dodging a searchlight.

At last she was back on the esplanade, weak and shaken, standing in front of the *Tatuta Maru.* Nothing had changed—

not the impregnable girth of the ship, the faint hum of traffic in the distance on the Bay Bridge, or the ticket booth, safely within sight.

"Good evening, Miss Nordby," a voice said.

She whirled around. "Who are you?"

His face was shrouded in shadow. The red glow of a cigarette flashed in his fingers. "May I escort you aboard?"

"Wait. I know your voice."

He snuffed out the cigarette beneath his foot and started for the gangplank.

As he passed, she peered more closely. "You're Mr. Okamura's chauffeur, aren't you?"

"He is aboard. Follow me."

Don't be a fool, she thought, yet she hurried to keep up behind the man's long steps. How much had he seen? How much did he know?

He led her to a reception room filled with stately, stiff chairs and ornate tables. Minutes passed excruciatingly slowly. She paced, straightening her skirt and hose and running her fingers through her disheveled hair. And then, in an instant, Tokido was striding through the room, concern written on his face. He wore an elegant tux as naturally as other men wore sweaters and slacks—the luster of the material as black as his hair, the crease of the pants knife-sharp.

"Lily, this is so unexpected. Are you well?" He reached for her hand, his fingers glancing hers.

"Of course." She plunged her hand into her coat pocket. "I'm perfectly fine."

"Your hand is freezing. I'll order tea."

"Don't bother."

"It isn't an inconvenience. In fact, I like to close my day with jasmine tea. I would like you to join me."

"In that case, I accept." She flopped into a high-back chair, crossing and uncrossing her legs, jiggling her foot.

He broke away and spoke into a receiver hanging on the wall. When he returned, he took a chair across from her.

"You've been celebrating," she said.

"Yes, we've just returned." He looked at the face of his wristwatch. "Not thirty minutes ago."

She blinked at him.

He smiled pleasantly. "It is Christmas."

"For some people."

"There were parties all over the city. I had hoped our paths would cross."

She struggled for an answer. None came.

"I remember what you said about this holiday."

"What was that?" she asked.

"'Christmas is for children,'" he said gently. "I wondered if you were in the company of children."

She waved aside his question. "Do you have a cigarette?"

He quickly withdrew a small, thin silver box from his pocket and offered her a slim cigarette. She brought it to her lips. He bent close and flicked a lighter. As she inhaled, her hand shook uncontrollably.

"Let me take you somewhere less formal," he suggested. "It's where I like to spend the final hours of the evening. I was there when you came aboard." He held out his hand. "We'll have our tea there."

She refused his hand—was he a worldly diplomat, or was he an enemy? She burned with a hot, hard flame to know the truth. He waited; she stood. He led her silently through the ship, toward the bow. At the end of the passage, he opened a door.

A glow warmed the interior of a small salon, and, through wraparound windows, the brilliant lights of the city blazed against the skyline. Nearby, the island's high, sculptured walls were covered with a gray, opaque haze.

Tokido pointed to two deep club chairs flanking a low, burnished table. "Please."

Lily folded into a chair. A knock sounded on the door. A demure woman in a dark kimono entered, carrying a lacquered tray that contained a pot of steaming tea and two cups.

"*Arigatou,*" Tokido said.

The woman placed the tray on the table, bowed, and left the room.

Tokido served, and, as if in silent agreement, they sipped the tea without a word. Lily was acutely aware of his presence, but she dared not look at him. She felt his eyes studying her.

Finally, she sighed, placed the empty cup on the tray, and approached the windows. "I wonder if the city will be the same after the Expo."

He came up behind her. "Nothing remains the same. Such is the nature of all things."

He stood so close that his proximity radiated heat. A deep ache rose up in her. She turned to him. He filled her vision, only him. With his finger, he lightly touched her chin and searched her eyes, as if to ask permission. His hand circled her neck strongly. She closed her eyes and tipped her head back. He kissed her mouth, his breath filling her lungs, his body enveloping her being, his desire answering her longing.

CHAPTER SEVENTEEN

Tokido

The streets of Japantown glistened with a sheen of fog lit by the headlights of passing cars. On Post Street, Tokido stepped from a limousine and walked up Buchanan. People passed by in twos and threes. Wind chimes tinkled a muffled greeting. Automobiles were parked along the curb, their rounded bumpers dripping with moisture. The scent of charcoal stung his nostrils. Through the window of a restaurant, flames leaped from a hibachi. His mouth watered in anticipation: crispy duck, pungent fish, juicy pork-and-cabbage *gyoza,* hot sake.

An alleyway, bordered on either side by shops and businesses, appeared ahead. Just before he turned to go into the alley, he heard his name being called. He watched as a small figure hurried toward him. It wasn't until she was upon him that he recognized her.

"Chizu, what is it?"

"Forgive me, Tokido-*san*."

"Yes?"

"The reporter from the *Examiner*." Her voice trembled. "She went into the alleyway and through your gate. She did not return."

"There is no cause for alarm." He reached out and gently touched her arm. "It is best that you return home now."

She dropped her eyes. A tear hovered on a lower lash and cascaded down her petal-soft cheek. "As you wish."

"I'll see you tomorrow," he called, as her small steps spirited her past shops and doorways and she disappeared into the night.

* * *

"I SEE YOU found the key," Tokido said.

"It was easy." The light from a rice-paper lantern fell on Lily's face. She sat at a low table, the collar of her coat spread open and draped over her shoulders. The room was furnished simply: tatami mats on the floor, a shoji panel over the window, a futon covered with cotton quilts, a *tansu* against the wall.

"Perhaps I should make it more difficult."

"Perhaps," she said.

"Shall I reward you for your skills?"

"How would you do that?" she asked.

"There are ways."

"I like it here."

"I'm hungry," he said.

"So am I."

He reached for her hand to pull her to her feet, and her coat slipped to the floor. Her warm lips were moist, her eyelids heavy with desire. The taste of her flooded his senses, and he lifted her off her feet, carrying her to the futon, laying her down, kneeling at her side. She was tearing at his shirt, fingers fumbling with the buttons.

They undressed each other in a flurry, clothes slipping from their bodies, until it was skin on skin, their hearts pounding. He was intent, moving on a different plane, waiting, until her yelps of pleasure told him she was ready and he burst inside her.

He stroked her hair, traced the shape of her lips with his finger, and kissed her brow. The branch of a tree in the courtyard scratched against the glass of the window. "Still hungry?"

She lay in his arms. "Ravenous," she sighed. "Simply ravenous."

* * *

HE LED HER through back alleys, over cobbled streets, and through the door of a small noodle shop. In a private booth, the entry covered by an indigo fabric panel, they sat opposite each other, bent over steamy bowls of miso ramen. Chopped scallions, ginger, garlic, a slice of hard-boiled egg, and pork floated atop the golden, aromatic broth.

"I had no idea how delicious this would be," Lily said, stabbing at the noodles that swam beneath the fragrant liquid.

"Go ahead and slurp the noodles. It's a compliment to the cook."

She leaned over the bowl, trying to manipulate the chopsticks. The noodles slipped, and flecks of broth flew over the tabletop.

He laughed. "Don't give up."

She shook her head. "Easy for you to say." She bent her head and tried again. "I've never been to this part of town. How long have you lived here?"

"Since I first arrived. On occasion, the *Tatuta Maru* returns to Yokohama. I was given an apartment on Nob Hill, but I prefer this part of town. When the ship docks at Treasure Island, I have a choice of where to stay. My quarters here are private, quiet, and simple. Exactly the way I like it."

"Do you miss home?"

He looked up at her, waiting before he spoke. "I do. I have an uncle who is very old. I hope to see him before he dies. When I was young, he taught me many things, like how to fish and grow bonsai and tie knots. Our family would take the train to the mountains. We stayed in *ryokan*, somewhat like your lodges, and bathed in hot springs and ate until we could eat no more. The air was pure, white birds flew over the river, and my brothers and I laughed and played until we were tucked side by side under quilts and sleep claimed us."

She was the first to look away, and they ate until their bowls were drained and their faces were flushed with satisfaction.

She broke the silence. "I'd like to take you somewhere that you may not know about."

"Where is that?"

"The lookout on Mount Tamalpais in Marin County. There's a view of the Pacific Ocean, the bay, and San Francisco. It's breathtaking."

"Tonight?" he asked.

"No, not tonight. You must see it during the day. There are trails everywhere. Impossible, given our schedules. But I'd like to try."

"Then we'll find a way." He reached for her hand and kissed it. "Come back with me now. It's hours before dawn."

* * *

BEHIND THE LOCKED door of the Japanese Pavilion's office in the frigid mid-January predawn, Chizu unfurled a set of plans from a bolt of silk fabric.

"As you requested, Tokido-*san*," she said, laying them on a desk. She smoothed the sheets with the palm of her hand and anchored the edges, which had begun to yellow and crinkle, with four smooth rocks.

Tokido stepped forward and bent over the drawings; Kiyoshi joined him. A faint smell of ammonia lifted off the blueprints. The title page read: "Golden Gate Bridge. Construction Drawings. Firm: Strauss Engineering Company. Signed: Chief Engineer, Joseph B. Strauss." Beneath this insignia, the engineer's seal was stamped in black ink.

"Well done, Chizu," Tokido said. "You have shown great resourcefulness."

"*Hai*," Chizu said, weaving her hands into the sleeves of her kimono and bowing slightly.

"Kiyoshi, let us confirm that we have a complete set."

Side by side, the men examined each sheet, upon which line drawings depicted anchorage structures, main piers, towers, deck, and cables. Each sheet was numbered, and all the sheets were stapled together.

Tokido peered at Chizu. "Did you receive calculations or specifications?"

"No, my contact assures me this information is forthcoming."

"I see," he said. "Utmost discretion is practiced at every turn?"

"*Hai*," she answered.

"Did you receive anything else?"

She reached inside her obi and withdrew a small envelope. "Here are photographs taken during construction. The quality is poor."

Tokido opened the envelope. The two-by-three-inch black-and-white glossy photographs were perforated by sprocket holes running down one side. The images of the bridge's ironworkers erecting two towers, stringing cables, and building the concrete deck were out of focus.

"These may not be useful," he said, slipping the photos back into the envelope and handing it to Kiyoshi. "Store these."

He turned to Chizu. "This part of our mission is close to completion. My compliments."

"May I wrap the blueprints for you, Tokido-*san*?"

"Yes; then carry on. The time is short before opening-day ceremonies. I must go. My car is waiting."

* * *

CONSUL GENERAL MOTO eyed Tokido with a cool, unblinking stare. "We shall dispatch the plans immediately. Your work is commendable."

Tokido silently held Moto's gaze. Outside the office, he heard footfalls, hushed voices, and jangling phones. Inside, the air was as still as the hour before dawn. The consulate felt as impenetrable as the black Matsumoto Castle, yet a sharp band of tension ran down Tokido's spine.

"Tell me. Operation Blind Warrior continues?" Moto picked at the remnants of his breakfast: grilled white fish, miso soup, rice wrapped in nori, and sour pickles.

"Ship movements in the bay have not accelerated. There is no change in traffic. Now, the details of opening day need attention. We are anticipating thousands of visitors in the first month."

"Of course." Moto drained the last of the miso soup and burped. "The parade on Market Street requires my involvement. As do all dinners and events." He grinned broadly and wove his fingers together into a web, resting them on his belly. "Mayor Rossi has declared April 29 Japan Day. The tide of favorable opinion has turned our way." He fixed Tokido with one eye as if squinting through a gunsight. "And what have you learned from the newspaper reporter?"

"I have verified the batteries and gun emplacements in the military forts on both sides of the bay."

Moto nodded. "Exactly. Intelligence advises that, in the Marin Headlands, a powerful military fortification has been built. Last spring, we heard the explosions of dynamite and saw dust clouds rising into the sky. Then the blasting stopped. We have been unable to penetrate the top-secret nature of the installation."

"Are you suggesting I pursue my source on this matter?"

Moto managed a smirk, and then his eyes went cold. "Spare no opportunity. The reporter's recent articles about the pavilion are favorable. Advise me when you receive new information. I will be in touch."

Tokido rose carefully from the chair. "As you wish." And, departing with a bow that could only be interpreted as one of the utmost respect, he let himself out.

Leland Clifford Painting the Tower of the Sun
on Dorothy Drew's Back

CHAPTER EIGHTEEN

Woodrow

Woodrow's remorse tormented him. Never did it cross his mind to offer Lily an apology—too easy, meaningless, even crass. He was sure she was jammed into the after-hours crowd at Shanty Malone's, where dry martinis flowed, or Lucca, where sixty-five-cent, seven-course dinners with wine sold out.

Newspaper headlines were touting the Exposition like the Rapture, and Lily's stories ran in the *Examiner* daily. Woodrow tried to read between the lines for any personal slant upon which to heal their spat. Her reporting ran the gamut between academics who were hypnotizing women's clubs with lectures about glorious European art treasures and a dress designer who devised a Treasure Island women's wardrobe: leather vests and high-heeled boots by day, and, by evening, a frock called the Coit Tower, a cylinder of pleated chiffon. Woodrow shook his head at such nonsense, declaring to himself that any female visitor to the island would need Eskimo skins not to freeze. San Francisco seemed on the verge of hysteria.

He set upon a solution to make amends with Lily and simultaneously roamed the island to drown his misery.

A cold snap had dumped snow on Mount Diablo and Mount Tamalpais and Skyline Boulevard. He wondered if the koi at the Japanese Pavilion's lagoon had frozen, but avoided the wretched place. Meanwhile, gardeners and workmen on the island were planting and painting in a final flurry while dozens of pretty, nubile women paraded around in one-piece bathing suits.

They marched up stairways and under arches, gesturing grandly for the camera toward the architectural wonders of the ersatz Chichén Itzá and Ankor Wat. Goose bumps as big as gumballs rose on their arms and legs. No one seemed to mind.

One brisk morning, he rode his bicycle down to the north end of the island, where a twelve-thousand-car parking lot had been graded over the muck. The projection was five folks per car. *Imagine that,* he speculated—sixty thousand people streaming onto the island in cars! Add the white ferries lurching over the bay at fifteen-minute intervals, stuffed to the rails with passengers, and the orange Key Route electric trains, marked "X" for "Exposition," rolling over the Bay Bridge from the East Bay, depositing even more fairgoers onto the island. Why, there could be two hundred thousand people on opening day! His mind boggled at the number.

On the way back, he saw chamber of commerce mucketymucks, consulate dignitaries, army and navy brass, and foreign delegates being ushered over the island like royalty. In a small contingent huddled in front of a column at the electricity and communications building, he recognized Adolph Schuman. He circled back and pulled up outside the knot of men.

Schuman turned as he approached. "Hello, Woodrow. Good to see you."

"Likewise. Haven't met you since our poker game."

"When you skunked us?"

Woodrow offered a modest smile. "The cards don't lie." He peered between the men's pant legs. "Say, what's going on here?" An artist in a beret and a white smock was dabbing paint onto the naked back of a brunette stunner who perched on the base of the column. She mugged for the camera, looking over her shoulder, hand on hip, crossed legs dangling.

"Leland Clifford is painting the Tower of the Sun on Dorothy Drew's back. Another publicity stunt the press won't resist."

"Who's Dorothy Drew?"

"One of Sally Rand's girls."

Woodrow shrugged. "You mean the fan dancer?"

"The very one. She's operating the girlie show in the Gayway. Rand has the women gussied up in cowboy hats, holsters placed in strategic spots, and boots. Apparently, that's all. They cavort behind a glass wall, feeding lambs, sitting on donkeys, that sort of thing. She calls it the Nude Ranch."

Woodrow shook his head. “Not my kind of thing.”

“Nor mine, but not all tastes run to European art and flowers. Vanderberg and his PR staff will do anything to entice visitors. I think the stakes are so high their brains are addled.”

“I guess I’d better get myself over there before the island sinks under the weight of the masses.” Woodrow shuffled his feet, smoothing the brim of his hat between his fingers. “May I have a word with you”—he nodded to a landing farther down the steps—“in private?”

“By all means,” Schuman answered.

They eased away from the group, walked to the landing, and stood side by side.

Woodrow swallowed repeatedly. Adolph crossed his arms and waited, peering out over the bay as if he were waiting for a Clipper to drop out of the sky and land at their feet.

Finally, Woodrow cleared his throat. “Have you seen Lily lately?”

“Can’t say I have. Why?”

“I’m afraid I insulted her.”

“How is that?”

“When we saw her at Forbidden City, it was quite a shock.”

“You mean a white woman with a Japanese man?”

Woodrow flushed in anger. “I’ve traveled all over the world, lived and worked alongside men and women of every stripe and color. The color of one’s skin has nothing to do with integrity. I’m not a racist.”

“What is it, then?”

"When Lily came into the club with Okamura, you caught my eye."

An icy emotion hardened Adolph's expression. "And?"

"You looked at me like you seemed to know something that I didn't know. As if you were warning me off."

"I don't know what you're talking about."

"Is that so?" Woodrow asked, holding Schuman's gaze. "Then my error."

"Sounds like you have a romantic interest in the woman."

"Don't take me for a fool, Adolph. She's a friend. I'm a realist. I know my limitations."

"Well, I wouldn't worry. Lily can take care of herself."

"That's what I'm afraid of," Woodrow said. He tripped down the stairs, jumped onto his bicycle, and sped away.

* * *

BY THE TIME Woodrow zoomed onto the grounds of the Gayway, he was sweating profusely and still hopping mad. "That son of a bitch," he mumbled. "The suave businessman and humanitarian shows his true colors. If it kills me, I'll find out what he knows."

When his vision cleared, he found himself in the midway, flanked on either side by false-fronted buildings. Other than workmen hammering nails into stages that hovered off the ground next to the buildings' facades, the midway was deserted. It was like waking up in the middle of a movie set before the director called, "Action!"

He propped his bike against one of the starburst light

poles and wandered toward an establishment that stated simply DOUGHNUTS. As he drew closer, a delicious, sugary aroma rose on the wind. On tiptoe, he peeked in the window. No one appeared. *Perhaps the bakers are testing their skills over ovens, getting ready for opening day,* he thought.

Signs on other buildings advertised an array of temptations. In front of an attraction called *Stella,* he read how, for fifteen cents, a visitor could peek at a painting of a nude woman who appeared to breathe. At Ripley's Believe It or Not, photographs showed a man about to drive an eight-inch spike into his head with a hammer and a woman poised to swallow neon glass tubes. A movie promised nudists playing volleyball. Woodrow shook his head at such foolishness. He could only imagine what the other wonders of these emporiums had up their sleeves or down their throats. No doubt women would be sawed in half, monkeys would drive race cars, and King Kong would beat his chest. Incubator Babies and Palace of Monsters turned his stomach. *The puerile taste of man knows no bounds,* he thought.

Farther down the midway, a towering neon sign, two stories high, read SALLY RAND'S NUDE RANCH. Farther yet, two Ferris wheels side by side were etched against the sky. Nearby, a giant crane stood ready to welcome passengers into pods that hung from its Y-beam and would spin them to oblivion.

Here indeed stretched Forty Acres of Fun—a carnival fairyland for starry-eyed innocents, a playground for raunchy pleasuremongers, an amusement park for thrill seekers. Toss in a little sugar to rot teeth and grease to churn stomachs, and you could spend day and night here. If the front of the island was highbrow, the back of the island was pure lowbrow. Woodrow envisioned mothers covering their children's eyes, hurrying them along before they spotted a heaving bosom or a naked cowgirl, and teenage boys stealing their older brothers' IDs to sneak into the nudie shows.

Just then, from a distance, he noticed the tallest man he had ever seen step from around a corner. He looked as if he had been hewn from a slab of granite. When he saw Woodrow, the man's eyes, sunken under a heavy brow, lit up. The giant seemed friendly indeed, but Woodrow wasn't in the mood for idle chatter, even with a giant. *What a pair we'd make,* he thought. Two ends of the spectrum. The giant raised his hand in greeting. Woodrow turned to leave, but he could see that for every six steps he took, the man would easily overtake him with one stride. Woodrow held his ground.

"Name's Rosy," the giant called. He was coatless, pink skin flushed with good health, hair Brylcreemed to his huge skull.

"How do you do? I'm Woodrow."

"You with the miniature Western village?"

"No! That is an abomination."

The giant's uncomprehending eyes starred down at Woodrow like headlamps.

"One hundred dwarfs in cowboy outfits reenacting pioneer days. No thank you."

"You mean the midgets? What's wrong with that?"

Woodrow turned on his heel and walked away as fast as he could.

Rosy stuck to his side. "What, then? You in a freak show?"

"No, my good man—not that, either."

"You talk like some educated man."

"If you'll excuse me, I have an appointment."

The giant halted, as if weighing his options. "I was right. You're important for sure. I'll be keeping a lookout for you." He shouted to Woodrow's departing figure, "See you around, Boss!"

* * *

AS WOODROW PUTTERED down Commonwealth, passing the parade grounds in front of the federal building, devoted to housing exhibits that showcased government in action, he saw a figure signaling to him at the edge of the lake in front of the immense, forty-eight-column structure. *What now?* he thought. He stepped on the brakes and straddled the seat, squinting toward a man walking toward him along a path. As the figure drew closer, he saw Timothy Pflueger, who hailed, "Come on over!"

A sudden inspiration matched his realization that escape was impossible. Woodrow wheeled the bike toward Pflueger and stopped at his feet.

"My friend, haven't seen you in an age. What do you think of this achievement? I'm damn proud to see it finished."

Woodrow nodded enthusiastically. The building was like Pflueger the man: upright, civic-minded, bred for success.

"When do you sleep? I have the impression you bunk here on the island."

Pflueger chortled. "No, a preposterous idea."

"You still live in the Mission district?"

"That's true. I live in the house where I grew up. Wouldn't trade it for a penthouse on Nob Hill. Everyone knows everyone else. A community all to itself."

"It sounds ideal for a busy man like you."

"When you're ready, I'll show you around the neighborhood. Salt-of-the-earth types, blue-collar and hardworking.

"I understand you know Lily's family?"

"Where'd you hear that?"

"She told me when I took her home after the ball at the St. Francis."

Pflueger rubbed his hand over the pale stubble on his chin. "I feel pretty bad about that, poking my nose into her business."

Woodrow kept silent, watching Pflueger.

"I was being friendly, telling her about my aunt who remembers her as a child, and how my aunt knew her mother."

"So I heard."

"I had no idea she believed her mother had died." Pflueger shook his head. "Lily comes from a rough breed. Let's say I wouldn't call her father if the pipes burst in our house and flooded the basement."

"Her mother?"

"Apparently she was a beauty in her day. Then she packed up and left. Now rumors circulate like flies on pie."

"What rumors?"

"After the poker game at Hotaling's, we passed by the International Settlement on our way to Forbidden City."

"I remember."

"It's rumored she's there. Singing for her supper. She calls herself Sweet Sadie."

* * *

WOODROW PAUSED ON the one-block stretch of Pacific Avenue that ran from Montgomery Street and ended at Kearny. The arched sign, INTERNATIONAL SETTLEMENT, straddled the thoroughfare. Its lights blazed into the night sky. The buildings sported stucco facades and gleaming windows. Nightclubs and restaurants lined both sides of the street. Patrons wandered up and down the avenue like tourists slumming on the wrong side of town.

Woodrow had no idea where to start, so he picked the first club closest to him, the Pago Pago. He walked through the swinging door into the dark interior of a seedy Polynesian setting. A tiki bar ran one length of the long room, and tables surrounded a small dance floor. A few couples sat at tables. They eyed him curiously. Billie Holiday's voice crooned "Strange Fruit" from the jukebox.

He hopped up onto a barstool. The bartender, thin as a blade, peered down from the far end of the bar, where he was polishing glasses. He tossed the cloth over his shoulder and walked toward Woodrow. Slapping down a flimsy cocktail napkin that portrayed a Tahitian dancer in a grass skirt, he asked, "What'll you have, mate?"

Woodrow fingered the napkin. "What's the specialty of the house?"

The bartender looked bored. A fringe of hair lined his bald head. "Mai tai."

"I'll have that."

When the bartender set down the pale yellow concoction, Woodrow lifted the glass and took a sip. The rum was weak, the pineapple juice thick and sweet. "Kind of quiet tonight," he said.

The bartender stared at Woodrow. "It's Tuesday. What do you expect?"

"My expectations may surprise you."

"I've heard it all."

"I'm looking for someone."

The bartender leaned back on his heels and lit a cigarette.

"A woman, probably in her late forties or early fifties. A singer by trade. Goes by the name Sweet Sadie."

The bartender removed a flake of tobacco from his tongue and took a drag of the cigarette. "Tell you what, mate—some of the clubs up and down this street play live music, some don't. But whether they do or not, singers don't last past their prime."

"You don't know her?"

"I didn't say that."

Woodrow removed a roll of bills from his coat pocket. He peeled off a fin and slid it onto the bar.

The bartender rolled the bill into a thin column and stuck it behind his ear. "Try Spider Kelly's. Down the block on the other side of the street."

"Appreciate it," Woodrow said, pocketing his bills and hoisting himself off the seat.

"Watch yourself. Strangers asking questions are suspect. Especially ones like you."

Out on the avenue, fog had coated the sidewalk like oil. Woodrow walked under the striped awning of the Sahara

Sands. The marquee advertised Edy Rich, Bobby Dee, and Noel Terry. The names meant nothing to him. He passed by the Arabian Nights cocktail lounge, the Gay 'N Frisky club, House of Pisco, and the Moulin Rouge. A neon sign of a cancan dancer's leg hung above the door.

Despite their flashy names, all the clubs had the faded air of high times gone sour. Then he saw Spider Kelly's. He stopped outside before going in and read a poster behind a glass enclosure: EPICURES AND CONNOISSEURS OF GOOD THINGS IN LIFE SAY THAT AN HOUR SPENT IN SPIDER'S IS A SURE CURE FOR THE TIRED FEELING AND WILL REMOVE TO OBLIVION ALL FORMS OF MELANCHOLY. ALL RACES WELCOME! Another poster featured a picture of Spider Kelly and the caption YOU COME TO SPAR WITH SPIDER KELLY?

He wrapped his hand on the rusted door handle and pushed. Inside, he was surprised to see a cavernous saloon with a large dance floor. Tables ringed the floor, and men and women two deep crowded up to the bar. Woodrow paused before deciding to take a seat at one of the tables. He surveyed the room. Here and there, couples nursed drinks and single patrons sat in corners or along the wall. No one paid him any attention, and no one came to take his order.

He decided to approach the bar and walked over the floor. "Pardon me. May I get through?" No one moved. He spoke more loudly: "What does it take to get a drink around here?"

Two gents turned and peered down at him. A skinny gent elbowed a burly one, who wore a thick coat and work boots. "Ain't no half-pints in this joint." He laughed. "Right, Mick?"

"You got that right. But where are our manners? Maybe we ought to offer the little guy a seat."

Woodrow held up his hand. "No need," he said. "I can fend for myself. Just came in for a friendly drink."

"Is that so? Well, where's the other half of you?"

The crowd turned toward the ruckus. A woman yelled, "Leave the midget alone."

"Yeah, send him my way," another woman shouted. "I'll take care of him."

Laughter erupted; catcalls rang out.

The burly gent shouted, "She wants him! She gets him!" He reached down, grabbed Woodrow by the lapels, and lifted him off the floor. Woodrow kicked his legs, thrashing and twisting. Suddenly, the man's mouth slackened and his eyes widened. The room went dead quiet.

"Put him down," Woodrow heard. He craned his neck.

"Hey, Boss," the giant said. "Nice to see you."

A bottle sailed over their heads and crashed. Woodrow's feet hit the floor. He scrambled on his hands and knees through pant legs and thick-soled work boots.

Fists flew, screams pierced the air, bodies scuffled, and the giant took on each contender, flattening them with a punch or a shove. "Get out of here, Boss!" he yelled.

Woodrow made a dash for the door. In the corner, a woman lifted her head off the table. Just before he could escape, her sunken eyes bore into him. It wasn't until he was safely down the block, out on Montgomery Street, struggling for breath, that her ashen face came back to him with such force that he stumbled. *Sadie,* he thought. *That was Sadie.*

* * *

"HEY, BOSS, WAIT up!" Rosy's voice rang out, echoing off desolate walk-ups wedged between brick warehouses.

Woodrow swung around. Rosy lumbered toward him, arms swinging, catching up in jig time. He rubbed his swollen knuckles and sported a red gash on his cheek.

"Keep walking," Rosy said. "Those lug heads may be on my trail. Say, what's the big idea of showing up in a rat hole like Spider Kelly's?"

"I could ask you the same question."

"But I asked you first, Boss."

"It's a long story," Woodrow said, trotting alongside Rosy's long-legged strides, trying to keep up.

"Well, I got time." The sidewalks were deserted except for shadowed figures that hurried past them, hats pulled down, collars up, coattails flapping. "Turn here," Rosy ordered.

"Where're we going?" Woodrow squinted up at a sign that read GOLD STREET.

"My place. It's up here."

Woodrow stopped. "Your place?" The dark alley was narrow. Low-slung buildings abutted one another. A light standard at the far end cast a halo onto the wet pavement. A rat scurried off the curb and disappeared down into a sewer grate.

"Yeah, this is my neighborhood. How'd you think I found you, anyway?"

Woodrow shook his head. "I have no idea."

"You look a little done in." Rosy's deep-set eyes radiated concern. "Come on. I'll make coffee, get you back on your feet."

Woodrow hesitated. He'd rappelled into caves, clamored over snake-infested ruins, and floated down rivers on pontoons, paddling away from alligators. *But this?* he wondered. *I must be deranged.*

"You coming or not?" Rosy asked.

Woodrow glanced back over his shoulder. No one was in sight. A few automobiles rumbled along, headlights flaring, red taillights disappearing. When he looked up, Rosy was striding up the alley. Woodrow hurried behind, hopping puddles and avoiding bits of suspicious flotsam.

Halfway up, Rosy stopped in front of a low, one-story building. Woodrow waited. Flecks of green paint peeled off the brick. Rosy slipped a key into the lock of an iron-gated door. The door creaked open. "Home sweet home," he said, ducking under the header. He flicked on a switch. A bare lightbulb hung from the plaster ceiling on a chain. "Welcome," he announced, with a sweep of his hand. "It ain't much, but it's all mine."

Woodrow stepped in, and Rosy locked the door. "Have a seat," he said. "I've got to clean up."

Woodrow scrambled up onto a chair, wiped the sweat off his forehead, and rearranged his shirt collar and jacket. The room was barren save two wooden chairs, a square table, and a single, neatly made bed against one wall. Black grates covered a high, narrow window. The worn wood floor was swept clean.

Rosie came out of the bathroom and stepped up to a white porcelain stove. "Boss, I hope you like your coffee camp-style."

"I do."

"Use the facilities if you like." Rosy pulled a tin of Hills Brothers coffee off a shelf and shook grounds into a pot.

"No, thanks. Maybe later."

At the sink, Rosy cranked on the faucet and doused the grounds with water. Switching on a burner at the stove, he set the pot over the flame and took a chair opposite Woodrow. "Okay, now tell me why a gentleman like you is prowling around the wrong side of town."

"First, I haven't thanked you. You saved my life. I'm grateful."

"Ain't nothing, Boss. I was passing by and figured there was a disturbance. Sometimes I'm a bouncer, so it wasn't no big deal."

"A bouncer? I thought you worked in a sideshow."

The scent of coffee bubbled from the stovetop. Rosy leaped up and grabbed two chipped mugs, splashing coffee into them. "Sometimes I do. Sometimes I work the docks. A little bit of everything. Keeps it interesting." He set the mugs down on the table. "Speaking of interesting, I heard you're one of those guys who work down in Mexico, digging up treasure."

"How'd you find that out?" Woodrow sipped the oily, bitter brew, scalding his tongue.

"I inquired. You're a big shot on TI." Rosy tapped his temple with his finger. "But not too smart on the other side of the tracks."

Woodrow shook his head. "I shouldn't have gone in there, but I did. You see, I'm looking for someone."

"Ain't we all?" Rosy slurped his coffee.

"No . . . I mean, yes."

"Let me guess. A dame, right?"

"Right."

"I knew it." Rosy banged the table; it trembled on its spindly legs. "There's always a dame."

Woodrow hopped off the chair and started pacing. "Not in my case."

"Didn't mean to offend, Boss. You're a good-looking guy. A little small, but so what?"

"The point is, I came here tonight looking for a woman. She may go by the name of Sweet Sadie. The funny thing is, I think I saw her in the bar."

"What do you want with *her?*" Rosy scowled. His ears had turned bright red, framing his huge skull.

"You know her?"

"She's in the rough trade."

"What?" The question burst from his mouth before he could check it; he was well aware of the answer.

Rosy went to the stove and poured more coffee into the cups. "Sit down, Boss."

Woodrow slowly returned to his seat. "This is important. Otherwise, I wouldn't ask these questions."

"This isn't a pretty story." He scratched his head and rubbed his hands together. "I knew Sadie way back when. What a voice she had. A real looker, too. Then she started using. That's what happens to beautiful women who come to Tinseltown, hoping to make it big."

Woodrow shook his head uncomprehendingly.

"They don't get the breaks, they get older, and then they get hooked on Cadillac."

Woodrow's mouth gaped. "Cadillac?"

"Yeah, you know, heroin."

"Oh God," Woodrow moaned, clutching his forehead. "This will crush Lily."

"So, I was right."

Woodrow looked up at Rosy through webbed fingers. "About what?"

"Lily is the dame."

Woodrow waved aside his question mournfully. "Do you know where Sadie lives?"

"Why?"

"Can you take me to her?"

"Don't look at me like that. No, Boss, I can't. Don't ask."

"If you don't help, who will?"

"Aw, shit. Don't put it like that."

"Then you *will* help."

"I didn't say that."

CHAPTER NINETEEN

Lily

"Well, look who's here," Maxine said, standing over Lily, who was tangled in a black lace slip under a mound of covers in their bedroom. "A rare appearance."

Lily squinted up at her with one eye. "Don't give me any baloney," she moaned. "My dogs are killing me. Fiesta Week will be my downfall." She flung the covers back and propped herself up on one elbow. "The opening of the Expo can't come fast enough. I haven't had a shower in days, and all my clothes are filthy. What time is it, anyway?"

"Nine o'clock, Lois Lane."

"Oh, for Chrissakes, I'm late," Lily said, hopping out of bed.

"What's wrong with you? Our fair city has turned itself

into a shoot-'em-up Wild West town, and you're complaining. You're not keen on covering our menfolk growing beards and walking bow-legged, women donning fringed cowgirl skirts and vests and lassoing dogs, and kiddies wearing satin shirts and snapping pop guns?"

Lily wobbled to a chair and scooped up her robe. "First I'm on Polk Street, where a merchant from Haight is staging a mock lynching of a shop owner; then I'm back to the financial district to catch Central Valley cowboys in Stetson hats who are riding down the middle of Montgomery Street, firing pistols; and then I beat feet down to Mission, which has morphed into the old Mission Trail. And this goes on day and night. Every citizen in every neighborhood thinks they're in the cast of a Roy Rogers movie."

"You're all wet. Dressing in costumes and getting drunk by noon is what saved us during the Depression. Retail sales are up twenty-two percent. We're honoring our Spanish heritage. Wagon trains are thundering down from Sacramento, and folks from all over the country are riding the rails to catch the fun. We'll leave New York in the dust!"

"Yeah, well, be a pal and let me borrow your underwear. I'm headed to the bath." Lily hot-footed out the door. "Get me a cup of coffee from the kitchen, and I'll forget what a pain-in-the-neck dame you are."

* * *

BEDLAM REIGNED IN the *Examiner* newsroom. Royal upright typewriters clacked; bells rang as carriages hit the end of a line; reporters and editors bellowed, "Boy!" for the copy kid. Lily pounded away at her desk in the middle of the room in the midst of men with their shirtsleeves rolled up to the elbows, suspenders cinched tight, and cigarettes hanging out of their mouths. The smoke was as thick as fog lying over the Great Highway. Glossy editions of the paper rolled off the presses in the basement in a delirium of round-the-clock coverage proclaiming Fiesta Week fever and the countdown to the grand opening of the Exposition.

Dudley leaned over her desk and stuck his nose in her coffee cup. "How can you drink this crap?"

She didn't look up. "Stubby makes it; I drink it. Unless you've got something better."

"Too soon for me, Nordby. But I'm happy to oblige." He pulled a cap low over his eyes and winked. "The guys will let you pull a swallow. Gladys, too."

"Light me a cigarette and quit pestering me."

"Why aren't you in one of those red fandango skirts? We could really cut a rug over at Sweets."

"Why aren't you wearing a black sombrero?"

"I got a great shot of Mayor Rossi in one of those monsters, decked out with silver braid and six guns strapped to his belt. Zoe Dell Lantis did backflips for the press the other day. Gee, she's a swell kid."

"It's the pirate hat and boots she wears that drive you crazy."

The phone on Lily's desk jingled.

Dudley saluted and stepped away. "See you at the Welcome Cavalcade Ball!"

She picked up the phone. "Hello!" she shouted into the mouthpiece.

"Lily, it's me."

"Speak louder. I can't hear you."

"It's Woodrow."

"Who?"

"Woodrow! I've been hoping to see you. I want to apologize."

"For what?"

"My outburst at Christmas."

"Oh, Woodrow, it was so long ago. Did you open my gift?"

"Yes. The gloves fit perfectly. Just the thing for this weather."

"Good." She pressed the phone to her ear so hard that the cartilage smarted. "Listen, I've got to go. It's nuts here."

"Wait! When can I see you?"

"I can barely hear you."

"It's important!"

"We'll have to talk later. Bye!"

Just then, Toth stormed into the newsroom, moving along the desks, clapping reporters on the back, and giving them thumbs-ups. He passed by Lily's desk and tossed down a memo. "Parker Maddux is over at his bank in a mock holdup. You know who he is?"

"President of Fiesta Week."

"Right. Get yourself over there. The tellers are holding him hostage with toy pistols. Right up your alley, kid."

"Yes, sir," Lily said. "On the double."

* * *

ON THE LAST night of Fiesta Week before the Exposition opening, the directors staged an electronic marvel. They wanted to show the world that San Francisco was the city that knows how, as well as demonstrate that Pacific Basin architecture and unity had indeed been realized on a spit of mud in the middle of the bay.

From Bombay, India, they worked with engineers to set up a photoelectric cell that would catch sunbeams precisely at noon—10:30 p.m. West Coast time—to transmit a radio signal across the vast Pacific. At that exact moment, the populace of San Francisco became the unexpected recipients of splendor.

The radio signal flipped a switch at Treasure Island that turned on all the outdoor lights. The Exposition glowed like a jeweled kingdom, casting beams into the night sky. Then the heart-stopping clanging of the forty-four-bell carillon pealed from atop the Tower of the Sun, playing "The Bells of Treasure Island."

The percussive sound rushed in through the open doors and windows of the grand ballroom in the Mark Hopkins Hotel. The band members stopped playing Cole Porter's "Begin the Beguine" and looked inquisitively at one another. Revelers on the outside of the dance floor forgot the jokes they were telling, and waiters who held champagne bottles cocked their ears.

Bunny and Adolph Schuman paused midtwirl in the center of the dance floor. All around them, couples froze in place. Instantly, Adolph peered up at the chandeliers, from which sparkling crystal teardrops hung in shimmering stillness. "Thank God, it's not an earthquake."

"The powers that be have been hinting about something grand that would happen tonight," Bunny said. "This must be it. Let's go up to the Sky Lounge."

Everyone had the same idea and rushed for the elevators, laughing and shouting and bursting through the doors into the Top of the Mark. Hurrying to the windows, which afforded a 360-degree view, they stared eastward, toward the heavenly sight of Treasure Island. The reverberation of the carillon faded, trembling over the rooftops.

"They have really outdone themselves this time," Bunny said, transfixed by the sight. Scanning the faces in the halflight, she said, "Lily must be here."

"I just saw her."

"Why didn't you say something?"

He shrugged off her question, and, taking her hand, elbowed with her through the exuberant throng, exclaiming "hello" and "isn't it wonderful" to friends and strangers alike, until they came up behind Lily, who was standing to one side of a group of people crowded around Timothy Pflueger, congratulating him on the opening.

"Darling!" Bunny gushed. "Isn't this spectacular?"

Lily turned and embraced them both in turn. "How good to see you!"

"Timothy's star is shining once again." Bunny nodded toward him. "He's lapping up the praise like a cat over a bowl of cream. Rightfully so, but really, the man can be insufferable."

"Now, now," Adolph, said, guiding them back to the windows. "This is a perfect night. Just look at Treasure Island. My God, we did it!"

Once again, they swayed in unison toward the sight, captivated by the distant but mesmerizing sweep of lights that washed over the Exposition's golden facades, sculpted arches, and enchanting gardens.

"All these years of planning, finance, and building," Adolph said. "Tomorrow is opening day!"

Bunny smirked. "Leland Cutler is apoplectic that the island will sink under the weight of visitors."

"Between the multitudes and the threat of rain," Adolph said, "he may come undone."

"Did you hear his radio message telling people to beware of traffic jams?" Lily asked. "He said to leave their cars at home, ride the ferries, and pack a bag lunch in case the concessions run out of food."

Suddenly, Bunny shivered. "Let's go back downstairs. I'm starving. All this excitement has given me an appetite, and I'm very thirsty."

A frown pinched Lily's brow. "I would love to, but I can't."

"Whoever it is can wait." Bunny insisted.

"No, that's not it."

"You expect us to believe that, my dear?"

"Believe what you will. Deadlines are my nemesis."

"Your friend Woodrow is here," Bunny said. "He's been asking for you."

"I really can't stay."

Bunny narrowed her eyes. "There's something different about you. Don't you think so, Adolph?"

Adolph appraised Lily with a mixture of consternation and tenderness. "Perhaps," he said. "She's definitely a lady with a purpose."

"It's something else," Bunny said. "What is it?"

"I'm the same," Lily insisted. "Dying for sleep, but who can sleep in this town?" She hugged Adolph, squeezed Bunny's hand, and dashed toward the exit. "See you tomorrow at the Expo!"

* * *

A BLACK LIMO idled at the curb. Lily opened the door and slid in. "Good evening, Hayato."

With a nearly imperceptible nod of his head, he acknowledged her presence and pulled into traffic. Lily watched the lights flicker past the window. She had tried to arm herself against Bunny's interrogation. Women's intuition was a powerful weapon used for either good or bad.

Yet the look in Adolph's eyes was disarming. She knew him to be exceptionally perceptive, as well as knowing. For the first time in her life, a magnetic force had overtaken Lily's every action. In public, she steeled herself against watching Tokido. In private, with him as her guide, she existed in a paradise of erotic discovery. She did not want anyone to expose her. She knew what she was doing, and she knew the risk.

The signals changed from red to green as Hayato navigated the streets smoothly. In minutes, he stopped at the curb on Post Street at Buchanan. "Thank you, Hayato," she said, exiting the limo.

Moving quickly along the street, she ducked into the alley. Glancing behind her, she stepped through the gate and found the key in a circle of rocks under a rain chain. She unlocked the door, returned the key to the place she had found it, and entered.

Here, in this room, the outside world fell away and she became the woman she had always wanted to be. The reedy scent of tatami mats peppered the air. The shoji lantern emitted a warm glow. The futon was perfectly made with cotton quilts.

She walked over to the *tansu*, less than three feet high, and ran her finger over its delicate wood. A compartment on the top was accessible by two sliding doors. She slid the doors open. The pungent scent of cedar met her nostrils. The compartment was empty. Beneath it were two drawers. She fingered the metal handle of the first drawer and peered inside. It, too, was empty. The last drawer, fitted with a tiny lock, was the deepest. She peeked inside. Empty. She paused, wondering why Tokido, so exacting in all his mannerisms, kept nothing in the exquisite *tansu*.

Turning away, she stepped out of her shoes, peeled away her jacket and gown, and slipped out of her lingerie. The anticipation of pleasure rippled over her naked skin. Draping the clothes across the chair, she folded her underthings into a neat bundle and laid them on the chair's cushion.

She tiptoed into the bathroom, half closing the door.

Two white towels were folded on a small bamboo table. She ran the water in the deep tub and submerged herself in the steamy bath, coming up slick as a seal, her dark hair plastered against her skull, her breasts floating above the surface of the water. She lay on her back and, with her toe, nudged a bar of sandalwood soap off the ledge, into the clear water. Its aromatic scent swirled into the warm, wet air.

She heard the door unlock. A soft footfall. The rustle of clothes. A shoe dropping to the floor. She lay still, barely breathing, eyes half open. A bead of perspiration slid from her forehead, curved along her nose, past her lips, and onto her chin, and softly dropped into the bathwater.

Tokido appeared in the doorway. He was naked, and she drank him in with her eyes. The musculature of his powerful legs, shoulders, and arms, the smoothness of his skin, were a constant source of mystery and wonder. Desire swept through her. She tilted her chin upward, beginning to rise out of the tub, water streaming off her shoulders.

"Don't move," he said, stepping between her legs. "You're beautiful. This is how I want to remember you."

CHAPTER TWENTY

Tokido

Hayato drove Tokido from the apartment to the island in the predawn. The number of cars on the road and people walking on the sidewalks at this hour always surprised him. The city never stopped. Lights flickered by the window as they crossed the bridge. Trying to settle his thoughts, Lily's scent lingered on his skin, pervading his mood. Arriving on the island, he decided to walk from the gate to the pavilion, and with every step through the courtyards and past the buildings, he breathed deeply, the cold air clearing his mind. Birds twittered, the wings of gulls flapped, sea lions barked.

Inside the pavilion, he hung his coat and umbrella and moved through the rooms, inspecting every detail. Sandalwood incense laced the air. All was in readiness for opening day. The staff and workers had created a masterpiece. In the silence before the crowds that would certainly descend, there was order and beauty.

Inside his office, at his desk, beneath his splayed fingers, he smoothed a thin sheet of manuscript paper and took up his pen. He paused before writing.

Akemi,

In this time when the cold winter gives way to signs of early spring and the promise of cherry blossoms and flowering quince, I send my regards. Thank you for your letters. I regret not writing more often, but my duties require my full attention and evenings are scheduled with diplomatic events that leave little time to attend to personal matters.

Did you visit the Kaneiji Temple to hear the 108 bongs of the bell on December 31? On that night, I, too, prayed for the health, prosperity, and safety of our family. My mouth waters to imagine the feast you had on New Year's Day and how delicious the mochi tasted.

Kindly give my greetings to the family and especially to Uncle. Is he well? I wonder if perhaps you are keeping unpleasant news of his poor health? Please extend to him my greatest respect and admiration.

It is a great honor to represent our country here in America. I do so in the spirit of humanity and philanthropy, with redoubled courage, knowing that I represent our revered emperor and our country's ancient cultural achievements, and that someday I will return home.

I send you and our sons my deepest regards,
Tokido

He folded the letter and placed it in an envelope. On the face of the envelope, he wrote his wife's name and address. He sealed the flap, placed the letter in the diplomatic pouch for delivery to the consulate, and returned to his desk.

He checked the time: 4:10 a.m. He opened the bottom desk drawer. At the back, behind accordion files, he removed a cardboard box no larger than a small tin of tea. Opening the top of the box, he removed a subminiature camera. MIDGET was inscribed on the shutter plate above the lens. From his desk drawer, he removed one roll of unperforated 35-mm film stored in a canister. Stepping inside the closet, with only the red darkroom light on, he sliced the paper-backed film lengthwise in two and loaded one strip into the camera. The Midget would take ten 14-by-14-mm images. He would have to shoot wisely. It would be impossible to load the camera in the field. Returning the camera to its box and the film to its canister, he left the closet and locked both items in the drawers.

He glanced around the office one last time. Stepping out onto the landing, he reflected a moment. A brimming stillness greeted his ears. A saltwater mist coated the rocks, trees, and plants with silvery, feathered brushstrokes. He would spend the remaining hour before dawn onboard the *Tatuta Maru.* As he moved along the path toward the mooring, he resigned himself. His duty had been fulfilled. The course was set. There was no other way.

Ferry Passengers to Treasure Island

Cars on the Causeway Opening Day

CHAPTER TWENTY-ONE

Woodrow

Woodrow's eyes snapped open, and he bounded out of bed. "Oh boy, oh boy, oh boy," he mumbled to himself, hopping on one foot and then the other as he pulled on his pants. The cold and rain that had gripped the city all month had miraculously evaporated. The sun rose and bathed the air in a luminous vapor that cleared to bright, liquid sunshine. All the cares and woes that had plagued him vanished instantly.

He finished dressing and peered out of the bedroom window at the silver-skinned Goodyear Blimp floating in the pale blue sky above Treasure Island. February 18, 1939—the opening day of the Golden Gate International Exposition! He felt like a kid again. Overcome with glee, he clattered down the stairs, gulped a biscuit and a swallow of tomato juice, and dashed for the front door. He flung it open and bumped smack into Rosy, knocking his hat off his head. Rosy scooped it off the stoop and handed it back.

"Rosy, what are you doing here? I thought you were avoiding me."

"Don't be asking me about that Sadie, Boss. We haven't got time. Not now!"

Woodrow looked up at him incredulously. "You're going to help me?"

"Not today."

"When?"

"Soon, Boss. It ain't as easy as you think. There's a lot of factors to be considered."

"As long as you give me your word."

"You got it. Come on, now! Let's go to the Expo!"

Woodrow hesitated. "I'm expected at a dedication ceremony."

"I'm expected, too. But we still got to get there. I'll be your escort!" Rosy opened the gate and started to bound down the steps.

"Wait!" Woodrow called. "I ordered a cab. It's up on the street."

Rosy ground to a stop, changed direction, and bounded back up the stairs. "I ain't never been in a cab!"

Woodrow jogged behind as fast as he could. At the top of the hill under Coit Tower, which gleamed crystal white in the morning light, he found Rosy standing beside the door of an idling cab. A radiant smile lit up his face. A two-seater plane buzzed high in the sky.

"Jump in," Woodrow called.

Rosy threw open the door, nearly ripping it off its hinges. He swung one leg into the cab, bent at the waist, and folded his body double onto the seat. Woodrow slid in beside him. As Rosy straightened, the top of his head pushed into the roof of the cab.

"Ferry Building, sir!" Woodrow ordered.

"I'll be damned," the cabbie said, squinting into the rear-view mirror. "Don't this take the cake?" He pushed back the brim of his cap. "I don't get many fares the likes of you two. But this ain't just any day. Hold tight, gents. I'll give you a ride you won't forget."

The cabbie tore through the congested streets. Fairgoers poured from their homes in their Sunday best, wearing hats, coats, and gloves, clutching ten cents in their hands for the ferry crossing. The cabbie dropped them off on a curb on Market Street mobbed with men, women, children, cops, and newspaper boys. Horns honked and streetcar rails squealed.

"There you go, gents. This is as close as I can get. See you at the Expo!"

"You bet!" shouted Rosy.

Woodrow paid the cabbie, and they jumped out. Instantly, Woodrow clamped his hands over his ears. Right outside the Ferry Building, two streetcar lines and two municipal bus lines converged in a roundabout, picking up and depositing hundreds of passengers.

"That was some ride!" Rosy exclaimed. "What's wrong with your ears?"

"It's the roar of the four," Woodrow mouthed. "The din bruises my ears."

Ordinarily, Woodrow would have been obscured in the tangle of trousers or hemlines walking through a sea of humans, but with Rosy it was otherwise. He cleared a path like Moses parting the Red Sea. His black boots gleamed, heels pounding the pavement. People stepped aside, staring up at him, before nearly tripping over Woodrow. The ferries blasted their shrill horns, and they charged ahead to board the Key System ferry, which puffed smoke from its two stacks. They stood alongside charter patrons and fairgoers on the decks who shouted and waved as the ferry churned away from the pier to deliver them to the Magic City.

Streaming across the bay toward Treasure Island, they saw the Tower of the Sun piercing the sky and the Elephant Towers glowing in pastel shades of golden cream and coral pink. Beyond the gates lay the promise of opulent gardens, sparkling fountains, exotic courtyards, and pavilions from strange lands. Housed in the many halls and buildings, industrial exhibitions and wonders of the modern world awaited inspection. For fairgoers weary of grand art and lofty architecture, the lure of the Gayway beckoned with its carnival enticements, forbidden pleasures, and mouthwatering foods.

Rosy and Woodrow held fast to the top railing. The ferry plowed through the strong currents, and the spray of marine air filled their lungs. Whitecaps scalloped the seawater, and sunlight sequined its surface. Around them, passengers surged and fell back, shoulder to shoulder, laughing and talking. Seagulls cried *caw, caw, caw,* diving from the sky.

On the lower span of the Bay Bridge, the Key System rail lines delivered patrons in endless pursuit of work and play. Today the trains would make a maiden stop at Yerba Buena Island to deposit thousands of patrons to the Exposition via a connecting road.

"Ain't it grand, Boss? Just look at it. Right out of a fairy tale," Rosy said. "I can smell the flowers from here."

Indeed, as the ferry grew closer, a magical carpet of rainbow-hued ice plants bloomed along the western flank of the island. Along the rock seawall, palms seventy feet high, interspersed with shrubs and tropical grasses, waved their fronds. American flags rimmed the Avenue of Palms, rippling and snapping in the wind.

"Yes, it's a fine sight, Rosy." Woodrow swiped an unexpected tear from his eye.

"Something in your eye, Boss?"

"No, it's just the wind."

"I want to see it all. I hear there's a Westinghouse robot that sits and stands and smokes cigarettes, and a see-through real-life Pontiac, and Pedro the Voder, a talking machine operated by punching keys. Imagine that! What won't people think of next?"

"That is the question." Woodrow turned and gazed at the orange towers of the Golden Gate Bridge in the morning mist. "Who would have thought that the Golden Gate could be spanned? The bridge is a miracle."

"Sure is, Boss. And look at the cars and rail lines humming across the Bay Bridge. Everyone is coming!"

"I expect you'll be spending some of your time in the Gayway, performing feats of strength?"

"Bending steel ain't too bad. Or hammering a spike through a board with my hand. But I'm not going to wrestle a croc again. No sirree. Not for me."

"I've seen men torn apart by those beasts."

"Down in the Mexican jungle?"

Woodrow narrowed his eyes as he remembered the cool, serene surface of a tropical lake broken by the snout of a twelve-foot crocodile. "Someday I'll tell you about it."

"Thing is, some of my friends are working the Gayway. The bearded lady is real sweet, and the Chinese lady that gets sawed in half is a trouper. Now, that Sally Rand—she's a live wire. She could tame a bull or make a pig dance. She told me to come by anytime to see her girls."

"Sounds like you're a fan of the ladies."

"You could say that. Say, will that lady Lily be here today?"

Just then, the ferry steamed up to the dock and the crowd surged forward. Rosy shoved Woodrow in front of him and plowed ahead. Their feet hit the landing as they were swept along with fairgoers toward the ticket stations. In the vanguard of seven thousand patrons who poured through the turnstiles in the first hour, they paused to stare up at the great golden walls. Civic pride swelled in Woodrow's heart. He was amazed that in a world where the drums of war pounded ever louder, Treasure Island could happen at all.

"We're here," Rosy said. "I'm so excited I could spit! Let's get you on an Elephant Train so you can make your way inside for the governor's speech."

"What about you?" Woodrow asked.

"My feet are itching. I gotta walk, Boss. I'm headed to the Gayway."

"No, sir." Woodrow exclaimed. "You're coming with me."

"Really?"

"Why not? Here comes a train!"

Rosy burst into laughter, and as the Elephant Train rolled up, they caught an outside seat. The usual stares aimed at the men evaporated in the grandeur of the moment. Suddenly, the train drove through the wind baffles and into the Pageant of the Pacific. All eyes focused instantly on the spectacular though puzzling nature of the architecture—what exactly was Pacific Basin style? Was it Cambodian, Mayan, Malaysian, Burmese, or Indonesian? And how did it fit with the beaux-arts courts and the campanile thrust of the Tower of the Sun?

The train circled the tower and stopped just outside the long Court of Reflections. Woodrow and Rosy joined the crowd filtering into the court, graced by a long pool, rows of towering Siamese umbrella lights, and dazzling beds of flowers. The view afforded a look from the court through a ninety-foot Arch of Triumph into the Court of Flowers.

Rosy gaped in wonder. "How many courts are there, Boss?"

"Too many. No one will ever be able to keep track of them."

"And promenades?"

"Miles and miles of them. You'll be able to walk your feet off."

"What about the naked-lady statues?"

"Same thing."

"This one is dressed. She looks like a goddess."

"She's called *Girl with Rainbow,* modeled in the Greek style. Quite lovely, really, holding a rainbow aloft. Wait'll you see the Pacific statues."

"Huh?"

"Massive, thick-lipped, native people meant to signify Pacific unity."

"Whatever you say, Boss."

They secured a spot against the circular base of a light, and Rosy gave Woodrow a boost up onto a corner to see over the heads of the multitudes gathered for the speech. Woodrow hopelessly scanned the faces closest to him. He knew it was futile to search for Lily, but he couldn't help himself. Even if he spotted her, there wouldn't be a way to reach her. *Somehow I keep trying to cross a divide between us that grows wider and wider,* he thought. *She's lost to me.*

At last, Governor Culbert Olson, decked out in tails and striped pants, stepped up onto the stage under the Arch of Triumph. A cheer went up, bouncing off the walls. Olson waved his tall hat and took the microphone. After a bout of flu, he looked a bit wobbly. He declared the Exposition begun by opening the central span of a small replica of the Golden Gate Bridge with a gold key encrusted with precious gems donated by the city's jewelers. The crowd clapped and shouted wildly, and as Olson stepped down, people emptied out of the court, streaming in different directions. At noon, the official ceremony was scheduled to begin in the Court of Nations.

Rosy put his hand on Woodrow's shoulder. "Let's wait."

"Good idea. It's going to be a long day."

"That was some key the gov used." Rosy watched two officials wrap the key in a bunting. One official tucked it under his arm and exited the stage. "The shine in those jewels is something."

"It's encrusted with rubies, diamonds, sapphires, and emeralds. I believe it's been estimated at thirty-five thousand dollars," Woodrow answered.

Rosy whistled. "Better keep their eyes on it."

"Are you suggesting it could go missing?"

"Ain't no one immune to slippery fingers."

"By Jove, you've got a point."

"How you doing, Boss?" Rosy rubbed his hands together. "Shall I get us a rickshaw?"

"Why not?" Woodrow agreed. "If anyone can snare one, you can."

"Great! You stay here until I come back. But the deal is, when we get to the next stop, I gotta get going. Don't be asking me to stay. Agreed?"

The logic of Rosy's request was undeniable, although it pained Woodrow to acquiesce. He knew the humiliation of gawking eyes. His presence on the stage would pose awkward questions. "You're right, Rosy. Agreed."

* * *

A SEA OF humanity jammed into the immense Court of Nations, spilling over into the Temple Compound near the lagoon. Forty thousand fairgoers had assembled to bear witness to the official inauguration of the Exposition, and they were still coming. Promptly at noon, bombs exploded and the blind virtuoso Alec Templeton unleashed the earsplitting power of the carillon's bells in the Tower of the Sun.

Leland Cutler stood on a large platform, surrounded by dignitaries, officials, and luminaries. Woodrow, hat in hand, found himself in the front row, wedged between Timothy Pflueger and Atholl McBean, chairman of Exposition's officers.

Cutler stepped up to the podium, cleared his throat, and, in a voice heavy with emotion, spoke into the microphone. "I have waited four years for this moment. Today, our Exposition, which we have been building, becomes *your* Exposition. Treasure Island is offered today upon the altar of greater peace and greater goodwill among all nations, among all the races." His message was broadcast over a public-address system to every part of the island and all across America.

Mayor Rossi, Governor Olson, and George Creel, US commissioner to the Exposition, each added their voices to the ceremony, until at long last the radio controls were switched to Key West, Florida.

The voice of President Roosevelt rang out. "Washington is remote from the Pacific. San Francisco stands at the doorway to the sea that roars upon the shores of all these nations, and so to the Golden Gate International Exposition I gladly entrust a solemn duty. May this, America's World Fair on the Pacific in 1939, truly serve all nations in symbolizing their destinies, one with every other, through the ages to come."

The right Reverend Edward Parsons, bishop of the Episcopal diocese, gave a benediction before the huge crowd, jammed shoulder to shoulder. With great fanfare, the band struck the opening chords to "God Bless America," and every voice, led by the chorus, swelled in joyful song.

On the stage, the entourage shook hands and clapped one another on the back. Woodrow felt stunned by the events and unexpectedly world-weary. He was entreated to join the festivities but declined. He tottered down the stairs onto the ground. The loudspeakers thumped out "Flat Foot Floogie (with a Floy Floy)." People were fanning out in waves into the courtyards and promenades, where fresh flowers were sprinkled. Chair boys in blue uniforms and visored caps rushed forward, offering rides in rolling chairs and rickshaws. Woodrow waved his hat as high as he could and flagged one down.

* * *

SLIPPERS ON HIS feet, robe wrapped around his body, brandy and cigar on the side table, Woodrow rested in blessed solitude. He had napped once he reached home and afterward warmed a delectable steak-and-kidney pie in the oven for dinner. A fire burned in the grate. He reached for a bundle of mail that he had brought up from the mailbox but had not yet bothered to sort through. He found an airmail envelope addressed in his father's hand, postmarked Philadelphia. *How unusual,* he thought. He slid the blade of the letter opener along the envelope's edge and opened a single sheet of onionskin.

February 10, 1939

Dear Woodrow,

Of late, I've had an interesting call from your Harvard classmate Fritz Hobart. He inquired as to your whereabouts. I told him, of course, about your work at Treasure Island and passed on your address. I suspect he already knew you were in San Francisco. Since then, a theory has been brewing in my mind. The European theater of war is intensifying. Roosevelt has been meeting Churchill on the Atlantic in secret meetings. There is talk that Roosevelt may be recruiting intelligence officers for special operations. My hunch is that Hobart, as their representative, will come to you. You may be strategically placed to act should the need arise.

Your mother and I send greetings.

With affection,
Father

The letter fell from Woodrow's hand into his lap. Night closed in around the house. Through the picture window, Treasure Island shimmered cobalt blue and deep gold. Beams of white light swept back and forth across the night sky. Woodrow lit the cigar, inhaled, and set it down on an ashtray. He lifted the brandy, cradling the bowl between his fingers, inhaling its intense aroma, and savoring the heat of it sliding down his throat.

Court of the Seven Seas

CHAPTER TWENTY-TWO

Lily

It was dusk as Dudley and Lily walked down the vast promenade in the Court of the Seven Seas, dominated by sixteen sixty-foot pylons along the walls of huge, rectangular exhibition halls on either side. On the top of each pylon, winged figures depicting adventure perched on ships' prows.

At the far end of the promenade, in the Court of Pacifica, the monumental form of *Pacifica* gazed outward. Behind the statue, a shimmering, one-hundred-foot-high metal prayer curtain rippled in the cool breeze, sending out a murmur of tinkling wind chimes. Nearby, and equally arresting, was a huge, bold relief mural, *Peacemakers,* done by the Bruton sisters, emphasizing the fair's underlying motif, Pacific peace and unity.

On the other side, the Hall of Electricity and Communications displayed the inventions of modern technology, and beside it, the Hall of Science exhibited the miracles of biology, chemistry, and physics in an eye-popping array of visual-mechanical demonstrations.

"Hey, Nordby, let's duck into the science building and check out Mendel's law of heredity. We can find out the color of our kids' eyes. It's a battle of dominant and recessive genes."

"Let's not. Those puppet dolls they use give me the creeps."

"How about I get a quick shave with one of Remington Rand's electric razors, and then we can neck at the television demo?"

"How about no? Let's double back to the Fine Arts Palace to see the European art. I'll never tire of looking at Michelangelo's and Donatello's paintings or Lalique's glass, and, oh, those tapestries from Aubusson, France."

"Heck, someday you'll be in Europe and you'll see all the art you can stand."

"Not likely," she sighed, "but nice of you to suggest."

As they drew closer to *Pacifica,* Dudley nudged Lily. "Look at Stackpole's mystery woman. What do you think of her?"

"Mesmerizing. Whether he meant for her to be Mayan or Oriental makes no difference. That placid expression, those upturned palms—she's all-powerful. She reminds me of those monolithic Easter Island statues."

"You could say so. I've seen little kids scream and cry when their parents drag them down here."

"You're jaded."

"Maybe so. There's only so much splendor a guy can take. Come on, Nordby. Let's get off this island and drive out to the beach in my pal's old Plymouth, eat It's-Its, and listen to Benny Goodman on the radio."

"What's gotten into you?"

"I'm punch drunk. Aren't you? After one nonstop week of

shooting people stuffing their faces with scones, Junket, and Coca-Cola, plus the Cossack choir, daredevils going down the ski jump, and the steer auction in the ag hall, I've had it."

They sat on a low wall by the sunken circular basin of the Fountain of Western Waters, which was flanked by primitive statues of native people reclining in various poses of play and work.

Dudley hooked his arm around Lily's neck and tried to nuzzle her neck.

"Cut it out!" she protested, pushing him away. She slipped off her shoes and began to rub her feet.

"Exhibition feet, eh?"

"They're killing me."

"I'm glad to be of assistance."

Just then, the floodlights switched on, transforming *Pacifica* into a marbled white goddess, the prayer curtain a scintillating copper backdrop, and the fountain an iridescent green waterfall.

"It's just all so beautiful," she said wistfully. "Not meant to last."

"What's with the dark circles under your eyes?"

"I've got a lot on my mind."

"Like what?" He wrapped his arm around her waist and pulled her close. "Tell me everything. I'll make it better."

She pulled on her shoes and jumped up. "No deal, Dudley. Come on, let's get out of here."

He looped his arm through hers then broke away to snap a picture of children running through the courtyard.

She watched him go, his good-natured, easygoing manner, trying to remember what it was like to be that carefree. Tokido's remark, "This is how I want to remember you," haunted her. The words had stung and burrowed into her mind. Several nights, she'd awakened in his bed to find he wasn't there. Reaching for him, her hand had grasped empty space, the sheet cold, the covers pushed down. Then she'd lain awake, listening to the hum of the street noise that never seemed to cease, wondering where he had gone, until she'd drifted into a fitful sleep.

When she asked him, he had the same response. "My work is never finished."

Was the apartment a setup? Possibly to snare her, possibly to what? There were so few personal items—an empty closet, except for a few shirts hanging on wooden hangers, no books or papers, no photographs.

Would a moment come when he'd reveal himself to be something other than her lover, other than a diplomat on a mission of goodwill? Were her early suspicions, confirmed by Schuman, a flight of fancy that had sent her on a wild goose chase? There was no proof of his deception. She had fallen into forbidden territory, and for now, the only thing she wanted, desperately needed, was for their affair to go on. There was no way out.

Dudley rushed back to her. "I've got an idea. Let me take you to the Argentine Café, and we'll do the tango."

"You're insufferable."

"We'll toss out your blues, and then I'll send you home. Unless, of course, you'd like to come to my place." He winked at her. "You're nuts about me. Don't resist. I'm your man!"

CHAPTER TWENTY-THREE

Tokido

The resplendent rooms of the Japanese Pavilion were adorned with ikebana and sprays of pink cherry blossoms in vases placed on low tables. Pale light from tasseled lanterns illuminated their fragile beauty. The Japanese community had turned out in force. On this night, the pavilion overflowed with dignitaries, their wives, and civic leaders. They lifted delicate cups of cool sake to their lips. Silk kimonos rustled, black hair gleamed, and voices rose and fell like ripples lapping at the koi pond below in the garden.

Tokido mingled among the crowd, pausing to speak with the guests and at the same time scanning the crowd. Kiyoshi walked patiently by his side, offering information and prompting him with cues about those whom he didn't recognize.

Tokido noticed Moto and Chizu in a far corner, apart from the others. Their heads were together, and Moto's ear dipped toward her painted lips. A searing flash of suspicion raced up Tokido's spine. Since the night he had turned Chizu away on the street near his apartment, she had been evasive, even aloof. In a confidential meeting when he had questioned her about securing the calculations of Golden Gate Bridge, she had reported that her contact was still active, but then she had gone quiet. He hadn't pressed her. Her performance as lead hostess was beyond reproach.

Kiyoshi lightly touched Tokido's elbow. "It is time now to speak." He acknowledged Kiyoshi's cue, excused himself from the group that had gathered around him, and moved toward a small dais that had been placed to the side of the front doors. He climbed onto the dais and faced the audience.

"Ladies and gentlemen"—he bowed respectfully—"please allow me to formally welcome you tonight." His voice rang out full and sure, and every person turned to listen. "The success of our presence on Treasure Island has been due to your support. As special envoy from Japan, I am honored to preside over the festivities. Thank you for your generous participation. Art displays have been presented for your viewing, and we trust you will find pleasure in their creation. Now, Consul General Moto would like to say a few words."

Tokido watched as the stiff form of his superior parted the crowd. When Moto stepped onto the dais, a thinly disguised aura of contempt frosted the air between them. Tokido stepped down and faded to the side.

"Good evening," he said. "The Golden Gate International authorities have been particularly considerate in allotting to us one of the best locations on the site of the Exposition. Not only that, but they have also extended to us every assistance and facility at their command, in order to make our part in the Exposition, which consists of properly introducing Japanese culture and civilization, a more significant and brilliant success."

Moto's words buzzed like an insect batting against a windowpane. Tokido's mind wandered as he watched the attentive faces in the audience. Chizu was not to be seen. Then he caught sight of Lily standing alone at the far end of the tearoom. He had not believed in falling in love. Love was earned through devotion. To dishonor one's family was fatal. Love sprang from order, from a mutual pledge to undertake responsibility and join together as the roots of a tree grow into the soil, its branches reaching toward the light and its leaves opening in season. He had tried to convince himself that what he felt with Lily wasn't love. It was wild, chaotic, ungovernable—a torment without purpose or reason. Why, then, had he allowed himself this passion? She had only to appear to answer his question.

As Moto concluded his speech, Tokido glanced at him. The slide of his eyes and inclination of his chin toward the hallway that led to the office were clear. Tokido waited for him to pass, and, after an interval of several minutes in which he engaged in conversation with Kiyoshi, he slipped away.

The office door was slightly ajar. Tokido opened it slowly.

"Come in," Moto said. "Lock the door." He was perched on the edge of Tokido's desk, with his arms folded. Without any civility, he posed a question cloaked in disdain: "What intelligence have you uncovered?"

"My attention has been on the opening of the pavilion and this event tonight. Details have required my total concentration. Thousands of San Franciscans and travelers from across the United States have poured through the pavilion. It is the most popular destination on the island. Are you not pleased?"

"Of course," Moto said grudgingly. "However, our mission must not waver."

"I have continued night surveillance and will speak to Chizu about—"

"Leave Chizu to me," Moto interrupted. "From now on, she is under my direction. Prepare yourself to gather intelligence about the high-security operation in the Marin Headlands. There is increased chatter about the installation of two sixteen-inch guns in Battery Townsley. The rumor is that either gun can swing in a 180-degree arc and hit a target twenty-five miles out to sea. As a naval coastal defense, it will be unparalleled. Find it," he ordered. "Record the topography, study its location, and report back to me."

"All the forts at the mouth of the bay are heavily guarded. Entry to Fort Cronkhite is through a tunnel that is protected by military police. How, then, do you suggest I gain access to the battery?"

Moto sprang to his feet and paced back and forth. "There are public lands called Tennessee Valley that abut the fort. Trails crisscross the terrain." He stopped dead and faced Tokido. A tight smile curved around his thin lips. "Perhaps a hike in those hills would suit you and your reporter?"

Tokido flushed with anger. "What are you implying?"

"Do not require me to ask where your loyalties lie."

"Is there any question?"

"Your association with her must reap more than personal rewards."

Quaking with frustration, Tokido clenched his fists in rage. "I beg your pardon?"

"Do not lose focus. Locate the battery. Move about the perimeters. Proceed with caution. If you are detected, the military will show its teeth. Act swiftly." Moto left without another word.

* * *

TOKIDO LEANED HIS shoulders into the damp wind that gusted, swirling high into the eucalyptus trees that lined the paved road in Tennessee Valley. He knew he must succeed, yet every step brought him closer to an outcome he dreaded. Basho's haiku rose like a ghost to accompany him.

> Fever-felled half-way,
> my dreams arose
> To march again . . .
> Into a hollow land

Binoculars, secured by a strap around his neck, hung on his chest. The Midget was strapped to his ankle inside his boot. Beside him, Lily held his hand loosely. Her head was down, the collar of her coat turned up against her cheek. More than once, he inquired if she was warm enough, but the wind whipped, making conversation impossible.

They had walked over a mile after parking in a nearly empty lot. Now and then, a hiker passed by. Tokido lowered his eyes and pulled his scarf more tightly around his neck. The camera dug into his ankle. A thin sun filtered overhead through the air, pungent with the scent of eucalyptus. Occasionally, when a gull or hawk appeared in the sky, he lifted the glasses to his eyes and peered through the lens.

He offered them to her. "No, you keep them," she said, her voice faint.

He had proposed over a week ago that they find a few hours to see the coast. "I can spare a few hours on Friday. Kiyoshi is capable of handling any contingencies. Our time together has been rare."

They lay side by side on the futon, the warmth of their naked bodies radiating against each other. Night pressed at the window, the room softly illuminated. "Long ago you said you wanted to show me Mount Tamalpais, but I would be satisfied to walk the headlands above the ocean." Immediately, he sensed her stiffen. He hesitated until there was nothing else to do but go on. "I consulted a map. There's a place called Tennessee Valley just north of the Golden Gate Bridge. We can walk there."

She turned her head away. He waited. Minutes passed.

"Lily." He cupped her chin, turning her face back toward him. He tried to ignore the sadness in her eyes. "Would you rather not?"

"Yes. I mean, no," she answered. "When would you like to go?"

He drew her into his arms then, starved for the sweetness of her skin and the silent union of their naked bodies, where he could pretend that he would never betray her, never have to leave her.

In the thin sunshine, they continued walking down the narrow valley. After a distance, he saw a steep trail leading south up a ridge. He stopped and consulted a map that he removed from his pocket. "Look," he said, indicating a thin black line. Lily leaned over the page, holding the fluttering edges in her gloved hand. "Here's a trail called Wolf Ridge." He pointed to the trail. "What would you say if we took this route?"

She squinted up toward the trail. "Is this where you want to go?"

He straightened the binoculars around his neck. "Why not?"

"Are you sure?" She addressed him with uncharacteristic solemnity. "Fort Cronkhite is somewhere in these hills."

"How far?"

"I couldn't say."

"We'll only go to the top." He consulted his wristwatch. "There's time. We're bound to see the ocean."

Deer scat littered the trail. They climbed single-file, up, up, up. Their breath came in short gasps. Here, on the roughshod open bluff, the ground was craggy, pebbled, and there was no sign of spring's benevolence, except for electric-green grasses bent sideways. Native shrubs, humbled by the unrelenting fog and wind, dotted the rocky landscape.

At last they crested Wolf Ridge and a clear vista opened to the west. A bank of fog lay on the far horizon, meeting the line of the gray Pacific. Through buffeting currents of air, he heard the hiss of the choppy waves breaking far below a cliff, against the jagged rocks.

Tokido's shirt was wet with sweat. His ankle ached. He estimated that the border of Fort Cronkhite lay close by. *Perhaps it's just over the rise ahead,* he thought. Moto's order thrummed in his head. *Find the location.*

Lily took two steps forward. "Look! Wildflowers." She advanced slowly to the edge of the hillside, before it dropped off into a gully. Stepping carefully onto a patch of grass where buttercups grew like a carpet of yellow, she bent to pick a flower. "This is so beautiful," she called, sprinkling blossoms over the front of her coat, flinging her arms over her head. She fell to her knees and rolled onto her back. Gulls called and swooped, *caw caw caw.* The sunlight began to dim as wisps of fog trailed in the sky.

"I'm going ahead," he told her.

"I'll wait here," she answered.

Quickly, he climbed to the top of the next rise. The ground leveled out, and, directly in front of him, not twenty-five yards away, a barbed wire fence loomed up. A sign was posted on the fence: KEEP OUT! MILITARY INSTALLATION. DANGER! His heart pounded in his chest.

Crouching down, he rushed toward the fence. Looking through the steel barbs, he saw a road that curved around the contour of a hill and into a man-made mound of earth large enough to conceal a fleet of tanks. *Battery Townsley! That's it!* Standing, he lifted his pant leg, unstrapped the Midget, and pulled it out of his boot. The wind whistled in his ears. He peered through the lens finder. *Click. Click. Click.* He aimed through the barbs, swinging the camera in several directions.

Estimating he had two remaining shots, he turned and rushed back to the rise just before it dropped. Diving onto his belly, he crept forward on his elbows to the edge, until Lily came into view. She was still on her back, her forearm shielding her eyes. He steadied his hands, aimed the camera, and took one shot of her. This picture was only for his eyes. He scurried backward, stood, turned, and edged back toward the fence. Not one person was in sight. With his last shot, he planted his feet wide and bent his knees for a long-view image and depressed the shutter release button. Abruptly, the mechanism locked. He swore, pushing the sound between his teeth, and dropped the camera into the top of his boot. No sooner had he straightened up than he felt a tap on his shoulder.

Lily stared at him. "What are you doing?"

He stopped breathing. In an instant, a veil dropped between them.

"My God," she whispered, looking over his shoulder and toward the fence. "Is that Battery Townsley?"

He grabbed her arm. "We've got to get out of here."

Her eyes bore into his, blazing with hatred. "This is what you wanted all along, isn't it?"

"No," he cried, lunging for her and trying to pull her away, his heels digging into the earth.

She resisted, fighting back with a ferociousness he didn't know she possessed. "Let me go!" she screamed.

Without warning, a voice shouted, "Halt!"

Tokido jerked back, as if electrified.

"Holy shit," Lily whispered.

"Turn around," the voice commanded.

Tokido pivoted slowly and came face-to-face with a six-foot soldier. He clutched an M1 rifle in his hands. Another soldier stood next to him, combat boots planted apart, holding the same weapon.

"What are you doing here?" the soldier barked.

"My mistake, sir," Tokido said. "We wandered off the trail. Taking in the sights."

"Who are you?"

"I'm a diplomat with the Japanese consulate."

Tokido steadied his hand as he lifted it toward his chest to take out his passport.

"Drop your hand!"

The soldier advanced and patted Tokido down. Opening his jacket, the soldier's rough fingers located the passport, lifted it out, and quickly examined it. "Hand over the binoculars," he ordered.

Tokido unwound the binoculars from around his neck and passed them to the soldier.

His eyes shifted between Tokido and Lily. A barely concealed look of disgust flickered in his eyes. "Who are you?" he asked Lily.

"A reporter with the San Francisco *Examiner.*"

He looked at her, stone-faced. "Show me your identification."

In his peripheral vision, Tokido watched Lily offer a press pass.

"Who's your superior?" he asked.

"Simon Toth, city editor."

Without a hint of recognition, the soldier broke away, walked off several paces, and spoke into a walkie-talkie.

* * *

CAPTAIN KOBLOS, IN military khakis, with two silver bars on his shoulder, waited behind a gray metal desk. Nearby, an MP stood stiffly at parade rest. The soldier marched Lily and Tokido in front of him, ordered them to stop, and came around in front of the captain. He saluted, passed their documents and binoculars over, and stepped to one side. Koblos set the binoculars on his desk and silently examined the documents.

Harsh light flooded the dank room. The American flag and a battalion flag hung limply in the corner. The smell of sweat and mildew hovered in the air.

Koblos raised his eyes, raking them back and forth between the pair. "You approached our restricted area. I could lock you up right now."

Tokido felt Lily start as if she'd been struck. He didn't move a muscle. The metal edge of the camera dug into his ankle, which throbbed with pain.

Koblos fixed his gaze on Tokido. "I've verified your identity with Mr. Moto." He clenched his teeth. His gaze slid to Lily. "Don't ever pull a stunt like this again." He paused. "Now, both of you, get out of here. We have a taxi standing by. Hutchinson, here's their papers. Take them to the main gate."

* * *

DUSK HAD FALLEN, and night was coming on hard. The MP pulled up sharply to the door of the taxi idling at the guard shack. Its headlights cut through the fog that rose from the ocean and poured down through the valleys and hillsides like fine rain. Lily leaped out and flung herself into the backseat. Tokido slid in beside her. She hugged the door, staring straight ahead.

He gave the cabbie directions back to the car. It was futile to attempt to talk; she was seething. Once they reached the parking lot, he paid the cabbie and opened the door for her. He weighed the question of whether she had seen him using the camera. If she had, why didn't she say something?

He drove out of Tennessee Valley, onto the highway, and over the bridge. The tires clicked over the bridge's roadbed. They rode trapped in hostile silence. Through the tollgate, into the Marina, and up Scott Street, he steered the car with precise execution.

Before the car reached the French boardinghouse, Tokido veered sharply around a corner, reducing the speed so that the car crawled like a great cat along the darkened street lined with stately houses.

"Lily," he began. "I—"

"Stop," she said. "Just stop." Her words, each delivered in measured cadence like a beating drum, came slowly. "Someday I'll give you back the hurt you have given me. You won't know when, you won't know where, but any peace you have will turn to dust, and you'll know my debt is settled." Her hand flew to the door handle. He braked, but not before the door swung wide. The gray asphalt, its surface razor-flecked, telescoped into view.

"No!" he shouted helplessly. She jumped, landing squarely, quick-stepping, regaining her balance, running, running, running, and disappearing in the rear window.

CHAPTER TWENTY-FOUR

Woodrow

In a darkened corner of the Family Club bar in downtown San Francisco, Fritz Hobart leaned back against a leather barrel chair and sipped a bourbon neat. Woodrow sat opposite him, fingering a cigar and nursing a French Bordeaux. Here and there, club members visited in pairs, smoking and drinking, some alone, reading the newspaper. White-coated gentlemen waiters held trays and proffered refreshments.

Hobart adjusted the knot of his navy blue and gold rep tie and regarded Woodrow with keen interest. "It's a pleasure to see you after all these years. You've done well, Woodrow."

"It never occurred to me that you wouldn't do well, Fritz. Law was a good choice?"

"Politics ran in my blood. A law degree was a place to start. As it turned out, Washington called and I answered."

"Providence plays its part. Right place, right time."

Hobart nodded and tipped the bourbon to his lips. "Precisely. Your work with the Carnegie team at Chichén Itzá is highly regarded."

"I appreciate that."

"Your contribution here at the Exposition hasn't gone unnoticed, either. I saw the hieroglyphics on many of the walls at Treasure Island. Fascinating stuff."

"Yes, and now it's time to move on." Woodrow inhaled and exhaled the cigar, the smoke circling over his head. "It appears that my work has come to an end."

"That may not be the case," Hobart said. He leaned in and placed the bourbon on the table between them. "I'd like to speak confidentially."

Woodrow nodded. "By all means." Hobart's remark did not come as a surprise. The curious letter from his father about Hobart lay visible under a paperweight on the corner of his desk. He was reminded daily of an imminent call.

"I'll be blunt. World events are playing out on a stage larger than is imaginable for the United States."

Without hesitation, Woodrow replied. "I, too, am concerned about the world's political situation."

"Exactly." Hobart leaned closer in. "Roosevelt's staff and top advisors are building a network of private citizens that keep him informed as the inevitable war in Europe and hostility with Japan unfold. Highly placed people believe you can help the country to stay informed from this strategic location on the West Coast."

Woodrow held Hobart's gaze, sensing what was coming.

"The presence of Japan on Treasure Island has not been overlooked," Hobart added.

"With good reason," Woodrow replied.

"I'm certain that if you joined this group, your ability to move widely would be invaluable to our country's effort."

There was no need for consideration. The reply was swift. "I'll do whatever I can to help. In fact, I already have information that may prove useful."

"Good man," Hobart said. "You'll be contacted tomorrow by a Mr. Johnson."

"Would you like to join me for dinner?"

"May I take a rain check?"

"Anytime," Woodrow replied.

Hobart stood and stepped around the table to clasp Woodrow's hand. "We're on the move. It's great to have you aboard."

* * *

WOODROW EXITED THE club into the bracing chill of fog. He was ravenously hungry and electrified by Hobart's proposal. By God, the fight was on! He pictured Roosevelt's leonine head, wide grin, and take-charge spirit that had pulled the country out of the Depression and set it working again. Not even the blow of polio, which crippled his legs, had stopped the man. Now his courage and cunning would prevail during these dangerous times.

All at once, Woodrow sought the camaraderie of good people enjoying a hearty meal. He hailed a cab that delivered him to the front door of Schroeder's Restaurant on Front Street. Inside the wood-paneled, high-ceilinged hall, he ordered a dinner of bratwurst, sauerkraut, potatoes, and a stein of excellent beer. All around him, diners ate and drank and conversed. Not for one minute did he feel alone. As his belly filled, his spirits held steady while he speculated about the future. Best to abandon the search for Lily's mother, he resolved. Lily was a grown woman, capable of fending for herself. Time to allow such folly to subside; there was new purpose now.

Gayway

CHAPTER TWENTY-FIVE

Lily

"Goddammit, Nordby, what in the hell were you thinking?" Every vein on Toth's forehead bulged as if it would burst. "Snooping near a goddamn military danger zone!" He flung a pencil down on his desk, stacked with papers and folders, and glared at her.

"Think about it, Boss. I found the site of Battery Townsley! What a story!"

"You *think* you found it." He yanked at his tie like he was having a fit. "And even if you did, it's a story we can't run. It's top secret! You know that. Don't give me any crap."

"Yeah, but—"

"In the company of a Jap, no less." The phone rang; he picked it up and shouted into the receiver, "Not now!"

Lily's cheeks burned. "I never took you for a racist."

"Don't be getting hot under the collar. He may be a diplomat, but he's still a Jap." Toth ran the heel of his hand over his bald head. "And take that indignant look off your face. You could have landed in the brig."

"I know, I know—"

"What you do with your personal life is your business, but get your head out of the clouds. People talk, Nordby." He lifted a lit cigarette from the lip of an ashtray overflowing with butts and took a drag. "Showing up around town gussied up, making googly eyes, but now you've taken it too far!"

"Shut up for one minute! There's something I need to tell you."

He squinted at her. "Hurry up. I've got a paper to put out."

"It's a bigger story."

"I'm listening."

"I have no proof."

"Cut to the chase, Nordby."

"Okamura told me he wanted to see the coast. I suggested Mount Tamalpais, but he chose the headlands."

Toth cocked his head to one side. "And?" He ground out the cigarette.

"Just before we were sighted, I think he was taking pictures."

"You *think?*" Toth repeated. He chewed on his lower lip. "Pictures of what?"

"Battery Townsley. I was too far away to swear on it, but I'm pretty sure he dropped something in his boot. Maybe a camera?"

He jumped to his feet. "*Too far away!*" Toth thundered. "A *camera?* This gets better and better. You *think* you saw him drop something in his boot, but you're not sure. But obviously you don't say anything to the captain. Because if there's really a camera or some other blasted thing in his boot, then you're dead meat."

"Right."

"Goddammit, Nordby. Get out of here! Write me a story on the Gayway!"

"What about Okamura?"

"Drop it! Christ, how many times do I have to tell you? Do the stuff you do. Freaks, carny men, nude cowgirls—I don't care. Readers slop it up with their Wheaties. And stick around. You're not planning on leaving town or anything?"

"Where would I go?"

"Dames like you, I never know."

"Sure, sure," she said and headed for the door.

"Hold on. There's something else." He flopped back down on his chair. The phone rang again. Voices yelled from behind the door.

She paused and glanced back at him.

The features of his face sagged like a hound dog's. "Don't do anything foolish."

"I wouldn't dare."

"That's what you say." He waggled his finger at her. "Stay out of trouble. I want you in one piece."

* * *

BY NOON THE Gayway was clogged with amusement seekers hungry for carny thrills, daredevil theatricals, and sugar-rich, greasy concoctions. Lily jumped out of a rickshaw, tipped the sampan driver double, and surveyed the teaming crowds. A murderous mood pervaded her consciousness.

Over the weekend, she had alternated between crying jags and stone-cold appraisal of her behavior. She slept the days away and skipped meals, preferring to slink down to the kitchen after everyone had gone to bed and filch food out of the refrigerator. She'd stand over the sink, shoveling leftover pie into her mouth, looking out the windows, lights flickering in the black night. Then, at 3:00 a.m. on Sunday, unable to sleep, she dressed and crept out of the boardinghouse. The houses along the street were wrapped in shadowed silence. Walking around the block, she stopped stock-still on the pavement. Something clicked: What would Tokido do with the camera? It was worth the risk to find out. She'd have to act fast. She bottled up her sorrow, replacing it with a fury that made her jumpy and reckless.

* * *

A GIGANTIC BUILDING sponsored by National Cash Register was positioned near the entry to the Gayway, billed as Forty Acres of Fun. The attraction, built in the exact shape of a cash register, flashed the daily number of each visitor to the island high in the dollar window for all to see. Lily stopped and watched the ticker roll from 149,201 to 149,202 and keep scrolling higher. She scribbled the figures down in her notebook. She supposed that many visitors, after sampling the highbrow culture in the front of the island, headed, tired and thirsty, to partake of lowbrow enticements at the back. The concessions were packed.

Despite the barkers in the shooting galleries crying, "Try your luck! Last chance"; the cries of riders on the giant crane, Tilt-a-Whirl, and dodger cars; and the whoosh of the Roll-O-Planes, an air of desperation soured the air. She drank a gin and ginger beer, snacked on a corn dog, felt a little woozy but mostly sick to her stomach, and kept going.

Strolling by Ripley's Believe It or Not! Odditorium, featuring a photo of the Mule-Faced Woman—a swollen, forlorn, pale-lipped creature—and an armless man who tossed knives with his feet at his wife, she picked up her pace. Nothing and no one seemed worthy of a story—not the fortune teller, the turbaned sword swallower, or the snake charmer who managed the reptile pits. *If this place doesn't rot your mind,* she thought, *it will rot your teeth.* Even stopping in to see if Sally Rand would grant her an interview struck her as garish and cheap. *Who in the hell really cares about nude cowgirls?* she decided.

On impulse, she considered striking out for the Cavalcade of the Golden West, a theatrical stage show in the northernmost corner of the island. If she hurried, she could see the two o'clock show. Until now, she had avoided it, perhaps because it reminded her of the tawdry concession that had installed eighty-two midgets dressed in cowboy outfits in a miniature Western village. She was sure Woodrow would be horrified by this vulgar ploy to parade the misfortune of another's deformity in order to make a profit.

A pang for her old friend gave her pause. Nonetheless, the cavalcade featured three hundred actors; two hundred animals, including a stampede of Herefords; covered wagons and steam locomotives; war-painted Indians, and soldiers on horseback—all on a stage that was four hundred feet wide and two hundred feet deep, with a painted backdrop of the High Sierras. Toth would give the story a thumbs-up. The Wild West lived on! Lily knew everything about it was big, but up close it was probably as fake as a wooden nickel.

As she headed for the exit, she noticed a crowd, whooping and hollering, under a sign: AMAZING FEATS OF STRENGTH! She elbowed through the spectators to the front. A barker stood off to the side. He shouted into a microphone, "You won't believe this, folks! Keep your eyes on the giant, now. He's about to perform the impossible!" The tallest man she had ever seen in the flesh was hammering a railroad spike with his bare hands through an oak board resting on his huge knees. She estimated he was nearly eight feet tall. But it wasn't only his height—his bones were as massive as a buffalo's. He wore simple brown work clothes that strained against his muscles and tie-up boots, and his shirtsleeves were rolled up past his elbows. The palms of his open hands, as thick as beef chops, were unbloodied but bright red. With each blow, the crowd cheered. She couldn't turn away. One last blow, and the spike pierced the wood. All the spectators shouted, "Hurrah! Hurrah!"

The giant peered out from under his brow, dripping with sweat, and threw the board to the ground, wiping his hands together. He lifted his arms into the air, clasped his hands, and let out a victory yell. A shiver went up Lily's spine. She was transfixed by his presence. His eyes swept out over the crowd, and when he saw Lily, a look of recognition flashed in his eyes. She stood glued to the spot. The giant turned away, lifted the board off the ground, and dragged it behind a red curtain. Gradually, the crowd dispersed. A barker swept aside the curtain and shouted, "Ladies and gents!" Come one, come all. See the Strongman perform amazing feats of strength!"

She began to approach the barker, when the giant swept aside the curtain and walked toward her. In a few long strides, he was upon her.

"I know you," he said.

"Really?" She tried to modulate her voice. "How is that?"

"You're the reporter."

"Right. I work for the *Examiner.* You've read my stories, then?"

"Nope. I don't read much." He scratched his ear. "I listen to the radio." He pursed his lips and swallowed. His larynx jumped, as if he had swallowed an apple. "The thing is, we have a mutual friend."

She shrugged. "We do?"

"Yep."

She waited for him to continue, but his eyes bore into her as if she were a specimen under glass. "I'd like to write a story about you. Do you have time now to talk?"

"Can't," he reported. "Next show is coming up quick."

"What about later today?"

"Tell you what. Come to my place tomorrow, after work, around nine. You can ask all the questions you want."

She lifted her notebook. "What's the address?"

"Seventeen Gold Street."

"San Francisco?" she asked, but he had turned away, tramping back toward the curtain, which he swept aside with one swat. "What's your name?" she called.

"Rosy," he boomed, giving her a final salute. "See you to-morrow night!"

CHAPTER TWENTY-SIX

Tokido

Tokido stepped from his apartment into the small courtyard. By force of habit, he glanced down at the circle of smooth stone. The key glinted in the morning light. He considered whether to remove it. Turning up the collar of his jacket, he unlatched the gate and rapidly walked away.

Over the weekend, Consul General Moto's wrath about the incident at Battery Townsley had not descended. But Tokido knew it would come. He was useless to the mission; it was only a matter of time before he would be stripped of authority. At the pavilion, he had circulated through the visitors, answering questions, engaging in conversation. He kept his distance from the staff, knowing that around him had been built a wall of silence that no one, not even trusted colleagues, dared to penetrate.

In the evening, he retreated to the apartment, alone and defenseless. He felt like a fugitive. He waited hopelessly, imagining Lily's return. Driven back into the night, he found himself again on Treasure Island. In the pavilion, he walked through the rooms, studying the displays and artifacts that he had come to relish with pride and pleasure. In the tearoom, he remembered the day he had argued with her. An ache for her rose up so sharply that he rocked back and forth to dispel it. On the bridge above the lagoon, he paused to gaze west, past the sparkling outline of the city, as the foghorns sounded their constant lament.

Morning brought determination. He recalled the saying "one must push to receive blessings," and so he prepared to meet his responsibilities. Activity was brisk on the street. He sidestepped around vendors delivering goods, shoppers scurrying along on the sidewalk, clutching straw bags, and children hurrying to school. Ahead, the consulate limo idled at the curb.

Hayato sat at the wheel, his gaze aimed straight ahead.

Tokido opened the rear door and slipped onto the seat. "*Ohayo gozaimasu.* I trust you are well."

"*Hai,*" Hayato replied curtly, pulling into busy traffic and accelerating cautiously.

Tokido watched the back of Hayato's head, waiting for him to resume their familiar banter, but neither conversation nor comment came. Unease bubbled in Tokido's stomach. He picked up the morning *Examiner* lying on the seat next to him and scanned the front page. Under a banner headline that read: "Mahatma Gandhi Fasts to Protest Autocratic Rule in India," he zoomed in on a feature article: "Festivities for Japan Day!"

He skimmed through the article, trying to decipher whether Lily had written it. "Mayor Rossi has proclaimed Sunday, April 29, as Japan Day to commemorate the 38th birthday of Emperor Hirohito. . . . Thousands are expected for a grand celebration. . . . Parades and floats will mark the grand occasion. . . . *Takarabune,* a treasure ship, will float in the lagoon. . . . Japanese Ambassador Censure Horinouchi will speak in a broadcast coast to coast and in Japan."

There was no byline. The content was boilerplate factual. It was impossible to know who had written it.

Abruptly, Tokido glanced out the window. This was not the usual course that Hayato took to the consulate. He was driving east, toward the rising sun.

"Hayato, are you taking a new route this morning?"

"No, Tokido-*san,* I am not."

"I have an appointment with Consul General Moto at the consulate this morning."

"With respect, Tokido-*san,* I have been directed to take you to Treasure Island. We are headed toward the bridge. I will have you there shortly."

In that split second, Tokido registered the blow that he had known was coming. The newspaper slipped from his fingers. Before it fell to the floor, he caught it. He wondered how much time he had left.

* * *

INSIDE THE OFFICE of the pavilion, Kiyoshi stood at attention as Tokido entered. Posture erect, suit and tie immaculate, eyes downward, he bowed quickly. *"Ohayo gozaimasu."*

Returning the salutation, Tokido removed his coat and settled at his desk. He ran his fingers over the polished wood, observing with detachment the ikebana of curly willow pierced by a single purple orchid.

With pristine formality, Kiyoshi offered him a file.

Tokido received the document with equal solemnity. *"Domo arigatou."* Inside, hand-printed pages were fastened by a clip. He flipped through them. As he turned the last one, an envelope with his name printed in ink appeared. It was stamped with the return address of the consulate. Without expression, he closed the file. "Are there any messages?"

"None," said Kiyoshi. A muscle in his jaw twitched.

"I see." Tokido surveyed the office—black phones, lamps, notepads atop ink blotters on each desk, prints on the walls, and, on the back wall, the glass-fronted display cabinet of netsuke. Nothing appeared out of the ordinary.

"Tokido-*san,* shall we continue?"

"Ah, yes, plans for Japan Day. It is essential that all steps are taken to ensure festivities for the emperor's birthday unfold without a flaw."

"Of course. I'm at your service."

Just then, a young woman whom Tokido had never seen before, dressed in a pale peach kimono printed with white blossoms, entered the office, carrying a tray laden with an earthenware teapot and two blue-and-white porcelain cups.

She placed the tray on Tokido's desk, poured green tea into the cups, and departed without a sound.

"Where is Chizu?" Tokido asked, lifting the cup to his lips.

"I do not know."

"When is she expected back?"

"I cannot say."

"Please," Tokido said, "enjoy the tea while it's hot."

"*Arigatou*," Kiyoshi said, taking the cup to his desk and sitting in his chair. A fleeting glance of worry belied his calm demeanor. "Shall we proceed?"

Tokido nodded, removing the schedule from the file, lifting his fountain pen, and unscrewing the cap. "Please continue."

"Here is the plan of the day. The opening celebration begins at nine a.m. in front of the pavilion," Kiyoshi began. "The ambassador will review the parade alongside Consul General Moto. Mayor Rossi, officials from city hall, and dignitaries from the Japanese community will also be present.

"First, hundreds of young girls wearing kimonos and hats intertwined with flowers will march alongside grand marshals. Some of the girls will carry paper umbrellas, and some will play flutes. Young boys will play drums."

As Kiyoshi spoke, Tokido could see how it pained him to uphold the pretense that nothing had changed between them. The greatest honor Tokido could show Kiyoshi would be to spare him further discomfort. "May I make a suggestion?"

"Naturally," answered Kiyoshi.

"Leave the plan with me. If additions are needed, I will make notes. You are free to go."

Kiyoshi looked startled. "Tokido-*san,* please allow me to finish."

A fragile balance, as fine as spider silk, stretched between them.

Tokido bowed his head and nodded. "As you wish."

Kiyoshi began again. "Next will come a procession of our countrymen in traditional costume, interspersed with many floats depicting village life, agriculture, and the arts. *Takarabune,* the treasure ship of the seven lucky gods, will end the parade.

"At ten thirty, His Excellency Censure Horinuchi will receive military honors. He will then speak from the Federal Plaza. The speech will be broadcast coast to coast and by shortwave radio to Japan. A formal luncheon will follow.

"In the afternoon, pavilion hostesses will offer special tea cakes and refreshments for all visitors. Origami cranes and *wagashi* will be offered as gifts. Cormorant fishing demonstrations will take place in the pond. The men, also dressed in native costume, will catch fish exactly as it is done on the Nagara River in Gifu Prefecture.

"In the evening, paper lanterns will be lit for a feast to honor the ambassador and spectacular fireworks will conclude the night." Kiyoshi placed the schedule on the desktop and folded his hands together.

Tokido fingered his pen. He hadn't made a mark on the plan.

Kiyoshi waited.

"Excellent. You have done well. I'm sure the day will be a great success."

"Domo arigatou gozaimasu."

"As it is, then, Kiyoshi-*san*. You may go now." He rose to his feet and bowed deeply. *"Sayonara."*

Kiyoshi whispered, "*Sayonara*," bowed, and departed with all the dignity and intelligence that had proved him to be an invaluable ally.

Tokido leaned against door. This was no time for regret. He pulled the letter from the file and ripped it open. His eyes raced down the page.

> *You are ordered to return to Tokyo on the Tatuta Maru, which departs San Francisco on March 15. In the interim, perform the diplomatic duties and community contacts required at the pavilion. Make no contact with the reporter Lily Nordby. Upon departure, leave all documents in the office. When you arrive in Yokohama, a car will take you to headquarters for a debriefing. Speak to no one about your departure.*
>
> *Sincerely,*
> *Consul General Moto*

Tokido moved rapidly to the display cabinet and ran his finger down the carved molding on the outside of the case to the head of the seventh carved bird. He pressed its head. The molding popped open. He peered inside. The cavity was empty. The hydrographic map of the San Francisco Bay, the land map of coastal defenses, and the black-and-white photos of the construction of the Golden Gate Bridge that Chizu had secured—everything gone.

His movements became automatic: leave nothing behind.

Close the cabinet, find the motorcycle key in the desk drawer, grab his coat, exit the office. He looked neither left nor right; figures moved by him in a blur. The doors were open wide. He leaped down the stairs and dashed for the motorcycle at the back of the pavilion. It leaned against a wall. He pushed it out, jumped on, and pressed the starter button. The motor sputtered, missed, sputtered again, and turned over. He revved the gas and popped the gearshift into first. The motorcycle growled and sprang forward as he steered it around the buildings and out onto the street.

He throttled the motorcycle until the engine screamed. He tore along the Avenue of the Palms, the bitter wind off the bay whipping him senseless. Up onto the bridge approach, he leaned into the curve and sped through traffic. The bridge cables whined in the wind. Maybe there was a chance that the camera wouldn't be found. They would confiscate his logbook. They were welcome to it. But the film in the camera. The one photo of Lily. That was his.

Ten minutes over the bridge, twenty minutes to his apartment. He bargained with the fates. Even though he knew he was too late, he rode as if his life depended on it.

CHAPTER TWENTY-SEVEN

Woodrow

Woodrow had no sooner pushed open his front gate than he heard, “Boss, hold up!” He turned to see Rosy running down the Filbert Street steps like a bull in charge.

Rosy skidded to a stop and clapped Woodrow on the shoulder. “I been looking for you everywhere,” he huffed. “We gotta get back to my place!”

“What are you talking about?” Woodrow demanded.

“That dame you’re crackers for is due there in short order.”

“Lily?” Woodrow’s hair stood on end. “Is she hurt?”

“No, Boss. Don’t ask me to explain. We ain’t got much time.” He yanked on Woodrow’s arm. “A cab is up on the street. Hurry up!”

The cab tore back through town and sped up Gold Street.

Its headlights beamed on Lily as she was peering through the iron bars on Rosy's front window. She pivoted toward the sound of the cab's screeching tires. Rosy was halfway out the cab before it stopped. Woodrow paid the cabbie and hopped out.

"Woodrow!" Lily said, "What are you doing here?"

"I'm not sure," Woodrow said sheepishly. But he wasn't being entirely truthful. His mind fled to one possibility.

Lily glanced at Rosy, who was unlocking his door. "You know each other?"

"Come in, Miss Lily. I'll explain."

Lily approached, peeked in, and crossed the threshold. The men followed behind. She refused the chair that Rosy pulled out for her. She backed against a wall and folded her arms across her chest. Woodrow dragged a chair out from the table and perched on its edge. He clasped his hands together to keep them from shaking.

Rosy paced. "You see, it's like this," he began. "I didn't get you here for the interview, or whatever you call it, and I'm real sorry about that."

"So why *am* I here? You've got about two minutes until I lose my temper, and then I'm out the door."

"Slow down, Miss Lily. What I have to tell you will take a little longer." He scratched his head. "You sure you don't want a seat?"

"Absolutely not," she snapped.

"For starters, you got to know this here is a real neighborhood where real people live. Unusual people like me who don't fit in with regular folks. You get my drift?"

"Of course. Hurry up."

"So, Woodrow, my friend, who I know from the Expo, comes looking for one of our people." He pursed his lips and nodded several times toward Woodrow, whose heart was slamming in his chest. "Where does he go? To Pacific Street, where the sleaze joints attract a clientele that's drowning in booze, the big H, and song and dance."

"Yes," she said impatiently, "I know it. The International Settlement."

"That's when I happen to come along. I pass by Spider Kelly's. I hear a commotion. Good thing. Bottles flying, fists swinging, knives flashing. Who's in the middle?" He nodded toward Woodrow. "That's right. Woodrow himself. Me, I know my way around a brawl. Him, well, not so much. So, I get him out of there before he gets his head bashed in. Later, I come to find out he's in there looking for someone because of you, Miss Lily."

Her eyes flew to Woodrow. "Why?"

"It was a bad idea," Woodrow stammered. "At Christmas, I let you down. I wanted to make amends. The business with Tokido. I lost my temper. Then I heard a rumor."

"What rumor?" Lily's face drained of color.

Woodrow couldn't speak. The words strangled in his vocal cords.

"Okay, Boss. I'll take over. There ain't no other way to say this than straight out. He was looking for a woman called Sweet Sadie."

"Sweet Sadie?" she asked.

"The name of a singer, Miss Lily. The name of the woman who's your mother."

Lily jerked backward, as if she'd been struck, and Woodrow jumped from the chair, rushing to her. She grasped his hand, steadying herself. "My mother. You know my mother?"

"For years." Rosy bent his head, as if it pained him to continue. "But I gotta tell you, Miss Lily, she ain't singing no more."

"What are you saying?"

"She's been hooked on the big H for years."

"Oh my God," Lily moaned. "How can this be?"

"Happens to the best of 'em, Miss Lily. But now she's clean." His face brightened. "I talked to her about you. She's ready to see you. Well, as ready as she'll ever be. But I gotta warn you: she's in rough shape."

"Take me to her."

* * *

THEY WALKED THROUGH backstreets, past industrial buildings and warehouses, to the edge of the old waterfront. Rosy stopped at a two-story building blackened by grit. A door lay partially open, its hinges rusted by salty air. Rosy leaned his shoulder against the splintered wood, and it creaked open. One bare lightbulb hanging from a cord lit a long, narrow staircase. The stench of urine and rot hung in the airless shaft. Woodrow heard Lily gag. They walked up the stairs, one at a time, holding their hands over their noses.

Rosy led the way down a hallway, walls streaked with brown stains, past closed doors, past the sound of coughing. He stopped in front of a door flaked with gray paint. He knocked twice. He turned the doorknob. "Wait here," he told Lily and Woodrow. The door lay half open. Lily reached for Woodrow's hand, gripping it hard, and when he looked up at her, terror glazed her eyes.

They heard Rosy's voice. "Sadie, she's here. It's Lily."

Woodrow drew Lily's trembling body closer, and together they squeezed through the opening. Across the room, the woman in the iron bed was a collection of bones covered by a thin blanket. The skin on her face was mottled; her thin gray hair was matted against her skull. A lamp on a table next to the bed cast shadowed light over the room. A sour, fetid odor hovered close.

"Where?" Sadie asked in a hoarse whisper.

"There," Rosy said, pointing.

Sadie turned her head toward Lily. Her eyes, clouded by disease, flew open, and she raised her hand, blotched with blood bruises. "My child, come closer."

Woodrow released Lily. She crept forward, knelt down, and took her mother's outstretched hand.

"Oh, you are more beautiful than I have imagined," Sadie whispered.

Woodrow watched, spellbound.

"There, there, don't cry," Sadie murmured. "Forgive me, my precious child, forgive me." Her eyelids fluttered, and she arched her back, straining for breath. Gradually she settled, her breathing became steady, and she drifted off.

Lily wept, still holding her mother's hand, until Rosy walked around the bed and helped her to stand. "She's fallen asleep, Miss Lily. We should go now."

"So soon?"

"Yes, it's for the best."

"Who'll take care of her?"

"Don't you worry."

"Are you sure?"

"Yes. And you can come back tomorrow."

* * *

BACK ON THE street, Rosy bade them good-bye. "That was mighty hard, Miss Lily, but you did good. Real good." He clapped Woodrow on the back. "Okay, Boss, see you later. Take care of Lily. I'll watch out for Sadie."

Woodrow found a cab and tucked Lily inside. He gave the cabbie Lily's address at the French boardinghouse. "You'll be home in no time. You need to sleep."

"I don't know what to say."

"You don't have to say anything."

"Oh, Woodrow, all the time that's been wasted."

"You've had a shock," he said, peeling her fingers from his hand. "Try to get some rest. I'll call you in the morning." He closed the door, tapped the window, and watched the cab pull away, its red taillights fading to pinpoints in the night.

CHAPTER TWENTY-EIGHT

Lily

Lily scrabbled in the dirt until her fingers unearthed the right-size pebble. She straightened, took aim, and threw.

Ping. The pebble bounced off the darkened glass of the second-story window. Dew dripped off the plants and trees in the garden. The silent world seemed to be sleeping. She counted to ten. Nothing. She found a larger pebble, jagged edges, heavier. Again, she aimed, threw, and waited. On the third try, a light blinked on. The window squeaked open. Woodrow leaned out. "Hello," he called, looking down. "Who's there?"

"It's me."

A moment passed. "Lily, what are you doing?"

"I need to see you."

"Wait there. I'll be right down."

Sleepy-eyed, hair disheveled, he answered the door

wrapped in a silk robe with a tasseled sash tied around his waist. *My,* she thought, *who but Woodrow wears a silk robe?*

"You're shivering. Are you all right?"

"Yes, and no," she answered.

"Come in," he said, taking her by the elbow. "Let's get you warm." He shuffled ahead of her, up the stairs, and into the living room. She followed, wondering how to begin to tell him why she had come.

"Make yourself comfortable," he said, switching on lights and straightening the pillows on the couch. "I didn't get a chance to tidy up tonight."

"It was an extraordinary night. I'll never forget it."

"Nor will I. I'll make tea."

"Thank you, Woodrow, but no tea."

He looked perplexed, shuffling on one foot and then the other. "What, then?"

"Please, come sit by me." She patted the cushion on the couch beside her.

Joining her, he tightened the sash around his waist and rearranged the robe, which draped over his knees onto his bare feet.

Timorous and uncertain, she clasped her hands together. "When the taxi dropped me off at home, Maxine was still awake and we talked. We hadn't really talked for so long. It's hard to hide anything from her." She pursed her lips, trying to smile. "She seems to know things about me that I don't know myself."

"She is a friend for life," he said.

"You're right. I told her everything that happened today. About the giant, finding my mother, and you."

Lily glanced at Woodrow and then quickly away. The room stilled, silent witness to their conversation.

"I've been thinking about my mother for months. Since the night Timothy told me she was alive."

"I'm sorry you had to see her like that. It wasn't what I had planned."

Her heart beat so quickly, she was sure he could hear it banging in her chest. "If you hadn't found her, I wouldn't have found her." She reached across the cushion and took his hand. His warm fingers circled around hers, cradling her hand in his strong grip. She never wanted him to let go. "Thank you, Woodrow."

"You don't have to thank me, Lily. The credit goes to Rosy."

"You're much too modest."

"Are you sure I can't get you something hot to drink? You're still shivering."

"Please, let me finish."

"Of course."

"And every question Maxine asked me about you led to the same answer."

"What's that?" he asked.

"Do I have to tell you?" She leaned over and looked into his astonished eyes. "I love you," she whispered, kissing him tenderly, slowly, and then kissing him again.

* * *

LILY AWOKE IN Woodrow's arms and dared not look at him. His beard was rough against her shoulder, and as she listened to his even and steady breath, she couldn't be certain if he was awake or not. As she slowly shifted her weight, the musky smell of love drifted from beneath the covers.

His bedroom was bathed in morning light. Slowly, she searched its every aspect—the claw-footed mahogany bureau topped with black-and-white family photos in gold frames, the bedside table stacked with books, and, through a window, a slice of unperturbed pale blue sky.

How like the room is the man, she mused. *Solid, cultured, refined. Who would ever guess the passion in his soul disguised beneath his gentlemanly exterior?* It made not one iota of difference that his limbs were shorter than those of a normal man, and as a vision of Tokido surfaced in her memory, she willed it away. *After last night*, she vowed, *I will never be the same. I will never go back.*

And in equal measure, overlapping with and invading this revelation, came the shock of finding her mother. The stench of death had hovered in each corner of that vile room. Although Lily had been overcome by shame and disgust, her mother's gesture of greeting had melted her heart.

Now she was driven by one thought: *I've got to get her out of that hovel.*

"Lily," Woodrow said, stroking her forehead. "I know you're awake."

She threw back the covers, wrapping the sheet around her body. "I'm late." She kissed his lips lightly and twisted away. Her feet hit the floor, and she grabbed her clothes, strewn about the room.

"Where are you going?"

"Back to my mother's place."

"Wait a minute."

"There isn't any time. She needs medical attention, and that rat hole she's in is an abomination."

"Let's think this through."

Lily ran down the hall to the bathroom and closed the door. After throwing water on her face and running her fingers through her hair, she dressed in a flurry. When she came out, she found Woodrow downstairs, fully clothed, talking on the phone.

Looking up at her, he covered the mouthpiece with his hand. "I'm speaking with a doctor. He'll advise us where to take Sadie. Then I'll make another call. You're not going alone."

* * *

A BREEZE CARRYING the tang of salt air blew through the hospital window, fluttering the white curtains and diluting the smell of disinfectant that seeped into every crevice. Lily cradled her mother's hand in her own, afraid to stroke the papery skin, for fear it would disintegrate beneath her fingertips. With her other hand, she adjusted the pillow under Sadie's head and drew the corner of a blanket over her bony shoulder. "Are you cold?" she asked.

"Just a little. Where am I?"

"St. Mary's Hospital, near Golden Gate Park."

"Oh dear, a hospital. How did I get here?"

"Remember Woodrow?"

Sadie blinked rapidly and then smiled. "Woodrow? You mean

the little man? Rosy's friend? I first saw him at Spider Kelly's."

"That's right. He was moving fast that night."

"He was running for his life." Sadie chuckled.

"He was looking for you."

"Why on earth me?"

"It's a long story, but the simple answer is that he wanted to reunite us."

"It's a blessing."

"Yes, it is, and he made arrangements to move you here in an ambulance."

"Goodness, what a generous man."

"In every way," Lily said, "and now you're safe."

Just then, a nun walked in, the skirt of her black habit rustling, a silver cross hanging around her neck over a white wimple. "Good morning," she said, a faint Irish brogue coloring her speech. Her pink skin was flushed with good health. She walked around the bed and touched Sadie on her arm. "I'm Sister Bridget. How are you feeling this morning, dear?"

"I'm not sure."

"Perfectly understandable," Sister Bridget said. A twinkle in her blue eyes, accentuated by a stark black headdress, radiated goodness. "We'll take care of you. Don't you worry one bit." She peered at Lily. "I see your lovely daughter is here to keep watch, too. Isn't that a comfort?"

Sadie sighed. "I'm so ashamed."

"Now, now, we're all God's children. His mercy is great." She carefully lifted Sadie's wrist and placed her fingers over the pulse. Closing her eyes, she listened. After a minute, she slowly returned Sadie's arm to the mattress and tucked it under the blanket. Her fingers lingered under the bedclothes. Then she stroked Sadie's forehead before walking to the end of the bed, where a chart dangled from the white iron bedpost. There, she jotted down a note. "Now, let's make you more comfortable. Your sheets and underclothes are a bit damp. I'll have you spic and span in no time."

Lily studied her mother's face while Sister Bridget deftly rolled Sadie to one side, quickly dressing her in a fresh gown, and then stripped the sheets and blankets and replaced them with clean bedclothes.

"I'll let you two be. Press this button on the wall if you need me. I'm only steps away."

"Thank you, Sister," Lily called.

"Oh, that's nice," Sadie said, her eyelids drooping, her chest rising and falling with each shallow breath.

Lily waited, her gaze shifting between her mother's face and a bronze crucifix above the bed. She prayed to a god she didn't believe in, for an outcome she knew wouldn't come, but still she prayed. *Tick, tick, tick,* went the minute hand of a clock on the wall. Footsteps echoed outside the door, distant voices called back and forth, horns beeped in the street.

Suddenly Sadie's eyes popped open. "Oh," she gasped. "I'm so thirsty."

"Here," Lily said, propping up her head and tipping the rim of a glass to her parched lips.

Sadie struggled to sip the water. "Oh, that's better. Thank you." She watched Lily as if she were an illusion.

"Can you talk?" Lily asked.

"I'll try."

"You were born in Vilnius?"

"How do you know such things?"

"Herman Oronoffski told me."

"Who?" Sadie asked.

"The grocer on Folsom Street. Across the street from where you lived with my father when I was a baby. He spoke of you with great affection. He said you used to bring him halvah."

Tears bloomed in Sadie's eyes, clouded with cataracts. "Such a sweet man."

"I promised him I'd come back, and I will. I'll tell him that I found you. Oh, please, don't cry," Lily said, blotting Sadie's cheeks.

"You are so kind to me," Sadie whispered, "when I've been so wicked."

"We won't speak of that now. Our time is precious." Lily reached for a bowl on the bedside table. "Taste this," she said, gently offering her mother a spoonful of soup.

"I'm not hungry, my dear."

"Maybe later, then."

Sadie squinted at Lily. "You asked me a question."

"Yes, about where you were born."

"Ah, what I remember would fill a thimble. Vilnius, a city of steeples, cathedrals, and synagogues blackened by soot, forbidding to a child's eye. But there was a golden summer after a winter so cold I thought my toes would fall off." She shuddered. "Snowdrifts piled higher than windows. My father was a tailor, never enough money to buy food or keep us warm. We fled. Everywhere, hatred and persecution. Borders shifting—turmoil, despair, war." Sadie shook her head. "Did your father tell you I was a Jew?"

"No," Lily whispered.

"Who told you?"

"Herman."

"Of course he would. Was it a shock?"

"The shock was finding out you were alive."

A tremor passed through Sadie's body. "I've done you harm."

Lily drew another blanket up to her chin. "What is past is past." She laid her hand on Sadie's arm. "Please, try to tell me more."

"We boarded a ship to Ellis Island. The crossing was miserable. Families carrying what they had in suitcases tied with rope. Children crying. Women wailing. An interminable wait on the island." Sadie squinted, as if trying to recall a past she had buried. "My parents lied about my older brother's health, fear draped on them like shrouds. Somehow we got through. The relief was joyous. My parents took the best of their heritage—laughter, food, music—and discarded the laws. Like many Jews, they gave up their identity to be free. It was a miracle to be in America. We took a train to Pittsburgh, where a cousin took us in."

"Pittsburgh?" Lily asked.

"A factory town where my father could get work. Our family crowded in with his family. I was no older than five. But it was too late for my older brother. He died of consumption. My father's heart was broken. His health failed, and he died, too. My mother carried on. A more courageous woman, I have never known."

"I wish I had met her."

"She brought me to this beautiful city." Sadie craned her head toward the open window. Rays of sunlight spilled across the windowsill and onto the floor. "I had never seen a sky so wide and an ocean so sparkling. And there was music in shanties and saloons, on street corners and halls. I remember my mother singing, always singing. Folk songs from the old country, and waltzes, too."

"And you sang."

"Like a Siren, music lured me. All of it—blues, ballads, love songs. Do you know 'Melancholy Baby'? I sang that with Bob Crosby's band. I thought I was headed for the big time." Her voice trailed off, and she seemed to collapse into herself. "It saved me from your father but tore me from you."

Lily stroked her arm and, without knowing why, began to hum. At first the notes were random, rising with each inhale, fading with each exhale. Then the melody from "My Funny Valentine" issued from Lily's lips, and in a faint voice she sang, "My funny valentine, sweet comic valentine, you make me smile with my heart."

Sadie cocked her ear, and, without opening her eyes, she began, "Your looks are laughable, unphotographable," in a pure soprano. The phrasing was sure, the pitch true. Lily lifted her chin, her voice growing sweeter and stronger, as together they sang, "Yet you're my favorite work of art."

The song ended, and Sadie drifted off to sleep, her mouth gaping in a hollow, half-open O. Lily was still suspended in reverie when she felt a hand on her shoulder and turned to find Maxine looking down at her.

"Hi, kid," she gulped. "So, this is Sadie?"

Lily smiled weakly.

Maxine pulled up a chair, sat, and threaded her arm through Lily's. "She's all done in, isn't she? I remember my mom and her friends talking about her. 'What a stunner,' they'd say. Then my mom would tell me to scram."

"You never told me."

"Somehow I knew it wasn't something to talk about." Maxine spoke in hushed tones, her face registering dismay. "She doesn't look so good now."

"When I met the grocer who lived across the street from us when I was a baby, he said I looked just like she did then."

Maxine hugged Lily. "If it's any comfort, you were always my mom's favorite. There wasn't a day when she didn't stick an extra sandwich or apple in my lunchbox. 'This is for Lily,' she'd say. 'Don't be eating it yourself or palming it off to anyone else.' Or, 'Set an extra place for Lily and bring her back for dinner.'"

"I wanted to live with your family."

"Over Chris's dead body, hey?" Maxine shook her head. "You got a bad break, Lily."

"Don't we all?" Lily answered.

Just then, Sadie stirred, opening and closing her hands, her mouth working furiously.

Lily pressed the button. Sister Bridget rushed in and took Sadie's pulse again. Looking up with tenderness, she said, "It won't be long now, love."

"Are you sure?" Lily asked.

"Take comfort. God works in mysterious ways. Shall I ask Father Corrigan to give her last rites?"

"Thank you, Sister, but I don't think so."

"As you like, then." Sister Bridget paused. "Mr. Packard and his friend are in the hall, inquiring if it's all right to come in now."

"Please tell them yes."

Woodrow and Rosy tiptoed into the room and stopped at the end of the bed. Woodrow gripped the brim of his hat between his fingers, glancing at Lily and then down at Sadie. The color drained from his face. He moved to Lily and wrapped his arm around her shoulder. Rosy stood close by, his sunken, dark eyes grave with sadness.

"Is it okay with you, Miss Lily, if I say good-bye?" Rosy asked.

"Certainly," Lily answered. "You were her friend."

Rosy inched forward to the head of the bed, laid his hand on Sadie's shoulder, and bent down toward her ear. "See you, old girl, on the other side. Be waiting for me at St. Peter's Gate. I'll need a song to get me through them pearly portals."

He stepped back, and the four of them, linked in unspoken agreement, waited. Sadie's breathing was labored, her eyelids fluttering. The minutes crawled. Rays of sun that had filtered across the floor dimmed, the tangy sea breeze subsided, the acidic scent of disinfectant clogged the air.

Sadie's face was waxen; her breath rose, ascending to a full, gasping throb, hovered, and held.

Maxine gripped Lily's hand.

Suddenly Sadie's eyes flew open, focusing straight ahead. "*Motino!*" she shouted.

Lily started and stared in wonder.

Sadie's eyes squeezed shut, followed by a long, slow exhale, and then her face collapsed into itself.

"*Motino?*" Lily whispered.

"That's Lithuanian for 'mother,'" said Rosy.

Lily gazed at Rosy in amazement. "She saw her mother?"

"Must be, Miss Lily. Sometimes that happens at the end. Her mother came to usher her to heaven."

Sister Bridget appeared and swept Rosy aside. She felt Sadie's pulse at her throat. "Praise God, love, your mother has been promoted," and she made the cross over Sadie's body. "In the name of the Father, and the Son, and the Holy Ghost, rest in peace." She glanced at Lily. "Take as much time as you like to say good-bye, love. When you're ready, let me know. I'll be out in the hall."

No one moved until Lily spoke. "Could I please be alone for a moment?"

One by one, they murmured condolences and shuffled out the door.

After a time, Lily slowly lifted a corner of the blanket and took her mother's hand, which, to her surprise, was still warm, and, although the skin was discolored, the fingers were pliant, the nails smooth. She marveled at the work they had done, the people she had touched, the musical scores she had handled. Then she forced herself to look at Sadie's face. All the lines and creases that had been etched into her skin before were wiped clean, and her face was as smooth as alabaster. She seemed at rest, her spirit taken flight, her body an empty vessel.

Lily closed her eyes and sought the words in her heart. After a time, she bent her head and whispered, "I forgive you, Mom. I wish we could have stayed together, but it wasn't meant to be. No matter what, I'll always love you."

* * *

SISTER BRIDGET WAS busy at the nurses' station as Lily approached. She patted Lily on the back. "Your mother is with God now. But she knew you were beside her. I'm sure that's why she went so quickly. You can go now. I'll take over."

They embraced, and Lily moved along the hallway, past a crucifix on the wall and, underneath it, a vessel of holy water.

Maxine, Woodrow, and Rosy waited in a clutch at the end of the hall.

"You okay, doll?" Maxine asked.

"Sure, I'm okay."

Woodrow stepped next to her, his eyes moist, his voice thick. "You showed great courage."

"That's right, Boss," Rosy chimed in. "Courage, pure and simple. Ain't easy. No sirree." Sheepishly, he hemmed and hawed. "Damn, I sure could use a stiff one."

Maxine's eyes bulged in surprise. "That sounds like just the ticket. All right with you, Lil?"

"Why not? I've got a hunch Sadie would approve."

"Approve?" Rosy boomed. "Hell, she'll be on the barstool right next to us. No doubt about it!" He grabbed Maxine by the arm and marched her out of the ward and toward the steps. "Come on with me. I know just the place."

Woodrow took Lily by the hand, and as they walked in silence, Lily moved his hand up around her waist, to her hip. "That's better," she said.

At the top of the marble stairs, she stepped down first and faced him so that they were face-to-face. She draped her arms over his shoulders and looked into his eyes. With her fingertips, she traced the bony orbit of his eye, beginning at the corner of his eyebrow, over its arch, down his nose, past his cheek, to his lips.

"This is feeling like good-bye," he said.

"No good-byes between us, only hellos."

"I want to believe you."

"I know," she said. "I know." And together they walked down the stairs, past a tall statue of the Virgin Mary at the high-ceilinged entrance, through the glass doors, and into the remaining afternoon. Momentarily blinded by the light, she breathed deeply, carved clean from the inside out, whole and free.

* * *

LILY PAUSED ON the corner of Market and Front Streets, clutching a briefcase. Midmorning traffic rumbled by—automobiles, trolleys, cyclists jockeying for position, pedestrians clogging the sidewalks, flower venders hawking carnations. A black sedan rolled up to the curb and stopped. Lily popped open the passenger door and slid in. Instantly, the clamor of the street ebbed. She laid the briefcase on the seat and patted it.

Adolph glanced at the briefcase, grinned at her, and pulled into the traffic lane, cutting off a cabbie. "Good morning, Lily."

"Same to you," she answered. "You look like the cat that swallowed the canary."

"Well, my dear, I've been waiting for your call a long time."

"Nothing escapes you, does it?" she inquired, a smile curving her lips.

"May I remind you it's been months since I suggested you join our efforts?"

"You mean the night at the St. Francis? That feels like eons ago."

"Exactly. But, as with many things in life, timing is everything, and you had to come to this moment your own way."

"I didn't have anything solid. I only had suspicions, and then, well, I let my guard down."

"We had our eye on you."

"Oh God, I guess you know all the gory details."

"No need to elaborate. I had faith you'd come through."

"Did Bunny?"

"Did Bunny what?"

"Have faith?"

"She admitted that the man had a certain charm and it was best to, shall we say, bide our time."

As Adolph drove along the Embarcadero, Lily silently watched the sights roll by: ships tied at the docks; trucks rumbling along, carrying loads of cargo; steamships plowing on the water. The sedan swept through traffic until Adolph turned in at a pier, where the dockworker saluted him and waved him on.

"Nice to have friends in high places," Lily commented.

"You bet. The clothes business has certain benefits." He pulled into a parking space that faced the bay. Before them, Treasure Island glowed in the sunlight. He turned off the engine.

"Tell me one thing," she asked. "Was I hand-picked?"

"Your activities signaled potential. Even before the Expo opened, you had a proclivity for causing disturbances—a news conference at the pavilion where you jumped into the fray, and a couple of break-ins. When I saw you at Forbidden City, I knew you were in over your head. That raised some eyebrows, as did a few motor trips." He regarded her with tender approbation. "Then at Christmas you took a turn, and we lost you for a while."

"But not completely."

"Dangerous exposure, my dear. We were concerned. So, what turned the tide? The excursion at Battery Townsley, then?"

"Completely," she admitted. "In fact, I've brought you a few items." She unsnapped the metal clasp of the briefcase and removed a black, leather-bound journal. "Here's Tokido's logbook. All in Japanese. I'm sure translators will have no trouble deciphering the information."

"Lovely," he said. "Well done."

"One more little item." She withdrew a small camera and placed it into his palm. "I saw him drop this into his boot before the MPs arrested us."

"You knew where to locate these items?"

She shrugged, looking smug. "I had a hunch that panned out."

"Well, well, quite the sleuth. Excellent work, Lily."

"I suppose there's no way to eliminate the one photo of my mug, so I'll swallow and say *c'est la guerre.*"

"That's the spirit. In fact, there's a contact in DC who wants to meet you."

"Really? You mean I'll be promoted?"

"Do you like to travel?"

"Hmm . . . It's on my list."

"Splendid."

"There's one more thing," she said.

"You mean your mother?" A shadow passed over his face. "Yes, we heard. How hard that must be. We're truly sorry about her passing."

"I'm still a little raw. It was for the best." She smoothed the folds of her skirt. "Then you know I'm a Jew."

His face brightened. "I had my suspicions. Welcome to the tribe."

"I'm not exactly sure what it means."

"Give yourself time. It will be revealed. You'll love the food."

"I already do." She hesitated, twisting her mother's ring on her finger. "I feel a little compromised here, but I suppose you know about Woodrow and me."

"He's an excellent man. He'll be one of *our* best."

She swung toward him and exclaimed, "I'll be damned. Are you saying what I think you're saying?"

"My dear, don't you know? Discretion is the better part of valor."

Lily gazed out the windshield to Treasure Island, which

appeared to float on the bay like a scene out of a fairy tale. "Look at it. The Magic City. It's every bit of that and more."

"I doubt we'll ever see such a vision of regal splendor rise in front of our eyes again."

"Yes, but will there be peace in the Pacific?" she asked.

"San Francisco is making a grand show of it. Festivities from now until the Expo closes in November."

"I wonder what will happen to the island afterward."

"It's anybody's guess," Adolph said. "Japan Day is in a few days. I suppose you'll be covering it."

"Yes, I'll be there."

"Mr. Okamura has returned to Tokyo."

"It had to be. I saw the *Tatuta Maru* when it pulled away from the jetty, heading back to Yokohama. I saw him on the deck, but he didn't see me. I made sure of that."

Suddenly, a Clipper at Treasure Island taxied away from its dock. Lily and Adolph spotted the great airplane as it began its gradual ascent, and both pointed in unison. "Look! It's taking off!" They watched it skim over the water, silver wings shimmering in the sunlight, and lift into the sky. Together they tracked the airplane, sailing higher and higher out over the orange towers of the Golden Gate Bridge, toward the open sea.

"Someday you'll be a passenger on that beauty," Adolph said.

"I can't wait."

"Just make sure you come back."

"You can count on it. I love this town."

Ralph Stackpole's Pacifica

A Historical Note

The Golden Gate International Exposition opened on February 18, 1939, and closed six weeks early, on October 29, at the stroke of midnight. For all its showmanship (never-ending parades, fresh-air concerts, and visiting foreign dignitaries) and all its beauty (acres of ever-changing gardens, shimmering fountains, and exotic foreign pavilions), the Exposition was a financial flop.

The Works Progress Administration had dumped nearly $3.8 million into the project, which included engineering the island touted as the future site of the San Francisco Airport. (This was never to be, in that by the time the Exposition closed in 1940, the proposed runways were too short for the size of commercial airplanes.)

Business sponsors pitched in almost $800,000 to make the Magic City a reality. Attendance at the Exposition had been grossly overestimated, and concessionaires lost their shirts because of high rents and penny-pinching fairgoers, who mooched free food or brought their lunches in paper bags. In the first year of the Exposition, the city was over $4 million in the hole.

But what it had accomplished in civic pride, employment of thousands, and demonstrations of the spirit of San Francisco as the city that knew how was inestimable. No one wanted to give up. The Pageant of the Pacific had celebrated the astonishing construction of two world-class bridges and signaled San Francisco as the Gateway to the Pacific.

What to do? grumbled organizers and politicians. Give the people what they want! What did they want? More fun! More razzle-dazzle! More entertainment! The Exposition reopened on May 22, 1940, to high hopes and renewed vigor.

Out went the $40 million Old Masters European collection, and in came a rotating "Art in Action" live event, featuring painters, sculptors, potters, and weavers. Visitors flocked to watch Diego Rivera paint a giant fresco for the library of San Francisco City College. Brilliant Billy Rose staged the eye-opening Aquacade in an enormous indoor pool. Eighteen-year-old Esther Williams and Johnny Weissmuller, a 1930s Olympic gold-medalist swimmer and Tarzan of the movies, glided, twisted, and flashed watery smiles while Aquabelles and Aquabeaux swam in synchronized formation beside them and Morton Downey crooned love songs. Free big-band concerts featuring Count Basie, Gene Krupa, Benny Goodman, and Bing Crosby packed the Temple Compound with thousands of fairgoers. The Cavalcade of the West, renamed as the Cavalcade of a Nation, a "Mighty Theme Spectacle," staged three performances a day, replete with steam-chugging locomotives, covered wagons, and soldiers on horseback. The show occurred on a four-hundred-foot stage, two hundred feet deep, against a painted backdrop of the High Sierras. A cast of hundreds, including actors and actresses in costume, livestock, and horses, cavorted across the stage in constant motion. Water jets surged thirty feet high over the dusty, thundering action.

Everything about the '40 Exposition was big, bold, and brassy. But by summer, it was apparent that the coffers weren't filling quickly enough. Despite the flamboyant entertainment and ongoing wonders of technology—like the model of the University of California, Berkeley, atom-smasher, television receivers, and talking robots—the Exposition continued to lose money. The redoubtable sensations at the Gayway, dubbed Forty Acres of Fun, continued to inspire indigestion, and not from the food alone. Even the Pan Am Clippers that docked at the island, where thousands of spectators watched the arrivals and departures of passengers who paid the $1,000 fare to Hong Kong, with stopovers for fuel and refreshment on Guam, Wake, and Midway, couldn't lure visitors through the turnstiles.

Suddenly, fun was out of fashion, nostalgia too empty an emotion for the terror of war across the seas. The grainy images of soldiers, tanks, and fighter planes on Movietone news were haunting filmgoers in growing numbers across America. When the Exposition opened in the spring of 1940, Hitler's army was pushing toward Paris through the Valley of the Somme. By September, Japan, Germany, and Italy had formed the Axis to conquer the world.

The Exposition closed on the night of September 29, 1940. Thousands of invited guests lingered on, clustered together, shivering in the chilly wind, and in towns ringing the bay, scores of people watched and waited for the beautiful lights of the Magic City to be extinguished. As the radiance faded, the age of innocence flickered into darkness.

When the bills were paid and the books closed, the Exposition had lost money. The directors ordered the demolition of the buildings. Newspapers published stories of the Tower of the Sun collapsing and the Japanese Pavilion in flames. Exhibits were packed away, and auctioneers sold displays. Even Ralph Stackpole's eighty-foot *Pacifica* and O. C. Malmquist's twenty-two-foot, two-and-a-half-ton cast-iron *Phoenix* atop the Tower of Sun were soon demolished. (For a complete listing of surviving art and architecture, please see the Treasure Island Museum's publication "Remains to Be Seen.")

The Administration Building, Hall of Fine Arts and Decorative Arts, and Hall of Aerial Transportation were saved and occupied by the US Navy as a temporary base.

Then, a year later, on the balmy morning of December 7, 1941, Imperial Japanese Navy pilots roared over the Hawaiian Islands in formation. In the emerging light, the skies glowed soft blue; warm trade winds blew steadily. When the pilots sighted Pearl Harbor, they aimed their Zeros, emblazoned with red suns, down at Battleship Row on Ford Island.

At precisely 7:48 a.m., the fighters fell from the sky, shouting, "*Tora! Tora! Tora!*" and rained down terror, mayhem, and destruction on the US Pacific Fleet. Three hundred fifty-three Japanese fighters, bombers, and torpedo planes came in two waves, deployed from six aircraft carriers in the North Pacific seas. They destroyed eight US Navy battleships and sank four. Cruisers, destroyers, and aircraft were crippled; 2,402 American soldiers were killed, and 1,282 were wounded.

Japanese losses were minimal. On the same day, the

Japanese military executed coordinated strikes in Malaya, Singapore, Wake, the Philippines, Hong Kong, and Borneo. Landings were made in every location except Hawaii.

The Light of Asia had spoken. From Manchuria to Korea, down through China, and across to Burma, their vision of unification extended to all countries in the Asia Pacific.

In Japan, the generals declared victory, Emperor Hirohito was honored, and the people rejoiced.

President Franklin Delano Roosevelt declared December 7, 1941, "a date that will live in infamy." On December 8, the United States declared war on Japan and joined Britain and Allied forces against the Axis. America turned her might and power against fascism and tyranny. The giant had awakened.

Acknowledgments

The birth of this novel was a long time coming—ten years of searching San Francisco's city streets and the labyrinth of my imagination, four years of research in libraries and writing in quiet rooms or on my bed, with papers and books strewn about me. The power of the World Wide Web was a mighty ally—you, too, can unlock the past with a keystroke.

The shape of the story emerged slowly. I could not shake my fascination about the contingent who came aboard the *Tatuta Maru* from Imperial Japan, the first foreign country to dock at Treasure Island, and then built the largest and most elaborate pavilion of any of the thirty-seven nations. The GGIE was devoted to peace and brotherhood among all countries whose borders touched the Pacific. Imperial Japan spared no expense in treasure or grandiose pledges of peace at a time when over one million Japanese soldiers were burning, looting, raping, and brutally occupying China. How could this be? I wondered.

Nonetheless, I want to state clearly that I found no evidence of spying or treachery at the Japanese Pavilion or among its representatives. Yet I have the advantage of hindsight. History has been my guide; there is no lack of evidence that Japan was plotting war against the United States. Before the war, from San Francisco to San Diego, there were reports of Japanese spies and conspirators swarming the coast. I have spoken to Bay Area residents who remember stories from their parents and grandparents about sightings of Japanese submarines outside the San Francisco Bay and Marin County beaches.

I grew up seeing a black-and-white photograph of my mother at the Exposition, wearing a suit, sunglasses, and a hat and sitting in dappled light with a few friends. The one thing I particularly remember was her saying it was "bloody cold" on the island. She thought my father, whom she did not know at the time, was running an audiovisual projector, but I prefer to think that he was playing sax and singing with one of the bands.

Additionally, I read *Unbroken,* by Laura Hillenbrand, the harrowing story of Louis Zamperini, an Army Air Force Bombardier in World War II, who crashed into the Pacific Ocean and survived thousands of miles of open water for forty-seven days, only to be captured by the Japanese forces in the Marshall Islands, imprisoned, and tortured.

When Louie was a star runner at USC, he and fellow members of the track team were befriended by Kunichi James Sasaki, known as Jimmie. Jimmie informed the athletes that he had degrees from Harvard, Princeton, and Yale. Widely accepted and liked by the team, Jimmie became good friends with Louie.

Not until years later did Louie find out the real story. During his POW internment in 1943, he was blindfolded and moved to Honshu, to a secret interrogation center called Ofuna that housed hundreds of starving Allied servicemen. When Louie's blindfold was removed, Jimmie Sasaki sat across the room. Jimmie explained that he was a civilian employee of the Japanese navy and the principal interrogator of POWs. Thus began another brutal period of beatings, deprivation, and corporal punishment at the hands of the most sadistic scum of the Japanese military.

Bingo! I had, if not proof, then justification that similar Japanese spy activity could have occurred in the San Francisco Bay Area.

I mention three journalists in the novel. David Warren Ryder, journalist and author, served a term in federal prison in 1942 for acting as an unregistered Japanese agent under the Foreign Agents Registration Act. Ralph Townsend, author and political activist, was also convicted of the same charge and imprisoned. Harry Cotkins, foreign editor of the *San Francisco News*, was implicated but not charged.

I also want to emphasize that the Japanese American community in San Francisco and the Bay Area were loyal and patriotic citizens and that their internment following Japan's bombing of Pearl Harbor was a national disgrace. Written accounts of these camps and the courage of the Japanese American families who suffered such hardships and deprivation are sobering and terrible reminders of how xenophobia can overtake reason and rationality.

This novel contains both imaginary characters and actual prominent individuals, like Adolph and Lillian Schuman, Timothy Pflueger, and Leland Cutler whom I hope I have treated kindly. Their genius and achievements inspired me.

Lily Nordby, Tokido Okamura, Woodrow Packard, and Rosy the Giant sprang from my imagination. It would be imprecise, if not cowardly, not to admit that there is some of my family's past in this story, but I leave it to you, kind reader, to divine fact from fiction. Many years ago, I saw a man in the audience of a Los Angeles playhouse who became Woodrow. He was one of the most handsome men I have ever seen, and over the years I could not forget him. Now he lives on in these pages.

The following authors and their books provided hours of knowledge and inspiration: Richard Reinhardt's *Treasure Island, San Francisco's Expositon Years*; Patricia F. Carpenter's and Paul Totah's *The San Francisco Fair, Treasure Island, 1939-1940*; Jack James and Earle Weller, *Treasure Island, The Magic City, 1939-1940. The Official Guide Book of the Golden Gate International Exposition on San Francisco Bay* with a full color map captured by inveterate collector and friend, Peter Oqvist, was the icing on the cake.

Finally, I must bow to the generosity of strangers who provided invaluable historic detail and the steady hand of my writing tribe, Betsy Graziani Fasbinder, Amy Peele, and Linda Joy Myers, who unselfishly gave of their talents and encouragement. Kudos to Patricia Araujo, luminous artist of the iconic images of the Exposition and inspirational friend. Heartfelt thanks as well to Brooke Warner, publisher of She Writes Press, and to Annie Tucker, copyeditor.

The librarians at the San Francisco History Center, the California Historical Society, the Dominican University library, and Marin County libraries, as well as the staff at the Treasure Island Museum, have been exemplary in every respect, and I praise them all.

Equally, thank you to the many friends and family

members who urged me toward the finish line. My unnamed mentor and wise friend was by my side the entire time.

Lastly, there is no greater love and support from one person than from my husband, learned editor, photography curator, adventurer, and soul mate, Ron Moore.

About the Author

photo credit: Tanya Constantine Photography

CHRISTIE NELSON is a third-generation San Franciscan, a graduate of Dominican University of California, a longtime Marin resident, and the author of *Woodacre*; *Dreaming Mill Valley*; and *My Moveable Feast.* She and her husband live in the 1880s brewmeister's home of the former San Rafael Brewery.

SELECTED TITLES FROM SHE WRITES PRESS

She Writes Press is an independent publishing company founded to serve women writers everywhere.
Visit us at www.shewritespress.com.

Portrait of a Woman in White by Susan Winkler. $16.95, 978-1-938314-83-4. When the Nazis steal a Matisse portrait from the eccentric, art-loving Rosenswigs, the Parisian family is thrust into the tumult of war and separation, their fates intertwined with that of their beloved portrait.

In the Shadow of Lies: A Mystery Novel by M. A. Adler. $16.95, 978-1-938314-82-7. As World War II comes to a close, homicide detective Oliver Wright returns home—only to find himself caught up in the investigation of a complicated murder case rife with racial tensions.

A Girl Like You: A Henrietta and Inspector Howard Novel by Michelle Cox. $16.95, 978-1-63152-016-7. When the floor matron at the dance hall where Henrietta works as a taxi dancer turns up dead, aloof Inspector Clive Howard appears on the scene—and convinces Henrietta to go undercover for him, plunging her into Chicago's gritty underworld.

Shanghai Love by Layne Wong. $16.95, 978-1-938314-18-6. The enthralling story of an unlikely romance between a Chinese herbalist and a Jewish refugee in Shanghai during World War II.

After Midnight by Diane Shute-Sepahpour. $16.95, 978-1-63152-913-9. When horse breeder Alix is forced to temporarily swap places with her estranged twin sister—the wife of an English lord—her forgotten past begins to resurface.

Eliza Waite by Ashley Sweeney. $16.95, 978-1-63152-058-7. When Eliza Waite chooses to leave a stagnant life in rural Washington State and join the masses traveling north to Alaska in 1898 during the tumultuous Klondike Gold Rush, she encounters challenges and successes in both business and love.

www.ingramcontent.com/pod-product-compliance
Lightning Source LLC
Chambersburg PA
CBHW022249211224
19369CB00003B/33